Mr. I Believe

Sean Morgan

Except where actual historical locations, events and characters are being described for this story, all situations in this publication are fictitious and any resemblance to living persons is purely coincidental

For my Sons, Dan and Colin

Chapter 1

Elgin, Illinois

The alarm went off at 6 a.m. with the usual noise and was greeted by the grumble and moans from Steve Michaels as he rolled over carefully so as to not disturb his wife of eighteen years, Michele. He turned off the alarm and went downstairs to begin his Sunday morning ritual of quiet time with his paper and his cup of coffee; he looked forward to it every weekend. The news was the same, just a different name to the horrors of the world that graced the headlines on the front pages of the two local Chicago newspapers that were delivered to his doorstep. As the coffee finished brewing, he heard the sounds of his fifteen-year-old son, Jim, coming down the steps to get ready for his day. Steve pulled out the sports pages, which he knew were the first things he would ask for.

"Morning, son," Steve said in his bright and too loud voice, which his son had learned not to comment on over the years. Jim had not turned out to be the morning person that his father was. "Seems the team didn't do too good last night in the football game," Steve added, referring to the home town high school team, the Rockets of Burlington Central.

"No, they got their butts handed to them again," replied Jim without looking up from the sports page.

"So, any plans after mass today? You're serving the 8 a.m. mass, correct?" Steve asked.

"No plans so far, but then Mom isn't out of bed yet, and that could change quickly!" Jim answered with a slight laugh.

"Oh? Who is not out of bed yet, young man?" Michele exclaimed, knowing she had surprised both of the men in her life.

"Oops…morning, Mom. Dad was just saying how late you keep sleeping as you get older."

"Oh, did he now?" she asked as she walked over to her husband and gave him a playful poke in the stomach and a kiss on the cheek.

"Son, can you still run the hundred in under twelve seconds?" Steve asked.

"Yes, you know I can. Why?" Jim answered.

"Well, if you don't get out of here quickly, I'll get you for that comment!" Steve replied as he moved to catch his son. Jim ran for the stairs while his dad reached for him, Michele stepping in front of him and laughing over their antics. She wrapped her arms around her husband and held on tight, kissing him while he tried to get away.

In another part of town, Bill Matters was getting ready for the 8 a.m. mass as well but for a different reason.

Bill had been troubled all of his life with pressure from peers or family to do something with himself. A brilliant artist who could draw anything but lacked the discipline to hold a job, he always seem to himself to be a failure. He found religion as a way to cope, but it became an obsession to him. He read all sorts of things but found himself drawn to the darker side, dealing with the judgment day and how to stop it from happening.

Today, he told himself, he would end this failure that his life was and take out the Anti-Christ who had manifested itself in the form of Father George, who was saying 8 a.m. mass at St. Paul's that morning. He had been reading a book about the judgment day that said if the Anti-Christ was killed in the house of the Lord while preparing the Hosts, the world would not end, and the savior would be vindicated of his sins. This obscure passage had become the focus of this plan to kill Father George after he had attended a lecture about judgment day that Father George had given at the church just two weeks previously.

At the lecture Father George talked about how we could prepare ourselves by doing good deeds and making ourselves shine in the eyes of the Lord. Bill took this to mean that a good deed would be killing the Anti-Christ, and then he would shine in the eyes of the Lord. Funny, Bill thought, how a simple lecture could change his life after all of the disappointment he had suffered and how one act could change his standing.

He had planned carefully, knowing that the 8 a.m. was the least crowded of the three Sunday masses; he should be able to kill the priest while he raised the Host during the consecration and then get away with no one catching him. He learned that the church had no security system or cameras after going there a few times once he had decided what to do. The only trouble was getting the 9mm handgun out of his dad's gun safe and finding a way to get the key lock off it. Once he had that figured out, he went over while his parents were at work and opened the gun safe with the hidden key he had found years ago while playing in his dad's study. He doubted that his dad even knew where the key was anymore. The 9mm fit his hand perfectly and was easily concealable under the tweed sport coat that he planned to wear so as not to look too suspicious on this cool Fall day. He took a magazine and loaded it, knowing that the fifteen rounds in the clip would be more than enough to kill the priest.

Chapter 2

As Steve showered and shaved, Michele came into the bedroom and let him know that she would be going to 9:45 mass that morning. She was meeting her girlfriend Elaine there and then going to brunch after.

"Do you want to join us at Colonial Café after mass?" she asked her husband.

"Oh, no, I promised Jim we could go out after mass and get a bite to eat. Funny how the only quality spend time I spend with him always revolves around food!" Steve exclaimed. Michele laughed at her husband, knowing that the time he spent with their son was more than most dads since he was also Jim's Boy Scout assistant troop leader. She found it unique that having a son had made her not a football widow, like most of her girlfriends, but a Scout widow.

While tucking in his shirt, Jim called out to his dad that he was all ready to go and would meet him downstairs. Steve yelled back a reminder to have black shoes on and not tennis shoes; that was his pet peeve for any altar server serving mass.

Jim yelled back, "I do," and ambled down the stairs, laughing at his dad.

"Why do you always have to remind about the shoes? It was only one time that he forgot," Michele asked.

Steve looked at his wife of eighteen years and smiled, which she knew meant either a long answer was coming, or he was going to chase her out of the bedroom. Steve did not answer, and Michele quickly ran down the stairs laughing, knowing she was going to be picked up and hugged by her husband like she always was when he caught her.

After the excitement was over, Jim looked at the two of them still so in love and said, "Get a room you two; it's so embarrassing!"

Michele just gave her son a dirty look and her husband a wink. "You two had better be going. Say *hi* to Father George for me. He doesn't have the 9:45 mass today."

"See you later, Mom," Jim yelled as he rushed out the door to get into his dad's car. Steve turned to face his wife and gave her a kiss and a swift pat on her butt, moving before Michele could react.

"Oh, I'll get you for that one later, fella!" Michele yelled as Steve raced to his car, laughing again.

"What's so funny, Dad?" Jim asked his dad, who was putting on his seatbelt.

"Your mom. She's getting a bit slow in her old age," Steve answered, still laughing.

"Well, we'll see at the Fall 5k Run," Jim answered. "I think she cleaned both of our clocks last year, Dad."

"Oops, forgot about that one, Jim," Steve answered and began wondering how much crow he would have to eat this year from his wife, who could still run her college cross country times.

As they pulled into the church's parking lot, Steve noticed one car all the way in the back near the parish office that seemed out of place but thought that maybe someone was at the office getting something.

Bill noticed Steve's car pulling in as well and smiled, knowing that in 40 minutes or so he would kill the Anti-Christ and save the world from judgment day.

As they exited the car, Steve gave his son's hair a tousle and reminded him to pay attention to the mass and help keep the younger altar servers from making any mistakes.

"Geez, Dad, I know what I'm supposed to do. You don't always have to remind me," Jim exclaimed. Steve just smiled, knowing that answer was the same one he gave Dad all those years ago when, at age fifteen, he served mass at the downtown church. After the little stroll down memory lane, he walked toward the doors of the church, still bothered for some reason he could not understand by the car that was parked by the parish office. As he entered, he said *hi* to the ushers and made the sign of the cross after dipping his finger in the holy water inside the doors.

Chapter 3

St. Charles, Illinois

Jim made his way to the sacristy to get prepared to say mass that morning. There, another younger altar server was having a bit of trouble getting the rope tied correctly around his alb.

"Here, let me help you," Jim said as the fourth grader look at him with surprise and bewilderment. Father George was sitting in the other room, praying to himself quietly as was his ritual before every mass that he concelebrated. Jim popped his head in and asked quietly if Father George needed anything out of the normal for this mass. Father George just mouthed *no*, shook his head, and then went back to reading his prayer book. Jim grabbed the younger boy and began getting the altar ready for mass. As he walked down the center aisle of the church, he noticed his dad was kneeling in his customary second pew on the right hand side, looking at the tabernacle with his hands together and straight up as he had been taught. Amazing how a simple act of reverence like making the sign of the cross and holding your hands in church can have such a lasting impression on a son or, for that matter, a father.

As he put the book, which would be used in today's mass, under the side table, he noticed his dad smiling at him, and he tried not to smile back. He knew he would hear about it later if he didn't keep a straight face on the altar. Funny, Jim thought to himself again, how he could get a lecture from the man that made him smile. Oh well, such was the way of life in the Michaels house. As he genuflected to go back up the aisle, his dad motioned for him to stop by a second.

"Almost made you smile there," Steve whispered while Jim leaned over.

"Yep, but I didn't, so no lecture today on the way home," Steve smiled back at his dad and went back to get another item to place on the altar.

As Bill entered at the back of the church, he noticed the altar server talking to someone in the front and surmised that it must be his father. Bill reflected that his own dad never even attended mass anymore, yet here was his son saving mankind from damnation and the fires of Hell. He entered the pew on the far right hand side, which would give him the best angle to kill the priest as he raised the Host over his head during the consecration. He had looked over all the available angles and, being a left-handed shot, this proved the best to achieve what he deemed to be his finest hour.

Steve did not notice the new man sitting behind him on the far right, but he began to have the feeling that all was not right in the church.

He put down the bulletin that he was reading and looked around to see what might be causing him to feel a bit edgy. Nothing looked out the ordinary, and he saw quite a few faces that he recognized from Boy Scouts or from the St. Paul's Men's Club that met at the church once a month. As a past President of the Men's Club, he knew most of the members, and it was a constant joke in their household that he never left church without saying hello to at least three members on the way out. If it was not Scouting, it was the Men's Club; Steve smiled to himself, knowing that he was a lucky man to have such good friends and to be respected for the work that he did in the community. But still the feeling of unease was there, and he could not shake it, nor could he figure it out. *Oh well*, he thought. *Just relax and see how many mistakes Jim makes during mass today.* He could tease him about them later.

He noticed the man again on his far right just looking ahead, almost staring at the center of the altar; Steve wondered who he was but turned back and began to say the rest of his prayers before mass.

Chapter 4

The music director stood up and announced over the PA system the number of the song that would be the entrance hymn today as the choir stood to welcome the priest and to start the mass. As Steve was not much for singing, he stood stoic, facing the front, wondering again how he was lucky enough to be so involved in the wonderful mysteries of the Church and to have his son involved as well. The greeting and the opening prayers went off without a hitch, and Steve noticed that Jim was a bit more on the ball today, correcting the other altar server's mistakes almost before they happened. He smiled to himself again, wondering if his late father had noticed the same about him all those years ago. The first reading and second reading ended, and Steve rose when the priest did as he walked over to read the Gospel. This was the best part of the mass to Steve, outside of the consecration of the Host and wine, as the reading was from one of the four Gospels. They were always consistent for the time of year, but it was the homily that he enjoyed the most, to see how the priest could tie it together to propose a new meaning to their faith. Father George was the best homilist that St. Paul's parish had at that time, and he never failed to deliver. Michele always commented that if Father

George ever gave up the priesthood, he would make a fantastic politician with how he managed a crowd and kept even the most mundane subject interesting. Steve wondered to himself if his lovely wife was making a comment on how he himself carried a conversation and could make his points clearer. After all these years, his wife was still so gentle in making her points to him and helping him change to be a better man and father.

As the homily began, Steve turned his whole attention to Father George, who started off with his usual light humor concerning the reading.

"In today's reading, we heard that the younger son wanted his inherence early and did not want to be bothered with the work that most men had to do. Funny…when I was younger, all I wanted was a piece of cake; my older brothers and sisters took slices that could feed an army so that all I got were crumbs that were left over." As Father George finished his first line, it brought the normal light laughter from the parishioners who had come to look forward to how Father George would be able to tie in the fact that he was the youngest of eight and never had anything when he was younger. His parents and siblings had been to St. Paul's to hear him say mass and had never disputed these facts. They had become the legend of Father George's upbringing.

As the laughter died down, Father George continued to explain the prodigal son and how we all must embrace those who have strayed from the faith and welcome them back with open arms when they ask for our forgiveness. He also explained in a very serious manner that all should be forgiven after a transgression if they are indeed sorry for what they have done.

This struck Bill as ironic: "ask for forgiveness and you shall receive it no matter what you have done." After he killed this priest, would anyone forgive him, not knowing that it was for their souls that he was doing this?

As mass progressed, Bill fought the urge to feel for the gun in his inside pocket and instead concentrated on the task at hand. *Not until he raises the Host will I shoot* was all that he thought to control his urge. As the Eucharist Prayer began, he said a silent prayer to himself: *Lord, the protector of light and the surge of darkness, prepare me, for I am about to heal the wound and save mankind from the damnation of the judgment day.* As Bill finished, he was smiling and at perfect ease with himself, ready to do what must be done.

The time was near. All of his senses were at a heightened alertness. He looked around to make sure no one had come up behind him who might stop him. As he did, the priest began to say over the Host, "At the time he was betrayed and entered willingly into his Passion, he took bread and, giving thanks, broke it, and gave it to his disciples, saying: *take this, all of you, and eat of it: for this is my body, which will be given up for you.*" With that said, Father George raised the Host over his head.

Bill jumped up, grabbed the gun out his pocket, and screamed, "Die, you blasphemer! Die!" The shot left the barrel before it even registered that he had pulled the trigger and headed straight toward its intended target.

Father George turned to his left at the sound of Bill's rant and never saw the bullet that struck him in his left shoulder. The bullet slammed into him with a furious force, knocking him down, and as he fell his head struck the base of the tabernacle. He was rendered unconscious.

Jim motioned for the other altar server to take cover behind the chairs as he crawled to Father George to see if he could do anything to help. The young altar server whom he had helped with his rope earlier was crying as he took cover, but he was staying put. As he reached Father George, he could not hear the screaming of the other parishioners; everything was moving in slow motion to him. All that he could think of was what to do and how to do it. *Think! Think what you learned in the Boy Scouts! Come on, you are an Eagle Scout! Think!* As he reached Father George, he made sure his airway was clear, checked to see if there was an exit wound, and then tried to stop the flow of blood from the gun shot.

Steve, seeing his son crawl to the stricken priest, got up and ran to his son's aid. He kept low since he did not know if the shooter was going to start picking off anyone else in the church. *Please*, he thought to himself. *Please let Father George be alive!* As he came up behind the altar, he saw that Jim had made sure the airway was clear and was applying direct pressure to the wound. He looked at his son, nodded, and smiled to give him some reassurance that everything was going to be okay.

"Dad, the bullet didn't go through. There's no exit wound. I need something to stop the blood. Grab me the towel from the table and get me the cloths from the altar," Jim said in a very grown up way. Steve did exactly what his son asked of him and knew that his Scout training was paying off in spades.

"Jim, listen to me. Keep the pressure on, and I will try to keep whoever is yelling out there away from you and him." He pointed at Father George.

"Dad," Jim said in a hushed tone. "Please do what you can; I don't think this alb is bulletproof!"

Steve smiled at his son and then noticed that the paten and the consecrated Host were lying by his side. He grabbed the paten and then very carefully put the Host that had Father George's blood on it in the center. He stood and placed the paten back on top of the chalice, making the sign of the cross to himself.

A certain strength came to him from this simple task, and he knew that he had to stop this mad man somehow, someway.

Chapter 5

Bill was now out of the pew, yelling at the top of his lungs, "You have been saved! This blasphemer has been silenced, and the damnation of the judgment day will not be upon you!" He was pointing the gun around him wildly at the parishioners seated in the pews. He began to yell again, "As you have been saved, you shall now exult me for being your second savior!" He then noticed that Steve was standing in front of the altar with blood on his hands and the shirt that belonged to Father George.

"What in the hell are you talking about?" Steve yelled so that he could be heard over the screams and the crying that were going on around him. "Who do you think you are, coming into this house of God and shooting His servant?"

"I am the savior, and you should be grateful that I acted today!" Bill yelled back at him. "Why should you care? What I have done has been foretold!"

Steve replied in a louder voice, "Care? Why should I care? This is my church and their church, and no man is my savior here on Earth!" Steve thought to himself that he sounded a bit like a Sunday morning tele-evangelist and might want to get off the soap box he was on.

21

Like Jim had just said, this shirt and his alb were not bulletproof! He needed to get this guy away from everyone and get him centered on himself. *Great,* he thought to himself. *Centered on me like a bullseye target!*

"Why did you shoot this priest? What has he done to you?" Steve asked as he began to move to his left and put himself in between this mad man and where Jim was caring for Father George.

"Done to me?" Bill replied in a serious tone "Done to me? He is a blasphemer who talked about the judgment day, not knowing that he was unleashing the fires of Hell upon whomever believed him. I heard him myself and took the guidance that was given to me to stop him and save us all!"

"Who gave you this guidance?" Steve asked, and as he did, those words left a bitter taste in his mouth.

"I was instructed through my readings and listening to those who know," Bill answered calmly. This man might actually care what he was saying.

"Oh," Steve exclaimed. "Those who know. And how did you meet these folks?"

"They are known to those who understand the teachings. This man was a pretender, an Anti-Christ who thought he knew better," Bill answered in a voice that was becoming stronger by the minute.

Steve looked at Bill and noticed that the gun was now at his side, that he was not waving it around anymore.

Good, he thought. *Maybe this was the key: let him talk, and hopefully the police would be here soon to take him out.*

He pondered the gunman's last answer and then answered in a very clear and crisp tone. "You have done nothing of the sort, my friend; all you have done today is shoot a man who has a vocation to serve his God. You dare call him an Anti-Christ for his service to our Lord? You are the blasphemer, not him!"

Bill raised the gun toward Steve, who was still moving ever nearer to him. "He is the Anti-Christ. He was the one talking about the judgment day and how we can be saved. Only Jesus can tell us this. Not this man nor those who listen to him!"

Steve looked down the barrel of the gun, which was now only five feet away, and wished he knew how to get this guy closer to him without making the first move.

"Father George was only discussing the judgment, not telling you what to do or how to prepare for it. You did not listen to the whole thing or only listened to what you wanted to listen to!"

Bill's rage was returning as this man, who was not his equal, questioned him about what the priest's intentions were. He did not know what Bill knew and could not be as well-read with the understanding that he had. No, not his man or any man or women here today could understand that he was right, and they needed to be grateful for what he had done.

23

"You think that you are like him, this Anti-Christ that I have shot?" Bill asked.

Steve was taken aback by this question. He knew that any answer was likely to get him shot.

"I only know what has been taught to me by men who are priests, like Father George. I have listened and made my own conclusions, and they do not coincide with yours!"

"So are you willing to die since you have listened to what this Anti-Christ has said?" Bill asked in a surprising way. "I say again, are you willing to die for everyone here? I will leave this building and not harm another person if you have the courage to say yes!"

Steve looked at the gunman, knowing that he was painted into a corner, but he needed to get closer to this guy to be able to stop him.

"I will die for everyone here if that is what it takes!" As the words left his mouth, he could only think about Jim and Michele, but he knew that this was the right way to go if he was going to die. It was his job as a member of the St. Paul's Men's Club, he reminded himself, to protect his priests and his church no matter the cost.

"You are willing to die for them?" Bill asked as he pointed the gun around him towards the other parishioners. "Why? Do you know them all? Do they know you?"

Steve answered loudly, "No, I do not know them all, but they are here with me, and I will die for them!"

"Why will you do that for people who would not even give you the time of day? Why would you do that?" Bill asked, not knowing what the answer might bring.

"Two words, my friend, and two words only: I believe," Steve answered in an even louder voice so all could hear him.

Bill rushed Steve and drove the barrel of the gun into his forehead. "You believe? Well, have you said your prayers, Mr. I Believe? Have you?" Bill yelled in his face.

"Have you said yours?" Steve answered in the same loud voice; then, amazingly, he winked at Bill.

As he winked his right hand pushed the gun upward over his head with surprising speed, and with his left hand, he struck the gunman's exposed throat. Steve struck the throat again, feeling his strike crush the windpipe of the gunman, all the while holding the gun far over his own head.

Bill grabbed for his throat, but before he could react, the second strike hit him. He began to gasp for air and was losing his grip on the gun, which this man had now snatched out of his own hand. *How could this happen?* was the last conscious thought he had.

As Steve took the gun out of the gunman's hand, he struck the gunman on the back of his head, knocking him down to the floor of the church. The gunman turned and landed on his back. Steve kicked him over onto his stomach and held the gun steady, pointing it at the back of the gunman's head. He looked at the choir director, who had gotten behind the piano for cover, and asked, "Got a cell phone that I could borrow?"

Chapter 6

As the music director reached for her cellphone, Steve looked at her while he asked her to dial 911 for him. After she dialed, she handed the phone to him and asked, "Is he dead?"

Steve replied, "Don't know and don't care. I just need help here now!"

"911. What is your emergency?" the operator asked with a neutral tone to her voice.

"Steve Michaels here. I am at St. Paul's Church and need to have the police here right away. There has been a shooting, and we have two injured. The gunman has been detained, but I need someone here now!" Steve said in the most normal voice he had at the time.

The 911 operator replied, "You say there has been a shooting and the gunman has been detained?"

"Yes, please, we need an ambulance and the police here now!" Steve exclaimed and handed the phone back to the choir director. "Tell them where we are and that I do not hear any sirens!" Steve ordered as he focused on the gunman to see if he had moved.

"Dad, you okay?" Jim yelled from behind the altar.

"Yes, there will be no more gunshots. How is Father George doing?" Steve yelled back.

"He is doing okay. The blood flow has almost stopped, but I don't want to take off the pressure. Is the ambulance on its way?" Jim yelled back over the noise in the church.

Steve looked at the choir director, who nodded and said, "Yes, we should hear them any second!" As she was talking, an usher came up to Steve and asked what he could do. Steve asked him to clear the aisle and have someone outside in the circle drive ready to direct the EMS squad and the police when they got there. Steve looked down at the gunman, not sure if his strike had done severe damage or even killed him, but he was taking no chances to check so as not to be caught in a surprise move from him. He heard a commotion from the back of the church and only then realized that a siren was wailing as it entered the circle drive. He could not make out if it was the police or the EMS, but he now knew help was on its way.

"Jim, can you hold on for a minute or two more? I think the police are here!" Steve yelled.

"No problem, Dad. I have it under control!" Jim yelled back.

Under control, Steve thought to himself. *This morning he was just a fifteen-year-old boy, and now he is a man handling the pressure of this mad world.* He smiled, knowing that this was one story Michele would never believe! *Oh crap*, he thought to himself. *She is going to kill me for sticking my nose into this. Well, better to ask for forgiveness than permission.* He smiled again.

The police started to come up the aisle toward him with their guns drawn, stating in a very stern manner, "Sir, please put the gun down on the floor and move away. Sir, please do it now!"

Steve did as they asked, saying out loud, "I am Steve Michaels. I was the one who called 911 and subdued the gunman. I don't know his state. I did not want to leave him uncovered." He lowered the gun, took it by the barrel, and stepped back. He then gently lowered it to the floor and backed up another few steps. "My son, Jim, is behind the altar with Father George, who has been shot by this man here." Steve spoke very clearly while pointing at the gunman.

"Thank you, Mr. Michaels. Please back away slowly so that we can take control."

As Steve backed away, the first police officer took out his handcuffs and placed them on the gunman, covered by his partner. Once they were on, he checked the vitals of the gunman and shook his head at his partner, indicating that he was dead. Steve looked at the police officer kneeling by the gunman and asked if he could go over and check on his son.

"Please do, but we'll need to talk to you in a minute." The officer keyed his mic to reply to command that the situation was under control and the coroner should be summoned to the church.Steve walked over to his son. The adrenaline was beginning to ease up, and he noticed that his hands were shaking just a bit.

"How is your patient doing, Dr. Jim?" Steve asked, trying to shake off the gloom that was beginning to set in upon him.

"He's doing good, Dad. Look! There's the EMS now!" Jim exclaimed in a relieved voice. As the EMS came up onto the altar and asked Jim to let them take over, he stood up. Jim walked up to the chalice with the paten and the bloody Host in the middle and placed it in the tabernacle for safe keeping.

"Dad," Jim said in a hushed tone. "This Host has been consecrated and cannot be allowed to be ruined. Think about it, Dad: a consecrated Host with blood on it. Now that is something you don't see every day!"

Steve smiled and recognized the man standing in front of him for the first time to be his son, standing tall, not knowing how impressed he had made his father. Steve grabbed him and gave him a big hug in front of everyone, hoping that no one would notice his eyes tearing up.

"Dad, what are you doing? You're not going to kiss me, are you?" Jim responded playfully to his Dad, but he realized just how lucky they both were to have made it through this ordeal.

"What are we going to tell Mom? She will never believe the truth," Jim commented with a serious face.

"I don't know, but we better think of something fast. She'll be here for the 9:45 mass. Knowing her, she'll be furious that we didn't stay out of the way and duck for cover!" Steve thought how he was going to explain to Michele that he had just killed a man in front of their son.

The EMS squad asked Jim to tell them what he did to administer first aid and if he had moved Father George after he was shot. Jim turned his attention to the EMS squad while Steve sat down on the steps of the altar and began to understand just how lucky they were indeed.

Chapter 7

As Steve sat on the steps of the altar, he noticed for the first time how the other parishioners were looking at him, some in awe, but most in disbelief. One young couple carrying their infant child came up to him, and the wife placed her hand on his knee, mouthing *thank you* to him. Soon more and more came forward to thank Steve as the reality of what had just happened began to take effect. The police came to him and asked him if they could take a statement from Jim since he was a minor and needed permission to talk to them. This question woke him from his stupor, and he rose to let Jim know what the police needed from him.

They led Jim to another part of the church to get the facts while they were still fresh in his mind. It was then that Steve noticed the pastor of St. Paul's, Father Rick, coming hurriedly into the church to see the condition of Father George.

"I got a call from one of the members on the parish council that there was a shooting and that one of my parishioners had stopped it. Steve, was it you?" Father Rick asked.

"Yes, Father, it was me," Steve replied seriously, which took Father Rick back a bit. "I stopped the gunman who had shot Father George.

I did not plan on this outcome, but something had to be done. He was going to shoot more people if I didn't act."

"Steve, are you okay?" Father Rick asked, realizing the gunman was dead in the aisle to his right.

"Father, my confession this coming Saturday will be a good one. So how many Hail Marys and Our Fathers for committing a killing in church will it be? Or should I begin to find a new faith to worship?" Steve asked Father Rick, who was amazed that Steve could still keep his humor at such a terrible time.

"Well, I do believe that you might have to see the Bishop about that one. It's a bit over my limit for confession!" Father Rick joked back to Steve as he leaned in closer and whispered to him, "I absolve you of this as you acted in the protection of our Holy Mother Church and her followers!"

Steve smiled, knowing that this was not going to be his last confession of what had just happened.

As he looked around, he noticed Jim walking back to him, still wearing his alb, which was covered in Father George's blood. Father Rick noticed it as well, and he almost gasped. He knew only that Steve had been involved in the shooting.

"Jim!" Father Rick called out. "Here, let's get you out of that alb before you are soaked in blood. How did you get this way?"

"I crawled to Father George after he was shot to check on him. I made the other altar server get behind the chairs to take cover in case there were any more shots," Jim answered. Father Rick took a seat, almost collapsing, in the first pew, holding the blood-soaked alb that he had just helped Jim remove. As this was his first time hearing the whole of what had just happened, the enormity of it was just now becoming evident to him. Jim continued, "I checked his airway, Father George's that is, and checked to see if there was an exit wound like I was taught in the Scouts. I applied direct pressure to his wound to stop the bleeding." Jim finished his answer with pride that he had indeed done what he was taught and took control of the situation at hand. Steve looked at his son, giving the account of what he had done, with amazement, wondering if this was the same person that he'd once caught drinking milk right out of the gallon jug from the refrigerator.

Father Rick asked how Father George was doing, and Jim answered, "He was knocked out cold. He hit his head on the tabernacle when he fell. He hasn't woken up, but his vitals are good from what the EMS guys told me."

With that said, the EMS guys came forward and asked if Steve and Jim could clear the altar; they were about to move Father George to the waiting ambulance.

As Steve and Jim moved away, Father George began to come around, not knowing what had happened to him. Father Rick came forward and told Father George that he would explain all to him in a bit but to let these men do their job.

"Was I shot?" Father George asked in a stage whisper.

"Yes," Steve answered. "But Jim here saved your life. He was Johnny on the spot, giving you first aid!" While saying this, Steve noticed how proud he was of his son for acting the way he did and reminded himself to have a chat with him later about taking cover next time. He chuckled to himself. He was going to get the same speech from his wife once she found out but in a bit more animated fashion.

Thank you, mouthed Father George to Steve and Jim as the EMS techs wheeled him down the center aisle.

There was a commotion at the back of the church that caused Father Rick, Steve, and Jim to look up.

"I don't care about a crime scene; you either let me in there, or so help me God, I will take all of you out!"

Michele had arrived.

35

Chapter 8

Steve called out to the police at the back of the church, "She's with me! Better do as she says, or she'll carry out her threat!" Both Father Rick and Jim were looking for somewhere to hide as a very pissed off wife, mother, and parishioner walked down the center aisle with a look on her face that could stop an army.

"Father Rick, I'm glad you're here to stop me from doing what I was going to do to this man once I got here! Please stay. I'd like a witness to make sure that he leaves here in one piece. What were you doing, Steve, standing up to a gunman with a one liner of "I believe"? Who do you think you are, putting my son in danger like this? I could just scream that you would do this!" Michele paused to take a breath and noticed that even the police were backing away and looking at Steve with sorrow at what was coming his way. She walked up to her son and noticed that his shirt and hands were still covered with Father George's blood.

"Oh my God, what the hell did you do, letting our only child get involved in this mess? Sorry Father, that just came out!" Michele exclaimed, knowing that everyone was looking at her.

"How did you know I said *I believe*?" Steve asked her.

"Ever hear of something called Facebook? Your mug and your lame brain speech are all over the internet, you idiot!" Michele yelled at him. "You stopped a gunman with a speech; you could have been killed! Or worse!"

"Or worse?" Jim asked knowing that this might break the tension between his mom and dad.

"You I will deal with later. Crawling to Father George's rescue? Have I not told you time and time again to take cover? Not run to trouble? God, you are so much like him!" Michele yelled at her son while pointing at Steve.

"Michele," Father Rick said, trying to defuse the next killing in church that was about to happen. "What do you mean Facebook and *I believe*?"

"One of the folks here at church had nothing better to do during this fun than to take a video, which is quite good by the way, of this knuckle head crawling to Father George and this one standing up to the gunman!" Michele exclaimed, digging in her purse for her cell phone. "Here, let me show you." She produced her cell phone and held it for all to see.

After the video had ended, Father Rick let out a low whistle and patted both Steve and Jim on their backs.

"I had no idea what you had done, the two of you. And you, Steve, standing up to the gunman like you did. All I can say is *wow* and that I'm so glad you're not a Lutheran!"

"Well, if *Mister I Believe* is done, I'd like to get them out of here before they both get too big of a head!" Michele exclaimed, grabbing her son and giving him a tight hug.

"Mom, someone might be looking. Geez, you're going to give me a mama's boy rep or something!" Jim squealed as he tried to get out of his mother's grip.

Steve looked on in amazement, now understanding the whole scope of what he had done and what the ramifications might be. He asked the police if they were done with them for now, and the officer in charge agreed that they could leave, but there might be some questions later for Steve. He nodded and asked Michele to take Jim home to get cleaned up, suggesting they leave through the kitchen since he was sure there were quite a few folks out front waiting for them. Michele told Jim to meet her there; she would pull the car around.

"What about you, Steve?" Michele asked. "Are you coming home right after?"

"I'm going to the hospital to see Father George after I take care of something with Father Rick here," Steve answered his wife, pulling her in for a quick hug.

"Ok, don't be too long. I'm sure the phone will be ringing off the hook now that you two are infamous!" Michele told him. She noticed that her husband was shaking just a bit while she hugged him.

"Infamous?" Jim asked. "Are you sure you got that right, Mom?"

"Oh, yes," Michele answered quickly. "Only someone like your father here would pull a stunt like that!"

Steve cringed. He knew he would never live this down, and he hoped that the guilt that was beginning to creep in to his conscience would soon leave.

"I'll meet you at home shortly," Steve said to Michele, who was gathering her purse and getting out her car keys. "Jim, please stay off the phone and listen to your mom; remember just to say *no comment* to whomever asks you a question. Let's keep ourselves very humble over this ordeal."

Jim nodded and understood; it was the same approach he took to soccer. *Humble is the man who succeeds* was one of his father's favorite dadisms.

"Father Rick, can I see you at the tabernacle, please?" Steve asked.

"Sure, Steve. What's up?" Father Rick asked.

As Steve walked up, he noticed the leftover packages and mess that the EMS squad had left after preparing Father George for the trip to the hospital. "You're going to need to close the church for the remainder of today and possibly tomorrow so you can get this all cleaned up, Father," Steve told Father Rick.

"I guess so; I have the entrance to the church blocked off; members of your Men's Club met me in the parking lot once the word got out," Father Rick said. "Funny how I don't have to ask, and they are there to serve!"

"That's who we are, Father, and that's what we do!" Steve exclaimed as he opened the tabernacle to discuss with Father Rick what to do about the consecrated Host that he had picked up and that Jim had placed there.

Chapter 9

Northern Italy

At the monastery where the ancient order of monks known only as the Brown Robes resided, two of the brothers were sitting down to their midafternoon meal. The oldest members of their order, along with the Abbot, they were discussing the preparations for Vespers that night. As they read from their prayer books, deciding on the reading for that night, the abbot of the monastery, Abbot Giuseppe, came into the room holding an iPad, smiling.

"We have finally, after all of these years, had the prophecy of St. Pius X come true!"

Brother Michael and Brother Angelo both dropped their forks and looked up at the abbot in amazement.

Brother Angelo looked upon his abbot and asked "Did you say the prophecy has come true?"

"Yes, as it was stated in the letter given to our Brothers of the Secret before us," the Abbot said in a very serious tone. "It would be recorded for all to see and understand that this man has the grace of God upon him!"

The abbot sat down next to Brother Michael and pressed play on the video that was queued up to play on Facebook.

As the video showed Steve Michaels telling the gunman 'I believe,' the brothers looked at each other and smiled. It had been over one hundred years since Saint Pope Pius X had written the prophecy, entrusted to monastery hands for safe keeping, six months before his death in 1914. These three were known as the Brothers of the Secret and were chosen for their devotion to their order and for their belief in what the Lord could do through His servants. They were the fourth set of Brothers to be entrusted with their present duties and had already begun the process of picking their successors as the abbot had almost reached the age of 65.

As Brother Angelo looked at the iPad, he smiled again and said in a somewhat trembling voice, "Who would ever think that a man from the United States would have the faith and the courage to stand up for his faith like this? I do not know if I could have acted with such belief in our Lord faced with a gun to my head. How could Saint Pius X know that this would happen? He truly was a man of God who understood what the world needed in its faith!"

Brother Michael, the pessimist of the three, looked at the video again and this time asked for all to be extremely quiet as he needed to concentrate while he viewed it again. When it was finished, he could not doubt any longer that this was the sign that the prophecy had indeed come true. Now, he wondered to himself, was the world ready for the pontifical orders that were one hundred years old from one of the most conservative Popes that has ever sat on the throne of Saint Peter?

None of them knew what was in these orders; they had often played a guessing game about what was in the package that their monastery had been entrusted with all of these years. Saint Pius X himself was the only person who knew; it was written by his own hand, placed in a wooden chest, and sealed with his pontifical seal in January, 1914, on the feast day of the Epiphany. He then gave it to his private secretary to give to the abbot of their monastery with his handwritten order of what to look for and what to do when the prophecy had come true.

The day was getting on, and they had to prepare for evening Vespers. They agreed to meet after and open the first envelope, which would give them, the Brothers of the Secret, their orders from a Saint.

Chapter 10

St. Charles, Illinois

As Steve left the church, he waved to his fellow members of the St. Paul's Men's Club, who were blocking the entrance to the church and explaining to those who asked why they were there. As they waved back, one of them approached him and asked if he needed anything. Steve just counselled saying a prayer since Michele was not done with him yet for doing what he did. His fellow Club member wished him well and smiled, knowing Michele was not a lady to mess with.

As he got into his car, he could see the vans from news stations lined up on the side of the road and hoped that he could get away without driving like a madman. *Oh well*, he surmised. *I guess this is what fleeting fame is all about!* He made a left out of the parking lot, the barricades of orange cones moved out of the way by his friends.

As he drove, he noticed that his cell phone, which he never carried into church, was blinking, and he could only begin to imagine the voicemails and texts he would have to go through tonight when he would try to relax a bit after the events of the day.

As he pulled into the hospital drive, he noticed another line of news vans looking for anything to get into their 5 p.m. newscast, to be the first to report that they did not know anything new. Steve laughed to himself that one of Michele's closest friends, Elaine, who was a community reporter for the *Daily Herald,* was probably camped at the end of their driveway, waiting for him to get home. Well, he would hate to disappoint his wife, but no newspaper reporters or television folks were going to be getting his side of the story.

He pulled into the side lot of the hospital parking lot to take the long way around the building to the emergency room where they had taken Father George. As he walked, he kept feeling a shiver and could not for the life of him figure out why he was feeling that way. Making his way into the emergency room, he got the attention of a young nurse and asked if the police were there and could she take him to them. She nodded and asked if he was indeed the "I Believe" man. Steve nodded back but asked her to keep it to herself, please. She smiled and patted his hand as she led him to the back where the police were waiting to talk to Father George before went into surgery. As he rounded the corner, one of the detectives recognized him, smiled, and motioned for him to come closer. He shook Steve's hand and asked what he was doing there. Steve looked toward Father George and nodded that he needed a few minutes with the good father if they did not mind. The detective ushered the other policemen out of the room to give Steve and Father George some time alone.

"Looking a bit peaked there, Father George," Steve said as he drew nearer to talk with him.

"Well, Mister I Believe himself has come to see me, and what, may I ask, is the reason for this great honor?" Father George quipped, even though the pain on his face told a different story.

"Came to see how you are before they go in and fix whatever that madman did to you," Steve said, looking down at Father George.

"Well, according to the docs, it's pretty messed up in there. They can fix it, but I will be on the sideline for a while recovering," Father George replied as he reached out for Steve's hand. "You make sure that Jim knows how grateful I am for the help that he gave me after I was shot! And who says that God does not work wonder in his deeds?"

Steve looked at this man of the cloth, still giving a sermon while in a hospital bed. "You know, with a speech like that, you might want to get out of the saving souls business and get into the political arena."

Both men laughed. Michele had said the same thing to Father George just last week during one of the classes that Father George taught on the mysteries of the faith at St. Paul's.

"Really, Father, no joking around or pontificating. How are you?" Steve asked, his tone serious.

"Well, they have me drugged up a bit, but being shot is not as bad as I thought it would be. I mean, I hit my head and blacked out, but it really doesn't hurt that much," Father George answered, but Steve knew better. He'd had a shoulder injury during high school that hurt just terribly at the time.

"Um, Mr. Michaels?" the detective said. "They need to get him to surgery."

"I'll be back tomorrow. You'll be out for a while after," Steve said as the young nurse came back into the room to get Father George ready to be transported to the OR. "Oh, and nurse? Please make sure he behaves!"

The nurse smiled at the statement, and Steve left with the detectives for what he was sure would be a bit of an interrogation about the events that had unfolded. As they moved toward the door, another woman came up to Steve in the ER and asked if he was the "I Believe" man. *What have I gotten myself into?* was the only thing Steve thought as he left to go outside.

Chapter 11

Northern Italy

The Brothers of the Secret met together after
Evening Vespers with much anticipation to read what
had been entrusted to them for one hundred years.
Abbot Giuseppe's hands were shaking; none of them
had ever opened the chest where the secret was
stored by the first Brothers who held it. The chest was
a simple one made of wood and strengthened with
hand-forged metal bands. It had no adornments, and
the clasp and lock were over a century old
themselves. As the abbot inserted the key that he
carried around his neck always, the other two sat in
deep concentration on this burdensome secret that
was finally going to be lifted from their shoulders.
When the lock opened and the abbot removed it, they
all said a silent prayer as the lid, with much effort
from ten decades of being sealed, was slowly opened
to reveal the package that they had helped keep
secret.

It was a very large package tied with a metal
binding that reminded the Brothers of the wire
strands that formed a cross on the front of the box.
Affixed in the center was a wax seal with the
impression of Pope Pius X's ring to mark it an official

pontifical document. On the front of the package, written in a flowing script, were instructions written in Latin: *Patefacio quondam oraculum est presto, Pius X.*

The abbot read the phrase out loud, "Open once the prophecy is fulfilled, Pius X." Brother Michael passed a letter opener to his brother the abbot with trembling hands. As the seal was broken and the wire rope untied, all three of them felt an inner glow, wondering if Giuseppe Sarto, Pope Pius himself, was with them tonight. The abbot removed the outer wrapping; there were four letters bound in the same wire rope, each affixed with the same wax seal of Pope Pius X. They examined each letter, and the writing on each was the same flowing script that was on the outer wrapper. Each was labeled with a number, but only the letter numbered *one* had any instructions on it. In Latin was written *Illis quisnam have been mando patefacio iam* — to those entrusted, please open now.

Again the abbot repeated the opening of this letter, being very careful to keep the seal as closely intact as possible for preservation's sake as this was truly now another miracle to be attributed to Pope Pius X. As he unfolded the letter, the script was very easy to recognize: the same as the wrapper, again proving to them that this was the writing of a saint.

He cleared his voice and read aloud for the other Brothers to hear, *"On this day of celebration of the Epiphany in the year of our Lord 1914, I have entrusted to you my Brothers to guard this until the prophecy that I gave you has come true. You will be asked to produce a certain item to prove that I am giving you this myself, and this item can be found near the main altar of your monastery. I've had it hidden there in the grotto that I gave to the church while I was still known as Cardinal Sarto, Patriarch of Venice. You will find that which I gave to this monastery for safe keeping under the side nearest the altar in the Grotto of our Mother Mary. Look for the sign of the fisherman near the bottom, remove the panel, and take out the box. This give to the man who currently sits on the Throne of Saint Peter after the third letter is read.*

"Go to Saint Peter's and give him letter number two along with the box. This must be done with great haste, for if my prophecy has been fulfilled, then the reading of letters two and three must take place within three weeks' time of your reading these instructions. Go with the grace of God, Giuseppe Sarto."

All three of the Brothers stared at the letter signed by a saint knowing that their task was not over yet.

Chapter 12

Elgin, Illinois

Steve took the long way home from the hospital, hoping against hope that he could get home with no one stopping him. As he pulled into his subdivision, he notice that there was a police car blocking the entrance to his cul-de-sac. He stopped and rolled down the window as an Elgin police officer approached his car.

"Sir, this road is blocked until further notice. Please move on," the officer said in a stern voice.

"Well, wish I could, but I live in the house with another of your cars in my driveway. I'm Steve Michaels," Steve told the officer who looked at him with a bit of surprise.

"Do you have some identification, sir? No one is getting in here, per my orders!" the officer answered.

As Steve got out his driver's license, he recognized the partner of the officer asking for identification and waved him over to his car.

"Brad, it's okay. This is the man that we're here to guard until relieved," Officer Paul Roberts of the Elgin Police Department, and a neighbor of Steve's, called out to his partner.

"Sorry, Mr. Michaels. I didn't recognize you. I haven't seen the video that has everyone excited," Officer Brad Smith said. "Please pull forward so we can re-block off this road."

As Steve pulled into his driveway, careful to leave some room between his car and the police car already there, he sighed. All was not going to be normal until this died down.

"Paul, what in the hell is going on that you're blocking the street?" Steve asked as he extended his hand to his friend.

Officer Roberts took his friend's hand and shook it warmly, leaning in to give him a shoulder rub as well.

"Since your little escapade at St. Paul's this morning, we've been blocking the road. The other neighbors started to complain about the amount of traffic that was building up," Paul explained to his friend. "You have become just another instant celebrity, and I for one could not believe what you did, Mister I Believe!"

Steve looked at his friend sheepishly and asked him in a very soft voice, "How mad is Michele at me, and would you come in to protect me from her?"

"Steve, my good man, you are on your own with that one, but I'll ask her to take it easy on you, a big celebrity and all," Paul responded, laughing as he said it.

Steve rolled his eyes at his friend and began to walk toward his open garage to face the only woman he had ever loved in his life. Funny, he thought, that after meeting in high school and being married for eighteen years, he was still scared of her. "Oh well. Time to face the hangman," he said to no one.

As he walked in, he noticed the phone had a note on it saying, "Do Not Answer and That Means You, Dad!" signed by Jim. He began to chuckle a bit when out of the corner of his eye, he noticed Michele standing there with a determined look upon her face.

"So, *Mr. I Believe*, have a good time trying to figure out on the ride home how you were going to get out of this one? Of all the lame brain things you have done in your life, exposing our son to a gunman and then standing in front of him saying *I believe*...if it didn't cost so much, I would divorce you right now! And another thing, you big idiot: you could have been shot like Father George and left me caring for you. You've got another think coming if you think I am going to care for a patient who wanted to play John Wayne and step in front of a gunman. You know, maybe divorce might be better than this!" Michele was so red faced that she almost looked like she would pass out from lack of oxygen.

Steve looked at his wife and smiled, thinking *well, that wasn't so bad.*

"What in the hell are you smiling at?" Michele screamed at him. "Do you think this is funny or something?"

"Oh, no!" Steve exclaimed. "I know I frightened you. I don't think this is funny at all. Just you have no idea how cute you are when you get all flushed."

Michele walked up to her husband and threw a punch at his chest, which he gladly took as he put his arms around her, and she broke down in tears.

"Look," Steve calmly said as he held her. "I'm okay. I didn't get hurt, and our son is okay as well."

Michele looked up at him and struggled to get out of his hug but knew it was useless. He would not let her go until she was done being mad.

"Okay, calm now? I'm going to let you go, but you have to promise no more punching. Deal?" Steve asked, knowing that she was not done but trying to get ready for the next round.

"Yes, I'm done for now. You can let go," Michele said as her tone began to soften. "But I'm not completely done with you yet, Mister I Believe!"

As Steve let her go, he saw Jim standing by the stairs, grinning while his mom tried to calm down.

"You know, she has a right to be angry," Jim said to his dad in a stage whisper that got a commiserating look from his mother.

"Are you okay, Jim?" Steve asked in a serious manner, which announced to both of them that he knew play time was over.

"I am, Dad. Thanks for asking. I felt a bit funny on the ride home, but I guess that was just the adrenaline wearing off. So, how was Father George?" Jim asked his father.

"He was getting ready to go into surgery when I saw him. He was in a good mood, but I think it was the drugs talking. I'm going to see him again tomorrow after work to check on him," Steve replied.

"Oh, okay, Dad. I'm going to do some homework and try to relax a bit. The phone was really busy when we got home, but it's slowed down a bit now," Jim told his dad and headed upstairs to his room.

"Jim, if you need to talk or anything about what happened today, please just grab me or your mom. Deal?" Steve said in a somewhat stern way.

"I will. Mom has been telling me the same thing since we got home. She's really upset with you by the way," Jim said with a smile.

"I know," Steve answered trying not to smile back at him. "Now get so I can have a couple of minutes with your mom!"

"Michele!" Steve bellowed in his usual loud voice. "I do believe you want another piece of me for something!"

Chapter 13

Northern Italy

As the abbot looked at the letter again, Brother Angelo was busy finding the keys to the monastery van. He didn't know when they were going to get ready to go to the Vatican.

"Abbot," Brother Michael asked. "Do we just show up and bang on the door saying we need to see the Pope?"

"No," Abbot Giuseppe laughed at his friend. "But I am going to call his Eminence the Secretariat of State who was at the seminary with me all those years ago."

"You never told us that you were there with him!" both of the Brothers exclaimed at once.

"In my class, there were five who became Cardinals, and one of them now sits on the Throne of St. Peter," Giuseppe said in a matter of fact tone. "I choose to be a monk; they chose to seek higher office. Funny how life comes back around in a full circle, my brothers. Now we get to tell the Pope that he has to do something!"

"Do you think he will believe us? I mean a prophecy that is one hundred years old and only we know about it...Let's hope what the good saint hid in the box will convince him that we are not crazy old monks who have spent too much time in a cave praying!" Brother Michael said with his usual doom of being the pessimist of the group.

"We will see," Giuseppe said. "We will see. Now, let's go find this box and make that call!"

As they left to go to the main chapel of the monastery, the Brothers were still in shock that this was finally happening. When they reached the chapel, they checked to make sure none of the other brothers were praying or mediating; then, they proceeded to genuflect to the tabernacle and go to the Grotto of Mary. On the bottom nearest the main altar, in the next to last panel, was the sign of the fisherman. It was so small that no one would have noticed it unless they found it by accident. The panel was not cemented in like the others, but only a light grouting had been used. This came out with the small hand chisel that Brother Michael had brought. Once the grout was cleared, the panel was easy to remove; there, as the letter said it would be, was a plain metal box sealed in wax to protect whatever was inside.

"Take a picture of this and the panel so that the Holy Father can see that we did not make this up!" Abbot Giuseppe told Brother Angelo. Angelo took the digital camera from his robe and took a series of

57

pictures of both the box in its hidden storage compartment and the panel that was next to it. "That should be enough. Please take the box out, Angelo," the Abbot commanded.

Once the box was removed, they noticed that the same lock that was on the box containing the letter was on this one as well. Affixed to the top of this box was the Seal of St. Pius X in the same brilliant red wax that was on the letters.

Brother Michael picked it up and commented, "This weighs so little. I wonder what is in it."

"We all shall see. You two are going with me to the Vatican as keepers of the secret; I could not take all the credit, my brothers, for a hundred of years of service to St. Pius X!" Abbot Giuseppe patted both men on the on their backs as he took the box from Brother Michael's hand. "Now let's go and call a Cardinal with the news that a Pope has given us Pontifical Orders to carry out!"

"One-hundred-year-old orders!" was all that Brother Angelo said as they left the chapel.

Chapter 14

Vatican City State

The office of the Secretariat of State of the Vatican City State was so expansive that it competed with the size of most conference rooms. Its size was used to show that even though he was not the Pope, he was the most senior Cardinal and the one who ran the day to day operations of the Vatican and its diplomatic missions as well. He was at his desk late into the night, as was his custom, so that the phone call did not seem out of the ordinary to him when his secretary buzzed him to announce that there was an urgent call for him.

"Cardinal Albani here, how may I help you?" Giovanni Cardinal Albani answered.

"Giovanni, it is I, Abbot Giuseppe of the Brown Robes. I need to have a private audience with His Holiness on Tuesday. Let's say before lunch?" the abbot said to his old classmate.

"Giuseppe, did you say a private audience? I did hear you correctly?" Cardinal Albani replied.

"What, has your high office affected your hearing, my old friend?" Giuseppe laughed.

"No, my hearing is fine. May I ask what is the nature of this most unusual request from the Abbot of the Brown Robes?" Cardinal Albani asked in a most curious way. It was extremely out of character for his friend but also a breach of Vatican protocol to ask for an immediate audience with His Holiness.

"I am under orders from St. Pope Pius X to meet immediately, if not sooner, with the current man who sits on the Throne of St. Peter!" Giuseppe informed his friend.

"Did you say St. Pius X?" Cardinal Albani asked in an unbelieving tone.

"Yes, let me come to your office Tuesday morning and tell you the prophecy of St. Pope Pius X and what my orders are," the abbot replied.

"I can meet you here at 9 a.m. on Tuesday. I have something planned, but I will clear my schedule to meet you. Until Tuesday morning then, Giuseppe!" Cardinal Albani told his friend.

"Yes, your Eminence, until then!" the abbot answered.

As the call ended, Cardinal Albani sat stunned that his friend and classmate from so long ago would call him at this hour with this request. What had a saint who died a century ago prophesied, and why was it given to the Brown Robes to hold? "I do not like mysteries," Cardinal Albani said out loud to himself. "I do not like them at all!"

Elgin, Illinois

The morning broke to find Steve awake in his den reading; he had not gone to bed the night before. The events of Sunday had left him emotionally drained, and the constant pressure from the media, friends, and family to talk about it was overwhelming. The phone had not stopped ringing, but he had handled that by simply unplugging it from the wall. His cell phone voicemail box was full, and he was not answering that either. Paul and the other officer had left by dinner as the fascination with what had happened began to fade just a bit.

Steve turned on his computer to find his email inbox overflowing but did not look at them; instead, he put them in a folder marked unread until later. He sent an email to his manager at work and informed him that he would not be in today. He needed some time; plus, he did not want to face the attention at work just yet. As he sat there with a cup of coffee, the events of yesterday unfolding over and over, he was grateful that he and Jim were unharmed and that they could face another day.

Michele came down the stairs quietly, not knowing if Steve had fallen asleep in his den chair, and as she turned the corner to check, she was greeted with a smile and wave to come and sit on his lap.

"Morning, you," Michele whispered to Steve. "Did you sleep even a wink?

"No, not a wink. I closed my eyes a couple of times, but what happened just kept unfolding over and over," Steve answered her softly, which was a bit unnerving to Michele.

"You okay with all of this, Steve? Do you want to talk to someone about this to help you deal with it all?" Michele asked but not in her usual, overpowering, mother-hen way. She could see with concern that the killing of the gunman was beginning to take a toll on Steve but did not want to press since he was famous for hiding his emotions from all.

"I might need to talk to someone but not today, Michele. Okay?" Steve answered her, again softly.

Michele immediately understood that all was not right with her husband. This was the man who had informed her, just a month ago, that if he ever needed to talk about his feelings, they would be putting dirt on him in a box six feet under.

"When you're ready, just let me know. I'll set it up and take care of it. In the meantime, you can wake me to talk anytime, Steve, or just come to bed and hold me. I don't mind," Michele informed her husband as she got up to make more coffee. As she got up, Steve gave her a playful swat on her butt, which caused a smile on her lips. How that man could still want to play after all that had happened to him in the past twenty-four hours was amazing, but then again it was him.

"Is Jim going to school today?" Steve asked as he followed her into the kitchen.

"I think so; he hasn't been as deeply affected by this ordeal as you have been. I mean that is a nice way, Steve. Please don't take it wrongly," Michele said to Steve seriously.

"I understand what you're saying, Michele. I'm just glad he didn't see what I did first hand. I still don't know how I was able to do it myself; I didn't think. I just reacted to the situation and tried to save those other people in church," Steve mentioned the killing for the first time since he had come home the day before. "I mean, this man just came out of nowhere and shot Father George. I just sat there while Jim ordered the other altar server to take cover and then he crawled up to him. When it finally kicked in what had happened, I got up and ran to help Jim. You should of have seen him, Michele. He was in total control of the situation and ordered me to get a towel and the cloths from the altar to stop the bleeding. He certainly has a lot of you in him!" Steve said, the last part making him smile as he grabbed Michele in a bear hug so he would not get punched again by her.

"Oh, and what do you mean by that? *A lot of me in him?* You had better not let me go, or I will deck you, mister!" Michele exclaimed as she tried to get out of the bear hug that Steve had her in. She was beginning to laugh; he always tickled her when he did this, and she was trying to keep quiet for fear of waking Jim.

"Geez, you two, why don't you take it somewhere else?" Jim said as he pushed his way around them to get a cup of coffee. "All you two ever do is act like high school freshmen on their first date. It is so embarrassing! I hope you both know that!" Jim exclaimed to his parents. "How are you doing, Dad? I know you didn't sleep last night. Are you okay?" Jim asked.

"I'm fine, buddy. Just got a lot on my mind," Steve answered his son as he let go of Michele who was fixing her robe, in disarray from the bear hug. "Are you going to school today? Are you up to it?"

"Yep, you guys taught me to tackle trouble head on, but I'm meeting with my counselor first thing. I emailed her last night, and she's meeting me before my first class this morning," Jim told his dad maturely.

"Well, it's good to talk things through, but you can talk to me or your mom anytime," Steve told his son, looking at him with the same amazement that he had felt when Jim was giving first aid to Father George.

"I know, Dad, but this is about school and coping with it and the teasing I'm going to get. Just want some help with that.

Not every day you save a man's life and your dad becomes an internet sensation. By the way, you are at over one million hits this morning. I checked. I know you haven't looked at it except on Mom's phone at church," Jim told his dad as he left the kitchen with his coffee.

"Hmm, wonder when he became so grown up," Steve said to the wall.

"Well, having you for a dad does put a little extra pressure on him, you know?" Michele piped up from the table where she was enjoying her coffee.

"Don't you have to go to work or something?" Steve jokingly laughed back at her.

"Umm, not today; I took it off thinking Jim was going to stay home. But since you're off, I get to babysit at least one of my men!" Michele said, smiling at her husband who never asked her to take care of him even when he was sick.

"Thanks, darling. But I will ask if I need something," Steve replied. Then, in a serious tone he said, "I mean that. This is a totally different thing that I'm trying to deal with in my life. Thanks for being there, Michele." He finished his statement and winked at her as he left the room.

Michele wondered if this had done something to him. He hadn't come to bed last night, and the last time that happened was when his father passed away.

"Well, I'm here if you need me!" she yelled, knowing he was already upstairs getting ready for the day.

Chapter 15

Northern Italy

Abbot Giuseppe, Brother Michael, and Brother Angelo were loading the monastery's van with their travel bags when Brother Michael asked if they could visit the Sistine Chapel again. Both of his Brothers winced; they knew they could never get him out of there in less than four hours as he talked about his obsession with the frescos of Michelangelo, whom, he reminded them again, he was named after. The abbot just smiled and politely reminded him of why they were going to Rome.

"So his Eminence is willing to see us at 9 a.m. Tuesday? Do you think he has doubts, Giuseppe?" Brother Michael asked.

"Oh, Giovani Albani has doubts about everything, Michael. He even doubts daily the outcome of the last conclave election!" laughed Giuseppe. "He has always thought that he would be the Vicar of Christ someday!"

"What did you think you would be, Giuseppe, when you took your vows?" Angelo asked as they were pulling out of the grounds.

"To be honest, just a servant of God. The Brown Robes fascinated me even as a boy. My father would bring me here to this same monastery for Sunday mass. I was intrigued even as a little boy by the faith and devotion that the brothers before us had. Did you know that when Cardinal Sarto visited and donated the Grotto of Mary that my grandmother was here to witness it? And this was right before the conclave that elected him Pope!" Abbot Giuseppe told his brothers.

"So your grandmother saw him, Pius X, in person?" Michael asked.

"Yes. She bragged about it her whole life. He did it in such an unexpected way that the whole town was taken by surprise. She always thought that he would have donated something beautiful to his home town of Riese, which is now known as Pio X for him," Abbot Giuseppe answered.

"So, if he donated the Grotto then, how did he affix the panel with the sign of the fisherman and place the box there? I mean the Grotto of Mary is in our main chapel. Certainly someone would have seen him do the work," Michael asked.

"The Grotto of Mary was placed next to the altar before World War I for safe keeping; it was originally outside in the cove next to what is now our main living quarters. The abbot had it placed there in 1914, the same year of the prophecy, so it had to be placed there during the dismantling and moved to its present location," Abbot Giuseppe answered his friend.

As the three began to watch the hills of Northern Italy fade in their rearview mirror, they each began to wonder how Saint Pope Pius X could have orchestrated all of these moves with all of the turmoil in the world at that time.

Abbot Giuseppe broke the silence by adding, "You know, he is not a saint for nothing!" At this all three of them smiled and settled in for their long trip to Rome.

Chapter 16

The Vatican

Giovanni Cardinal Albani paced nervously in his oversized office, which allowed him to walk a full thirty paces from his desk to door. *What,* he thought to himself, *would cause a man, dead a hundred years, to leave a prophecy, and why only now is it coming to light? Why does it have to be now when I am in this position of Secretariat of State? Why?"*

As he paced, his private secretary, Father Palo, came in with coffee and tea and noticed how upset His Eminence was.

"Your Eminence, what is troubling you?" Father Palo asked. "After that call Sunday night from the Abbot of the Brown Robes, you have not been yourself."

"I'm going to need you to take a little extended break once the dear abbot gets here, Alphonse. Please leave and lock the outer office once you show the abbot in," Cardinal Albani told his secretary.

"As you wish, your Eminence," Father Palo said to the Cardinal as he bowed and moved toward the door.

"Oh, another thing, Alphonse. Do not bow when you leave after you show the good abbot in.

He is an old classmate of mine from my days in the seminary, and he is always teasing me about my present position. No need to add more fuel to a fire!" Cardinal Albani said with a laugh.

"I will not, your Eminence," Father Palo said with a strange expression on his face. This was extremely out of the ordinary for the Cardinal.

As Giovanni kept pacing, he looked up and noticed the clock on the desk read 8:55 a.m. He walked around to his phone and pressed the intercom button. "Please escort the Abbot of the Brown Robes in as he is just standing there waiting for the clock to strike 9:00 a.m.!"

The door opened into his oversized office, and in walked the Abbot of the Brown Robes and his two assistants, one carrying a very old-looking wooden chest. Their brown robes were exquisite, made from one stretch of cloth with almost no visible seams. On Giuseppe's last trip to the Vatican, Cardinal Albani remembered asking how they were made, and his old friend had just looked at him and smiled. That always stood out in his mind, an abbot who could turn a smile into a thousand words and then finish the story with a nod. Giovanni wondered if, had Giuseppe not entered the Monastery of the Brown Robes, he would be sitting on the Throne of St. Peter instead of the current Pope.

"My good friend Giuseppe, how are you? Was your trip good?" Cardinal Albani asked warmly, moving forward to embrace his old friend.

"My dear Eminence Albani, how nice of you to receive us on such short notice!" the abbot replied.

"Well, not like you gave me much choice, my dear abbot!" the Cardinal answered back with a look of worry on his face. "It is not every day that the Abbot of the Brown Robes asks to see His Holiness. Father Palo," Cardinal Albani said, turning his attention. "You may leave, and thank you for seeing in my friends."

"Yes, your Eminence. I will be leaving as you requested," Father Palo said, catching himself almost bowing. As Father Palo closed the door behind himself, he wondered what was about to happen.

"I see your secretary does not know how to leave the office of the Secretariat of State. What, no bowing to his Lord Eminence?" Abbot Giuseppe teased his friend.

"I asked him not to bow since I knew you would tease me, and yet I still get teased," the Cardinal laughed out loud, still shaking his friend's hand. "Please, would you all like a seat? My brothers, please pull up those chairs there and bring them to my desk. Now, my dear abbot, who have you brought with you today?" the Cardinal asked.

"Your Eminence, may I introduce the other Brothers of the Secret, Brother Michael and Brother

Angelo? We have been entrusted with the Prophecy of St Pope Pius X, which is why we are here," reported Abbot Giuseppe.

"You say the Prophecy of St. Pope Pius X? I don't know of what you are speaking," the Cardinal said in an inquiring voice.

"Well, my Eminence, let me start at the beginning," Giuseppe stated seriously. "We, the Brown Robes, were given this chest, which was sealed with the pontifical seal until yesterday, by the private secretary of Saint Pius X in January of 1914."

"How do I know that it was sealed?" asked a very curious Cardinal.

"Brother Angelo, would you please show his Eminence here the video on your iPad?" asked Abbot Giuseppe.

Brother Michael had thought up this little bit of evidence, being the pessimist of the three. Brother Angelo queued up the recording, which showed the reading of the prophecy and the seal on the lock of the chest for all to see. The seal was clearly that of St. Pius X as it could be seen on all of his papers in the Vatican archives. As the video continued, it showed the opening of the lock and the letters inside. The wire wrapping on all of them was intact with the pontifical seal in the middle of each them.

"This is some very impressive evidence, Abbot!" the Cardinal exclaimed. "Nice idea to record it to show that it has not been tampered with!"

Brother Michael smiled smugly, which the other two brothers knew would be repeated the whole way back to their monastery.

"As you can see, your Eminence, this is the real thing, and our orders are that we need to see His Holiness with this matter now!" Abbot Giuseppe said sternly, not wanting to get caught up in the usual, infamous Vatican politics.

"Will you allow me to be there for the reading of what is in the letters, my dear abbot?" the Cardinal asked.

"That is not my decision, your Eminence, as we both work for the same man, and he can have stay whom he wishes," said Giuseppe with a wink to his old classmate.

"You always were smarter than I, Giuseppe!" the Cardinal exclaimed.

"Maybe, my friend, but I do not wear a red hat! So when can we see His Holiness?" the abbot replied.

Cardinal Albani knew that he would not win in this exchange with his old classmate, who was an excellent debater, so he reached for his phone. "Let me call His Holiness's private secretary right now and see what we can do!"

Chapter 17

"Yes, your Eminence, may I help you this morning?" came the cheery voice of Father Tommaso Antonelli through the speaker phone.

"Tommaso, I have the Abbot of the Brown Robes, Abbot Giuseppe, here in my office, and he needs, or excuse me, *wishes* to see His Holiness," the Cardinal said in a very uncertain voice.

"His Holiness is attending to a meeting but will be free in fifteen minutes if you wish to walk over then with my dear Abbot Giuseppe," was the reply from His Holiness's private secretary.

"Thank you, Tommaso. That will be great," the Cardinal answered.

"May I ask what this is pertaining to, your Eminence, if the Abbot of the Brown Robes is with you?" Father Antonelli asked.

"Father, this is Abbot Giuseppe. Let's just say that it is official business for His Holiness, and I am under orders to report to him at once," Giuseppe interjected.

"Hmm, orders to see him at once? But His Holiness did not ask me to set this up," Father Antonelli answered cautiously, not wanting to sound like he had forgotten something.

"I did not say the orders were from him, did I?" Abbot Giuseppe asked and winked at the Cardinal as he did.

"No, you did not, Abbot," Father Antonelli answered. "See you in about fifteen minutes then." Father Antonelli hung up the phone, intrigued by what was going on and whose orders Abbot Giuseppe was following.

"Well then, we are off to see His Holiness, Abbot. Brothers, please follow me," Cardinal Albani motioned to the door as he got up from behind his desk.

"Brother Michael, please bring the chest and your iPad with you. I have a feeling we will need both for His Holiness," Abbot Giuseppe said as they walked the thirty paces to the door.

As they walked, Abbot Giuseppe smiled, knowing that after one hundred years, the burden of the secret would soon no longer be his to worry about; no need to pick replacements or wonder what this had been all about. He just hoped His Holiness believed their proof and listened to whatever St. Pius X had written. It could be nothing, or the prophecy could be a sign of things to come, a new idea of a new order that could set his Church on a different path. As he wondered, he looked at his companions and smiled, knowing that their part was almost done, and they all could go back to their simple life of devotion and prayer to Mather Mary and her Son.

He wondered out loud if this feeling that was coming over him was relief or grief that the secret was going to be exposed after all of these years.

Cardinal Albani asked the brothers a simple question: "Do you believe what is in that chest is real?"

All three of them nodded and answered in unison, "Yes!"

Then Abbot Giuseppe added, "We have more proof, but that is for His Holiness only, your Eminence."

Cardinal Albani just smiled, knowing he had been played by his old friend, and wondered exactly how good this man would have been playing the politics of the Curia. As he walked, he wondered if his job as Secretariat of State was in jeopardy or if whatever was in that blasted chest would change their world.

When they reached the outer door to the pontifical offices, they were met by a guard in plain clothes who looked at them rather harshly; he did not like surprises, and the Brown Robes were surprises.

Chapter 18

As the four of them entered the outer office, led by the Cardinal, they were greeted warmly by Father Antonelli. "Your Eminence, my dear Abbot and Brothers, welcome. All I can say is that His Holiness is a bit mystified to hear that you needed—oh, excuse me, *wanted* to see him this morning. He has asked that you be escorted in right away."

"Thank you, Father, and sorry to put a wrinkle into the schedule that you keep for His Holiness," Abbot Giuseppe said warmly.

"No bother, my dear Abbot. He was rather surprised when he heard you were here. Kept commenting on how you were the smartest one in his class at the seminary so many years ago," Father Antonelli said with a bit of awe in his voice at the knowledge that the Cardinal and the abbot were classmates of His Holiness. *What a class that must of have been*, he thought to himself. As Father Antonelli led the way, he knocked very softly on the door to the inner office and waited to hear the customary response of His Holiness Pope Alexander IX.

"Who needs to bother me now, Tommaso?" Pope Alexander IX called out in a warm and amused fashion.

"Your Holiness," Father Antonelli said as he entered the room and bowed. "May I present his Eminence Cardinal Albani, Abbot Giuseppe of the Brown Robes, and his companions, Brother Angelo and Brother Michael?"

"My Brothers, please come in," the Pope exclaimed. Abbot Giuseppe was an old and dear friend, but this was puzzling to him. He knew his friend would not come to the Vatican unless it was something very urgent and very important.

Led by Cardinal Albani, each went forward and kissed the ring of the Vicar of Christ. Abbot Giuseppe went last. As he stood up after bowing and kissing the ring, he was grabbed in a huge embrace by His Holiness who was so glad to see his friend from so long ago.

"Since it is not time for your *ad limina Apostolorum* visit, I take it that it is something very important to get you out of your comfortable monastery," the Pope guessed.

"Yes, your Holiness, it is," Abbot Giuseppe said in a voice that showed much respect to his old classmate.

"Well then, let's hear what made you and your brothers travel to see me today!" the Pope exclaimed.

"I would like to start by reading to your Holiness the prophecy of St. Pius X, which we, the Brown Robes, have been holding in secret for the past hundred years," Giuseppe said in a voice that made even His Holiness sit up and take notice.

Abbot Giuseppe began to read an aged letter that had been carefully put into a clear view page for safety: *"I Pius X, on the day of our Lord's Epiphany, this January of 1914, do hereby give to you, the Abbot of the Brown Robes, this prophecy for safe keeping and what is in the sealed chest. This chest is not to be opened until the prophecy has come true. Please keep this safe from all, and follow what is in the chest after it has come true to the letter, and that, my dear Abbot, is my pontifical order to you and your successors.*

"The Prophecy of Giuseppe Sarto, Cardinal Patriarch of Venice and Bishop of Rome. Faith and belief is the steadfast vision of our Lord Jesus Christ, whom I have tried to follow all of my life. But, something has been given to me by our Lord that I must write down for the world to see when this comes to pass.

"There will be a man from the Americas who will display great faith and have the utmost belief in our Lord. He will withstand a great pressure of faith and will follow his belief in our Lord to do the right thing. He will be faced with death for his beliefs but will not let it sway him, and he will triumph over this, and this will be recorded for the whole world to see. He will win this fight on his beliefs and his beliefs alone.

"Once this has come to pass, you will open the chest and follow the instructions inside; then, you will take my prophecy to the Bishop of Rome and present him with the chest and what is inside for him to follow.

This I declare motu proprio, and it shall be followed with no excuse or divergence.

"Signed this Day of our Lord 06 January 1914.
Pius X pp, Bishop of Rome."

When Giuseppe finished reading the prophecy, His Holiness and Cardinal Albani both looked stunned at what had just been presented to them.

"How did you make the determination that this has come to pass?" asked His Holiness.

Abbot Giuseppe reached out to take the iPad Brother Michael was holding out as if they were reading each other's minds. The abbot queued up the video of Steve Michaels, "Mister I Believe." Once the video was finished, His Holiness sat there stunned and agreed without saying a thing that the prophecy had indeed come true.

"How and when did this happen?" His Holiness asked with the stunned expression still on his face.

"It was uploaded Sunday to YouTube, and it happened in St. Charles, Illinois, in the United States of America. This man, Steve Michaels, is a parishioner there and a member of the St. Paul's Men's Club. From all accounts he is a leader in his community and his church," the abbot answered His Holiness.

"What is in the chest? I agree with you that this man has faced death and that his belief carried him through. Who would have thought that this could happen in today's world with what is going on around us? And for this all to happen in the United States of America of all countries!" His Holiness exclaimed.

"Your Holiness, we might want to reconsider. This is completely out of character for St. Pius X, who as we all know was one of the most conservative Popes of the twentieth century," Cardinal Albani said in his most unofficial political view.

"Always looking out for the Curia and the Political angle, aren't you, your Eminence?" Abbot Giuseppe said, a stern tone to his voice.

"Now, now, my brothers, let's leave the political aspects of this alone for the time being. I am sure that Giovanni would love to debate you on that matter, Giuseppe, but then again he would lose just like the last time you two went at each other if my memory serves me correctly!" Pope Alexander said with a wink to his two longtime friends. "How about we do what we have been ordered to do? By a saint no less!"

Brother Michael brought the chest forward and opened it to reveal the one opened letter and the four still sealed, as well as the box with the pontifical seal on the top. He handed the letter marked *number two* to his abbot, who in turn gave it to His Holiness as the directions told him to.

On the top of the letter in the script of Pius X was marked *Letter Two, to be open by the Vicar of Christ* and signed *This day of our Lord, 06 January 1914."*

"Well, it looks official, doesn't it, your Eminence?" Pope Alexander asked his Secretariat of State.

"It does, but fakes of the pontifical seal have been known to happen before," Cardinal Albani said, beginning to sound like a doubting Thomas.

"Enough, Giovanni. You will be respectful of these matters, or you shall leave. Do you understand, or do you need to leave right now?" Pope Alexander asked.

Both Brother Angelo and Brother Michael winced for the Cardinal, who sat there like a schoolboy caught doing something wrong.

"I shall be respectful, your Holiness, and beg your forgiveness," Cardinal Albani sheepishly answered the Bishop of Rome.

"So let's see what letter two says. My dear abbot, would you do the honors and open this for me? Tommaso, would you please get him the letter opener from my desk?" His Holiness asked.

Tommaso retrieved the letter opener and gave it to Abbot Giuseppe, smiling at him in recognition that the Cardinal was just dressed down in front of them all. As Giuseppe cut the seal open and untied the wire strands that held the letter together, a pin drop could be heard in the room, filled as it was with

the anticipation of what was in this letter. He
unfolded the letter and asked for Brother Michael to
record the reading of the letter so that there would be
an official record of it. His Holiness nodded his
approval, and Brother Michael positioned the iPad to
record the reading of the letter. As the letter was
passed to His Holiness, he put on his reading glasses
and began to read it out loud for all to hear.

Chapter 19

*"Greetings to you, Vicar of Christ and Bishop of
Rome, from His most humble servant Giuseppe Sarto! If
you are reading this letter, then my prophecy has come to
pass, and the Abbot of the Brown Robes has sought you
out.*

*My thanks to the Brown Robes for keeping my
secret. I knew they could be trusted as their belief in our
Mother Mary is legendary and I base my belief in her.*

*I am issuing you the following pontifical order
motu proprio and will hold the Abbot of the Brown Robes
as my personal representative in this matter, which will
ensure that my orders are carried out. My dear abbot, by
my order, I now declare you to be elevated to Cardinal
Priest in my service and to have your successor take over as
abbot in your monastery immediately.*

*To the Vicar of Christ, I would imagine that you are
there with your Secretariat of State. I assume him to be like
all political men in his position who probably finished
second or third in the last conclave, so I ask you to dismiss
him from your presence and to keep only your private
secretary and the new Cardinal with you for the continued
reading of this letter.*

His Holiness looked up in astonishment. St.
Pius X was so accurate in his description of Cardinal
Albani, and this was written some hundred years ago.

"Cardinal Albani, you may leave this room, proceed back to your office, and await my call to come back by command of His Holiness St. Pius X," Pope Alexander said to his Secretariat of State in a stern, official tone.

"But, your Holiness, as this letter could deal with matters of state and policy, I implore you to let me hear what else has been written! My advice could be beneficial. Once this gets out, which it will, it could become a tempest quickly!" Cardinal Albani pleaded with his Pope.

"Cardinal Albani, this will not get out unless you leak it! I do believe that you have just stated that this will get out, so make up your mind quickly about your silence. Do I suspect that you are going against the orders of a Pope and one who has been declared a saint as well? Please try to impress us with your political savvy and get yourself out of this mess in front of these witnesses. Perhaps I should have placed a different Cardinal in your position, but I believe in keeping my enemies close by to keep a better eye on them!" Pope Alexander said in a loud voice as he rose to greet Cardinal Albani, who had also stood. "Do you rise up against me, Giovanni, the Vicar of Christ? Well, do you?"

Brother Angelo stood up as well. He was behind Cardinal Albani, for he was the lowest-ranking priest there in the meeting. He did so in such a swift and quiet manner that all it took was a nod from the new Cardinal Giuseppe to get him to move in front of Cardinal Albani and put himself in between him and Pope Alexander. When Cardinal Albani realized that he was outmaneuvered, he sought a quick and skillful retreat from the Pope's office, but before that could happen, Brother Michael blocked his retreat.

"I believe that you owe my Holiness here an apology, Cardinal Albani!" Brother Michael said in a voice that made even the Pope sit up and take notice.

"Your Holiness," Cardinal Albani spoke in a very soft and humble voice. "I do apologize to you and to everyone here for my conduct and actions." As he finished, he realized that he may have just ended his tenure as Secretariat of State and would perhaps be replaced by lunchtime.

"Tommaso, please show Cardinal Albani out and have him placed incommunicado by my guards. Cardinal, your cell phone, please," Pope Alexander said with an outreached hand.

As Cardinal Albani handed over his cell phone, he knew that he had no one to blame but himself for this. Being ordered held incommunicado was the worst possible thing to happen to him; he knew that his fate was undecided, but waiting to perhaps be fired would be the worst part of his punishment. As he walked out, he looked back at his old classmates and knew that each of them was smarter than he. It only registered a bit too late to save him.

When the door had closed, Father Antonelli returned to take his place again. The new Cardinal Giuseppe looked over to Brother Michael to see if the recording was still on. Brother Michael nodded, knowing that this outburst had sealed the fate of Cardinal Albani.

"So, my dear new Cardinal, it seems that St. Pius X knew more about everything than we could of have imagined! Funny how a man gone for one hundred years could, with a couple of sentences, make a decision that I had no idea how to make happen myself!" Pope Alexander exclaimed. "So let's continue reading the words of a saint, shall we?" And His Holiness began reading from where he had left off.

"I know that you must be startled by my frankness in having your Secretariat of State removed, but it is vital to what I am about to have you do. Please forgive my actions, but sometimes the fewer who know, the best, and in this matter, it is the best.

"I now command you to bring the man from the Americas to you there in Rome. Make him comfortable in his journey to you but make it with all due haste for what is to become of him depends on us.

"Once this man is in the presence of you and my dear new Cardinal of the Brown Robes, you may give him letter three to open. This is asked of you based on the belief

that what I have foretold is for our Holy Mother Church through the intersession of our Lord's Mother, Mary.

"*Pius X pp, Bishop of Rome.*"

As he finished reading the last word, His Holiness Pope Alexander IX let out a very loud gasp and exclaimed, "My dear abbot, I would have canonized Pope Pius for just the content of this letter alone!" As he finished he passed the letter to Brother Michael and asked that it be returned to the chest for safe keeping. "Now, let's do what the Pope has ordered us to do! Tommaso, please contact the Apostolic Nuncio to the United States immediately. I have a mission for him to carry out," His Holiness instructed. As he finished, he nodded to Abbot, now Cardinal, Giuseppe and said very softly to him, "I wonder what surprise is next from our revered Saint Pius?"

Giuseppe answered even softer so only His Holiness could hear, "I do not know, but it certainly has been worth the wait. Don't you agree?"

"It has, and I have only known about it for forty-five minutes or so; now go break it to Cardinal Albani that he is no longer the Secretariat of State for me!"

"Holiness, why don't you keep him? He owes both of us now, and with witnesses in Brothers Michael and Angelo, he can hardy go against St. Pius's wishes, no matter what they are," Abbot

Giuseppe said with a serious tone but with a whimsical smile on his face.

"I never would have taken you to understand and play this game of politics with the Curia so deftly, my dear abbot!" His Holiness said with a laugh.

As they walked, His Holiness asked Father Tommaso to get the phone number for St. Paul's Parish, which Mr. Michaels belonged to in the USA.

"Would you like me to make the call, your Holiness?" Abbot Giuseppe asked.

"Oh no, my dear Abbot. This is a call that only the Bishop of Rome should make. I know I would not believe anything that I am about to ask of these men myself if I had not read that letter," His Holiness exclaimed as they walked to the Secretariat of State's office to remind Cardinal Albani that he worked for the Pope alone.

Chapter 20

Elgin, Illinois

2 a.m. had come and gone, and Steve was at odds with his conscience and with what he should do; sleep was not an option, but he knew that he needed it badly. He grabbed an afghan from the couch and kicked up his chair to try to close his eyes for a few hours. As he settled into an uneasy sleep, the events of Sunday kept playing over and over in his mind. He knew that he had done the right thing in protecting all of those people, but he had killed a man to achieve it; he had killed a man, and even though he knew it was right, it still troubled him. Funny, he thought as he woke for the third time, how a man's conscience can control everything and make him understand what he has done right or wrong. He looked at the clock, and it came back to him with the number 4:30 a.m. More sleep would not come to him again this night.

He got up to find Michele looking at him; she took his hand and led him to the couch. As he sat next to her, Steve put his head on her chest and listened to her heart beating, thankful that she was there to comfort him.

As she pulled the afghan over them both, he drifted off to sleep with the demons of Sunday behind him, listening to the love of his life's heartbeat.

When Jim came down the stairs at 6:30 a.m. to get ready for school, Michele put a finger to her lips, motioning to her son to be as quiet as possible. Jim smiled and knew that his dad was finally asleep for the first time since Sunday. Waiting for his cup of coffee to brew, he very softly asked if she wanted a cup; she smiled and nodded.

Michele thought how much Jim had grown up since Sunday and how proud she was of her son. Without Steve's or Jim's knowledge, she had placed a call to the Boy Scouts to find out the requirements for the Honor Medal that the Boy Scouts gave to a Scout or adult leader who acted in a heroic way to save someone's life. She knew that this award was hardly ever given, but the way that Jim acted in getting the other altar server out of the way and then giving first aid to Father George, as well as taking command of the situation, she thought certainly warranted the attempt. She smiled at herself again as Jim put the cup of coffee down and kissed her on the top of her head, heading back up the stairs to get ready for school. *My men both acted in such a way,* she thought to herself, *that it was beyond belief, but belief is what made both of them come back unharmed to me again.*

Chapter 21

Washington D.C.

The Apostolic Nuncio to the United States, Archbishop Antonio Rucci, was startled when his cell phone rang while he was sleeping; as he fumbled for it, he was even more startled to see that it was 4:30 in the morning. When he answered, he was surprised to hear the voice of Father Tommaso Antonelli asking him to please hold for His Holiness.

"Antonio, it is I, Pope Alexander. I need you to do me a little favor," His Holiness stated.

"Your Holiness, I am at your command!" Archbishop Rucci answered in a very surprised manner.

"I need you to contact the Archbishop of Chicago and have him do the following for me quietly: arrange to have a first class flight from Chicago to Rome for a Mr. Steve Michaels of Elgin, Illinois, for departure tomorrow afternoon. I also need you to get him a passport issued by me as I am making Mr. Michaels an *ex post facto* diplomat of the Vatican City State as of this moment. Please issue the passport this morning and have it sent to the Archbishop of Chicago by this evening, if possible. I will have Father Antonelli send you an email to confirm all of this. Do you understand, Antonio?" His Holiness asked.

"Yes, your Holiness, I understand, but may I ask why?" Archbishop Rucci asked.

"You may, but you will receive no answer other than you are ordered to do this by me. And another thing: you are to tell no one of what I have ordered you to do, and you may pass the same order to my friend the Archbishop of Chicago as well. Again, Antonio, do you understand completely what I have ordered?" Pope Alexander asked in a very stern voice.

"I understand, Your Holiness, and my orders will be carried out to the fullest. Does Mr. Michaels know what this about, and if not, how do I go about telling him?" Archbishop Rucci asked in a very curious way.

"You will not tell Mr. Michaels anything, nor will you have any contact with him. My next call will take care of who talks to Mr. Michaels. Sorry to wake you, Antonio, but you do have some work to do. The email will be in your inbox within the hour." Pope Alexander hung up the phone on one very startled and surprised Archbishop Rucci.

Antonio Rucci sat in his bedroom, wondering what was going on and who this Steve Michaels was. He powered up his laptop and turned on the coffee pot, which he knew he would need over the course of the next couple of hours. After his laptop had powered on, he Googled "Steve Michaels, Elgin, Illinois" and was shocked at what came back in a split second. There were over five hundred listings for a Steve Michaels of Elgin, and all were proclaiming him to be "Mr. I Believe." As he played one of the YouTube videos Google suggested, Antonio let out a very soft but audible *wow* and replayed it again and again to understand what this man, Steve Michaels, had done to have His Holiness call him at 4:30 a.m. As he watched the video for the fifth time, he began to wonder what was going on at the Vatican. Why the sudden interest in the act of one man from Illinois?

"Well, I guess," Antonio said to the video screen, "I should get ready for my day, call the Archbishop of Chicago, and pass along the order of the Pope to him." But that did not stop Antonio from wondering what the heck was going on.

It was too early to contact the Archbishop of Chicago, so he began the paperwork to have a passport issued to Steve Michaels from the Vatican City State. He showered and dressed, knowing that the night crew would be at their stations since the office of the Apostolic Nuncio was manned twenty-four hours a day. He knew that he would need their help in getting the passport completed and ready to ship by special courier to be there that afternoon as ordered by His Holiness. As he dressed, he wished he could be a fly on the wall to listen to the person who was going to talk to this Steve Michaels.

As he went downstairs with coffee and laptop in hand, his staff was greatly surprised. He was a notorious late riser, and they knew something was up. He walked into his office, closed the door, put the laptop into its docking station, and began typing the order to create the passport. As he did he hit the intercom button on the phone system for his aide to come into his office immediately once he was dressed and downstairs. He smiled, knowing that his aide would be in disarray from being woken up two hours before he normally awakened.

"Good to keep things lively," he said to his laptop, which was becoming his closest advisor since the call from His Holiness.

Chapter 22

Rectory of St. Paul's Parish

When the phone woke Father Rick, he guessed that it was a parishioner calling to have him administer the sacrament Anointing of the Sick to a dying loved one.

"Father Rick speaking. May I help you?" He answered the call with the practice of being woken up at all hours of the night as a parish pastor.

"Father Rick, Pastor of St. Paul's Parish?" the question came back to him on the receiver.

"Yes, this is Father Rick. May I ask who's calling, please?" Father Rick answered in a somewhat serious tone.

"Father Rick, I am Father Tommaso Antonelli, private secretary to His Holiness, Pope Alexander IX. I am sorry to wake you this early, but His Holiness needs a favor from you. Do you have a minute to speak to him?" Father Antonelli asked.

Father Rick looked at his phone in disbelief and wondered who was playing a joke on him at 3:45 in the morning. "Um, sure. Put His Holiness on. Why not? It's only 3:45 in the morning, and I have nothing better to do at this time of the day!" Father Rick answered sarcastically. He was going to make sure that the person who was calling him at this time in the morning was going to get an earful from a very pissed off parish priest.

"Father Rick, I know you do not believe a word I am saying, but please go to your email box and open the one marked from me. I will hold while you do," Father Antonelli said calmly, anticipating the good father not believing him when he called. As Father Rick stumbled to his laptop, he put the phone down, and Father Antonelli could hear him swear softly that he was going to have whoever was on the phone by their balls. This got a laugh from Father Antonelli, which Father Rick heard through the receiver as he retrieved it from where he had laid it.

"Ok, my laptop is powered up. Who did you say you were again?" Father asked.

"Father Tommaso Antonelli, private secretary to His Holiness, Pope Alexander IX," came the calm reply.

"Ok, here you are," Father Rick exclaimed as he opened the email and let out a very loud "oh, crap!"

"Father, please excuse me again for calling you at this hour, but as you can see from my email, I am who I say I am," Father Antonelli said, hoping that the good pastor of St. Paul's would not drop the phone and disconnect the call.

"I am so sorry, Father! Please forgive me!" Father Rick pleaded into the phone as he looked at the email signed by Father Antonelli and affixed with the seal of His Holiness. "Again, please forgive me!"

"No problem, Father. It is I who should be asking for forgiveness from you for calling at this hour. Are you able to take a call from His Holiness now?" Father Antonelli asked again.

"Yes, please. Oh, wait…yes, Father. Oh, great. The Pope calls, and I don't believe his secretary. Hmm, this will not go over well with the Bishop of Rockford at my next review!" Father Rick said into the phone, which got a loud laugh back from Father Antonelli. "Sorry, Father, but you know how it is. You work with the man daily while I am just a lowly priest here in Illinois. What does His Holiness need me to do?" Father Rick said, flustered.

"Well, just listen to him and give him the benefit of the doubt as to who he is, Father Rick!" Father Antonelli said with a laugh to one very startled and shocked priest.

"Please, Father Antonelli was it? I am ready to talk to His Holiness," was all Father Rick could stammer as the Vicar of Christ waited to talk to him.

As Father Antonelli passed the phone to Pope Alexander with his hand over the mouthpiece, he smiled at His Holiness. He knew by the conversation with Father Rick that a parish priest was going to be given the shock of his life in taking a call from the Bishop of Rome.

"Father Rick, it is I, Pope Alexander IX, and I need a favor," came the calm and very clear voice of Pope Alexander.

"Your Holiness," was all Father Rick could muster. "What do you need?"

"One of your parishioners did something remarkable at mass on Sunday, did he not?" His Holiness asked in a roundabout manner.

"Are you talking about Steve Michaels and what he did with the gunman who shot Father George?" Father Rick asked, not knowing if there was a correct answer to any question at this point.

"Yes, Steve Michaels. Do you know him well enough to do me a favor?" His Holiness asked.

"I do know the family very well, your Holiness. What can I do for you?" Father Rick answered, a bit more sure of himself.

"I need you to contact him and have him come to your rectory tomorrow, say at about noon your time. Once he is there, please call me at the number that Father Antonelli will give you so that I may talk to him. Can you arrange this for me, Father Rick?" His Holiness asked.

"Yes, certainly, your Holiness. May I ask what this is all about?" Father Rick said before he realized that he was asking the Pope a direct question. "Umm, sorry, your Holiness. I guess once a parish pastor, always a parish pastor. Please forgive my directness with you," Father Rick said sheepishly.

"Please, Father, no need to ask for forgiveness. You are just protecting your flock. I'll tell you what: I will instruct Mr. Michaels to inform you of what our chat was about once we are done; for now, that is the best I can do," His Holiness answered with a slight laugh.

"Again, apologies, your Holiness. I will have Steve here tomorrow at noon, but we might have a bit of a problem with getting just him here," Father Rick answered, knowing how Michele would react to not being invited.

"What do you mean, Father?" His Holiness inquired.

"Steve's wife, Michele, is, let's say, quite the woman and will not take kindly to not being included in what happens with Steve and this incident. She was ready to take on every police officer there just to get to him on Sunday after the shooting," Father Rick said, already trying to figure out how to appease Michele once he told Steve what His Holiness had asked of him.

"Well then, please invite her as well. No need for you to have to face her alone for following my orders. I will speak to both of them, then, tomorrow at noon your time, Father. Thank you, and may God Bless you as well! Please hold for Father Antonelli," Pope Alexander said with a smile on his face. "Father Rick, I almost forgot: you will tell only the Michaelses that I have called. No one else.

And that is an order! I am sorry to make it one, and I hope you can forgive me!" Pope Alexander said in a way that meant nothing else needed to be said.

"I am always at your service, your Holiness," Father Rick replied, wondering why a Pope could not tell him all, but then again, nothing in this phone call was making any sense to him at this time.

Chapter 23

Elgin, Illinois

Steve woke a bit startled to find himself lying on the couch with Michele next to him; well, he was lying on her. He could make out the time on the television as 8:15 a.m. The talking heads on the morning show were going about their day. When the segment moved to local news, there was his picture above the moniker "Mr. I Believe."

"Oh no! The morning news is carrying this still?" was all he could say. "Is Jim at school already? Do I need to take him?" Steve asked Michele.

"He rode the bus and is quite fine, actually. We had a talk last night while you were down here, and all that he was worried about was you because of what you did," Michele answered, trying to keep the anger she still felt toward the two of them out of her voice and almost succeeding.

"So, does that mean that we are off the hook with you, my dear?" Steve asked in a pleading way.

"Umm, mister, you are not off the hook now or for the foreseeable future until I tell you otherwise. Got it?" she answered him, knowing full well that she had already forgiven both of them but wanting to see how long she could keep this ruse going.

The phone rang, which Steve took as the only way for this conversation to end, and he jumped up to get it. He noticed it was from the rectory. He had called Father Rick at the same number many times when he was on the church's advisory board.

"Hello, Father Rick?" Steve asked.

"Yes, it is, Steve. How are you?" Father Rick answered, glad that it was him and not Michele who answered the phone. "Do you have a minute, please?" Father Rick asked quickly to save the small talk.

"Yes, sure Father Rick. What's up?" Steve answered, knowing that this was not a social call from how quickly Father Rick had changed the subject.

"Can you and Michele be here at the rectory tomorrow at 12 noon? We have a call to place, and I need both of you here," Father Rick said.

"Yes, we both can be there, Father. Whom do we have to call?" Steve asked, grateful that Michele would be there. It would save him the time of trying to answer her questions after.

"Well, I cannot tell you. Let's just say it concerns what happened on Sunday and leave it at that, shall we?" Father Rick said in a *this is going no further* voice.

"Ok, Father. See you tomorrow at noon, then. How is Father George doing?" Steve asked, all the while trying to get Michele to quit asking question from behind him.

"Father George is actually doing really well. The surgery removed the bullet, and there was minimal damage done to his shoulder. He is milking the attention given to him from the staff at the hospital, and I'm a bit concerned about how big his head will be once he gets back here on Thursday, to be honest!" Father Rick joked.

"Well, we can have Michele here stop by to remind him how lucky he is and to be grateful that her son saved him. I am sure in her very meek and unassuming way she can handle that for you, Father!" Steve answered while avoiding the punch being thrown at him by his wife.

"I'll see you tomorrow and good luck with Michele, Steve. You'll need it!" Father Rick answered with a laugh and hung up.

"What the hell are you two talking about?" Michele asked, looking to land one in Steve's mid-section. He moved too fast for her to get a good shot at him.

"He wants to see both of us tomorrow for a call, and he couldn't tell me who the call is with, so don't ask!" Steve answered, looking for a hiding spot from Michele but coming up empty-handed.

As Michele came in closer, Steve quickly grabbed her in a bear hug and begged her to calm down as he had no answers for her.

"Steve Michaels, you better let me go if you know what's good for you!" Michele yelled at him, but he just kept her in his arms while she tried to get away. He smiled and wondered why she always wanted to hit him for just answering the phone. "And you better not be smiling behind my head 'Mister I Believe' or I'll knock that off too!" Michele yelled as she began to laugh, knowing that any more fidgeting or twisting would not get her out of his arms.

"Ok, I'm done for the time being. You can let me go, Steve," she pleaded with her husband, but Steve was not quite certain that she was through. As he began to release her, Michele turned quickly and was about to land a very quick punch to his stomach when he grabbed her and kissed her quickly, which took all of the fight out of her.

Chapter 24

Steve began to clean out his email and answer only the ones from his and Michele's closest friends. As he read, Michele came up behind, asking him again about maybe meeting with her girlfriend, Elaine, who worked for the *Daily Herald* part-time and was one of the reporters who handled special interest articles.

"I really don't want to give any interviews, Michele," Steve said to her again, but he knew that sooner or later he was going to have to talk to someone in the press.

"Look, Steve, you've stayed in this house and said nothing about what happened. Do you not think that a little of your side of the story might just make a great human interest story for Elaine? Please don't make me beg, Mr. I Believe!" Michele said to him, her foot tapping out a cadence as she stood near him.

Knowing that look and that there was no way out of this situation, Steve said, "Okay. Have her come to the house today, and I will let her ask me some questions. But I get to approve what is going to be put in the paper."

"Oh, sure, you get to approve everything!" Michele laughed at him, rolling her eyes and turning away to call Elaine.

As Steve sat there listening to Michele arrange the interview with Elaine, something kept tugging at him about the call from Father Rick. Could it be a meeting with the lawyers from the bishop's office in Rockford, or even with the police and the state's attorney? He did not like this hanging over his head, and now with Elaine coming over to interview him, he was going to make certain that what he said could not be used against him in any way possible. It seemed that being a good citizen and caring about his fellow man put him in the spotlight, and that was one place he was not comfortable being.

When Michele got off the phone, she informed him that Elaine would be by at noon and wanted to know if she could bring a photographer with her since this might make the cover story of the day. Steve grimaced at the thought but knew that they had already set it up, no matter what he thought, so he nodded his head as Michele mussed up his hair and smiled.

Chapter 25

The morning went too fast as far as Steve was concerned; he voiced his disapproval of the whole thing again to Michele but to no avail. She got out a nice dress shirt for him to wear and gave him the best little pouty face that she could muster, but he didn't fall for it. He refused to wear the tie.

"Michele, I am in my own home, and I was not wearing one on Sunday. I'm surprised you didn't make me wear the same dress shirt I wore Sunday to make this even more realistic!" Steve yelled down the stairs as his wife made coffee to enjoy with Elaine during the interview.

"Steve, I had to throw that shirt away. It was covered in Father George's blood from when you helped Jim!" Michele answered him. "You know, a little self-promotion might help you with this. You still are not sleeping, and just talking with someone other than me might help."

Steve came down the stairs and stood there watching Michele talk, make coffee, and get ready for what he was sure would be a disaster. *I mean, I can tolerate Elaine for only ten minutes at a time and now an interview? What did I get myself into?* he thought. He smile at Michele when he realized she was waiting for a comment or an answer, but he had not heard a word she had said, so a smile was the best she was going to get.

"Steve Michaels, did you even hear a word I said?" Michele asked, already knowing the answer as the doorbell sounded.

"I'll get that, Michele. And the answer to your question is *no!*" Steve said as he quickly got out of the kitchen to answer the door.

Elaine and her photographer were standing there holding their equipment, and they came into the house quickly, Elaine giving directions about where to set up and how she wanted the room to look. Michele came up to her and gave her a hug, asking what she should move to make the room look better.

Women, thought Steve. Even the photographer was one. "Stop moving my furniture and stop directing the traffic, Elaine! This is my interview, and I will handle this my way!" Steve said uncharacteristically rudely to his wife and her friend.

When all three of them looked up at him, they were startled at how Steve was looking at them and how he had taken control of the whole situation.

"Now, everyone please sit at the kitchen table and let's get on with this: no backdrops, no moving anything, and no nothing else, or you can leave now. Do you understand me?" Steve said in a very clear and strong voice.

Both Michele and Elaine looked at him again; Michele had not seen this side of Steve for quite a long while, but she knew that what he meant what he said. The photographer asked if they could leave one table light on, and Steve nodded as she got her camera out and said nothing else.

"Now, I'm sorry, but what happened on Sunday was a tragic thing, and I am not going to treat it like a three-ring circus. You have thirty minutes to ask me any questions, and I alone will decide what I answer. Are we clear?" Steve said to both of them.

"Yes, Steve. Sorry for acting like this is my house, but it is my job," Elaine said, not knowing how Steve would react.

"I appreciate that it's your job, Elaine, but this is my house. I also will tell you now that the ground rule is that I control everything that gets printed, not you or your editors. Are we clear?" Steve knew from the look on Elaine's face that Michele had not mentioned that caveat. Steve asked in a way that suggested only a *yes* answer would be correct.

"No, she hadn't, but it's not up to me to agree to that, Steve. I work for other people who make those decisions," Elaine said to him in a very soft manner, watching him while she answered.

"Then this interview is done. A man died by my hands, and this will be what I want it to be, not what someone who was not even there tells me it should be. Now, if you cannot agree, then please leave. Sorry for my outburst, but this is the way it will be. Your choice," Steve said to Elaine, who was only now beginning to understand how emotional this was for Steve.

Michele came up to her husband's side and closed her hand around his. She nodded at Elaine and then said, "Elaine, call you editor and tell him that you have an exclusive with Steve Michaels, Mr. I Believe. He has a couple of stipulations for an interview, and only you will be granted this interview for the world to read under your byline. Make the call, Elaine. You will never have this opportunity come your way again!" Michele finished speaking and turned to wipe a tear from her eye. She only now could see the emotion coming out of her husband and knew that what he was saying was right as she sat at his side.

As Elaine took her phone out, her photographer, Linda, took a couple of pictures of Steve and Michele standing there. Linda understood the emotions that were on display for all to see and knew that one of these pictures was going to be the one in the article. Steve smiled at her and mouthed an apology to her, but all Linda did was smile, knowing that raw emotions like these are what gives the edge to any picture.

Elaine hung up her cell phone, looked at both Steve and Michele, and said in a very meek voice, "My boss has agreed to your stipulations and that the final approvals rest with you, Steve. He did ask that the wording might be changed a bit for reading purposes, but you would see the final copy as long as you agree not to talk to any other news services or television stations. That is the best I could do considering the situation that we would like to have this out in today's edition."

Steve nodded and motioned all three of them to sit at the kitchen table to begin the interview. Michele looked at Steve and smiled while Elaine took out her recorder and positioned it in the center of the table between her and Steve. "Steve, I will be recording this as it is easier and far better to use your own words in the article. I hope you don't mind?" Elaine asked.

Steve looked at Michele, who nodded, and then added, "Fine by me, but I would like a copy of this for my records if you can arrange that for me. Michele can meet you and pick up the copy, and then you two can tell each other how terrible I am being about this whole ordeal!" Steve said childishly and without his customary smile.

"Okay, I would like to begin by having you tell me your name and residence for the record," Elaine said.

"Steve Michaels, Elgin, Illinois," Steve answered, now beginning to settle down.

"You have been labeled as "Mr. I Believe" for your actions at St. Paul's church this past Sunday; I would like you to tell me in your own words what happened that day," Elaine stated, knowing her normal line of questioning was not going to work in this instance.

"I would prefer to answer your questions, Elaine; I believe that the video tells everything very clearly that happened that day," Steve answered her, knowing that an essay on the facts was not what he wanted to do.

"Okay then, let me ask you my first question. Steve, what made you do what you did?" Elaine asked, not knowing if this was the line she should start with.

"I don't know to be honest. When I saw Jim crawling toward Father George, I just knew I had to do something. I mean, that was my son up there going to help, and I wasn't going to let my son get in harm's way while I just sat in a pew looking dumbstruck. I got up and ran toward the altar, not knowing what I would find. No one knew where Father George had been shot, but we knew that he fell.

"Jim was there, checking his back, looking for an exit wound, and found none. He looked at me and told me—that was funny, him telling me—to get the towel from the side table and to grab the cloths on the altar to help stop the flow of blood. I grabbed them. I looked at my son and knew that he was no longer my little boy but that he was a very determined young man who could handle anything." Steve took a sip of coffee that Michele had poured and then asked Elaine if this was what she needed.

"Please, Steve, continue. Maybe a firsthand report is better than an interview. Let's just see how this goes," Elaine answered him, knowing full well that Linda had her camera in video mode and had attached the extra battery pack to it. Elaine smiled; this was not going in the paper but on the paper's website and would be worldwide by dinnertime.

Steve continued, "Jim had everything under control, and the gunman was ranting, yes ranting, on the left-hand side of the church near where the choir sits. I knew I had to do something. When Jim asked where I was going, I told him I was going to do something about the gunman. He informed me to be careful because the alb that he was wearing was not bulletproof. I got up and noticed that the Host, which had been consecrated and was in Father George's hands when he was shot, was lying on the ground. I picked it up and placed in on the paten, then put it back on top of the unconsecrated cup of wine. Funny thing was that it was covered in blood spatter, and I'm sure that does not happen every day during a mass. I made the sign of the cross over the Host and then proceeded to go down and face the gunman who was ranting about killing the Anti-Christ and waving his gun around. I knew I had to do something, but what I had no idea. From there the video shows clearly that I was an idiot in trying to get the gunman

115

closer to me so that I could get the gun away from him.

"An 'idiot,' Steve? Why would you use that word?" Elaine asked him but not in a way that suggested she disagreed.

"Elaine, I was unarmed, not trained in hand-to-hand combat against an armed attacker, and had no idea what I was doing. Of course, Michele here was the one who called me an idiot, but it had to do with something about getting shot if it didn't work in my favor," Jim answered her and received a light punch in the shoulder from Michele, who was smiling at the attempt at humor.

"You said that you were unarmed and untrained in hand-to-hand, so you really were just acting on impulse then?" Elaine asked her first real question of the interview.

"Not an impulse, Elaine. I am a member of the St. Paul's Men's Club, and it is our duty to protect our priests and our church. I was doing my duty as a Club member, and no matter the outcome, I was going to do my duty!" Jim said forcefully to make his point known to all.

Michele just sat there, stunned, now fully realizing what possessed the man she loved to act this way, why he did what he did. Funny, she thought to herself, that this must what it feels like to be married to a U. S. Marine: they do their duty and defend this country when they do. Michele continued smiling but was masking her emotions as she knew that this might be the only time that Steve would open up about what happened and why he did what he did.

"So as a Men's Club member, you did what you did to protect the church and those in it?" Elaine asked.

"Yes, I did my duty, and if the outcome had been different and I did not make it here to talk to you today, I still would have done my duty. He was going to shoot other parishioners who were just going to church to worship like me. I didn't know everyone, but I knew enough that I had to do something. When he finally got close to me after I told him why I was willing to die for everyone, I just reacted and took whatever measures I could to take him out of the picture and get control of the gun. I have never hurt anyone intentionally in my life, Elaine, and even now this haunts my dreams. After I disarmed him, I didn't even think about anything but getting the police and fire rescue there to help Father George and to take this man into custody." Steve finished telling Elaine a condensed version of what happen and was not going to into any more detail; the video, he thought, took care of that for him.

"Wow, Steve," was all Elaine could say as she nodded at Michele "It's remarkable that you acted as a noble knight to come to everyone's rescue. I'm sure that the community is grateful for what you did to

117

save the parishioners at St. Paul's that Sunday morning."

"I understand all of that, Elaine. But I still killed a man, and that is the outcome of it all. I pray that his family can forgive me for what I have done, and I hope that someday I can come to terms with it as well. Thank you for coming and talking to me today and letting me tell my side of this tragic event. Thank you, Elaine!" Steve said to Elaine as he stood up to leave the table and turned to wipe his eyes from the emotions that were beginning to flow after finally talking about what happened on Sunday morning.

Elaine looked at Linda, who just smiled as she turned her camera off and took out the video card for safekeeping. Michele and Elaine made small talk while Steve asked if Linda needed any help in putting her camera equipment away. Once they were packed up, Elaine informed Steve that her editor would call him shortly concerning the article and its contents. Michele walked them out and reminded Elaine to call her to get the copy of the recording.

Steve was emotionally spent from finally telling why he had done what he'd done and was sitting in the den in his chair when Michele came in to check on him. He had a tear running down his cheek, and Michele just came and hugged him, knowing that he was going to sleep tonight after telling his side of the story.

Chapter 26

Steve slept through the night, having fallen asleep just after dinner and after talking with Jim. Jim was not as emotionally upset as Steve was but was still very worried about his dad. When his mom informed him at dinner that his dad had finally talked about what happened and to whom he talked, Jim was quite surprised as it was not in his dad's nature to talk about himself, but his mom told him that the whole interview had lasted only thirty minutes and that it would be in tomorrow's paper, which Elaine had called to tell her.

When Steve woke the next morning, he felt strangely calm for the first time since Sunday. Maybe this was all part of healing, but then again he wished it would be over quicker. He called work and informed his boss that he would be back in on Monday, as he was still dealing with a couple of issues, and that he would make it up to him next week.

As Michele came down the stairs, she reminded Steve that they were meeting Father Rick at the rectory at noon and to be ready to leave on time. Steve nodded; it was still a mystery to him why Father Rick would want to see both of them at the rectory. *Oh well*, he thought. *Let's just go and get it over with.* As the morning dragged on, Steve forgot about the worry of the meeting. He started a new book and was finally able to concentrate and enjoy reading again.

Vatican City

Brother Michael had just returned from his second visit to view the frescos of the Sistine Chapel and was already carrying on about something new that he found in them. Abbot Giuseppe just smiled as he went on and on about it, wondering if this is what infatuation was; if so, he was glad to be a Brother of the Brown Robes so that he didn't have to deal with it. As he was staring off into space thinking about that, he did not hear Father Tommaso calling for him.

"Your Eminence, it is time to place the call. The Holy Father wishes all three of you to be there with him when he calls Mr. Michaels in roughly ten minutes. Your Eminence, are you listening?" Father Tommaso asked in his very polite but professional tone.

"Yes, sorry Father, and please call me abbot. 'Your Eminence' is still taking me a bit to get used to," Giuseppe responded.

"Your Eminence, you know that protocol forbids me from not recognizing your position, and in a building that has eyes and ears everywhere, let's just say that I do not want to take the risk of not addressing you correctly. You know already what this place is like, but if I may say, you are the easiest of all of the Cardinals to talk to, and it was my privilege to be there when it was announced about your being elevated to your new rank!" Father Tommaso said as Giuseppe smiled at him, understanding everything.

"Well, let's go and see how Mr. Michaels handles a call from the Holy Father. I am sure this does not happen every day here in the Vatican!" Giuseppe said to his fellow Brown Robes as Father Tommaso led the way to the Pope's private office.

When they entered His Holiness's office, all three of them bowed and paid respect to the man who was currently sitting on the Throne of St. Peter. Abbot Giuseppe always smiled at how a man who was elected by his peers could be this gracious and humble as he continued in his service to the church.

"Father Tommaso, please place the call to the pastor of St. Paul's. It is time," Pope Alexander said. "So, my dear new Cardinal, are you ready for the next surprise from St. Pius X?" His Holiness asked Giuseppe.

"I am, but after the first two letters I do not think anything else could surprise me much more. But we will see!" Giuseppe replied.

121

St. Paul's Rectory

Steve and Michele pulled into the parking lot with five minutes to spare, went to the door, and rang the buzzer. Father Rick answered the door and showed them into the conference room for the meeting to take place. He did not show his hand, so to speak, and kept his face even, showing no emotions except for a slight tremble in his hand, knowing that the Pope was calling any second. He asked Steve and Michele if they needed anything and went to answer the call on his office phone. Michele reached for Steve's hand and said softly, "Don't worry. The state's attorney cleared you of any wrong doing; this might be just to talk to their insurance supplier to make sure their butts are covered." She said it smiling but with a look of concern.

Steve nodded and just sat there, not having a clue still what this was about. Back in Father Rick's office, they both could hear some talking but in a very hushed tone.

Vatican City

"Father Rick, it is Father Tommaso, His Holiness's private secretary. Are we ready to take the call from His Holiness?" Father Tommaso asked.

"Yes, may I put the phone on speaker for Steve and his wife, Michele? They are sitting in the conference room here at the rectory," Father Rick added.

"Yes, but please leave the room once you do as this must be a private call. So they don't know whom they will be speaking to?" Father Tommaso asked if the directions from His Holiness were followed.

"The directions have been followed to the letter, and speaking of letters, the package is here that you informed me about in your email. It is unopened as instructed; do I bring it to them when I set the phone up?" Father Rick asked.

"Yes, Father, but please tell Mr. Michaels to open it only once he is instructed to do so. After the call is over, I would like you to call me back at the number that is in my email, and His Holiness will explain the reason for the cloak and dagger nature of this call. Again, Father Rick, thank you for your understanding in this matter!"

"I am going to place our call on hold and set the call up with the Michaelses. You will hear me ask if you are there, and then I will leave the room after placing the package next to Steve," Father Rick said and placed the call on hold.

St. Paul's Rectory

"Steve, if you are ready, let me set the phone to speaker for you. I will not be in the room for the call per orders; also, this is for you. I do not know what is inside, so please don't ask me, Michele!" Father Rick said as he smiled at Michele and pressed the speaker phone button. "Are you there?" Father Rick asked.

"Yes, Father, thanks. Please let me know when Father Rick has left the room," Father Tommaso said very politely to both Steve and Michele through the speaker phone.

"He is gone, and who is this calling, please?" Steve asked.

"I am Father Tommaso. I am the private secretary to His Holiness, Pope Alexander IX. He is the person you will be speaking to. Father Rick was under orders to leave the room, but he will be told everything once this call is over. Do you have the package that Father Rick gave you?" Father Tommaso asked Steve, who was busy looking at Michele, her jaw wide open in disbelief.

"Umm, yes, I have the package, Father. Did you say the Pope ordered Father Rick? Did I hear you correctly?" Steve asked, trying to hide the surprise in his voice.

"Yes, His Holiness Pope Alexander IX," Father Tommaso said in his calm manner. "I am sorry to have sprung this on you, but these conditions were set forth by His Holiness himself. Please forgive me as I am just the messenger, Mr. Michaels."

"Oh, you are forgiven. This is just quite a shock to me and my wife. Never in a thousand years would I expect the Pope to call me with all of this cloak and dagger going on!" Steve replied as he heard a bit of laughter in the background.

"I am sorry for the laughter, but some of the folks here in the private study of His Holiness have the same feelings that you do, Mr. Michaels, about all of this," Father Tommaso said, himself trying to hold his laughter in.

"Oh yes, Father, please call me Steve. I do believe the formality of being called *mister* is a bit overrated with the present company on this call. Please start at the beginning and tell me why I am on the phone with the Pope!" Steve said looking at Michele. Her jaw was still open, but she was at least nodding now.

"Steve, this is Abbot Giuseppe of the Abbey of the Brown Robes. I am the reason that His Holiness is calling you, as I am the holder of the prophecy that brought you to us. Before you ask, the prophecy was fulfilled by you with your actions this past Sunday when you defended the parishioners of St. Paul's during the attack by the gunman. We have decided through these actions that you have fulfilled a prophecy that was given to us by Saint Pope Pius X in 1914. Please listen to what Pope Alexander has to ask you, and all of your questions will be answered to the fullest. If we can!" Abbot Giuseppe said, knowing full well that Steve did not believe a word of what he had just said.

"Do you have any proof to give me that you are who you say you are, Abbot? I don't mean to sound cynical, and I'm not calling you a liar, but come on! Really? Me, fulfilling a one hundred year old prophecy for what I did? I killed man; now how could that be fulfillment of a prophecy that a saint left you? Well, Abbot, with all due respect, what do you have for me?" Steve asked as his head was swirling, not understanding what was happening or whom to believe. Michele was no good to him at this point, and Steve started to laugh out loud about that.

"Steve, what is so funny? This is a serious issue that we are talking about," Abbot Giuseppe insisted.

"Well, I apologize for my laughter, but for the first time in my wife's life, she has no comment. I should really be thanking you as this is a first for me!" Steve said. He was trying to control his laughter, but he could not.

"Well, for that I guess you have us here laughing with you. Now, if you can regain your composure, His Holiness would like a word with you," Abbot Giuseppe replied, a little sterner now.

"Sorry, Abbot. Please, I'm ready," was all Steve could say not knowing what was right to say at this time anyway.

Chapter 27

"Steve, this is Pope Alexander speaking to you. Could you please open the package that was given to you by Father Rick?" His Holiness asked.

Steve opened the package and placed the contents on the table. Inside was a plane ticket and a passport from the Vatican City State. Steve opened the passport and saw his own name and address staring back at him.

"Steve, will that be enough proof for you to believe that it is I, Alexander, the Bishop of Rome, talking to you?" the Pope asked.

"Your Holiness, now you have me dumbstruck. What may I do for you?" Steve asked the Pope as he looked at Michele, who was coming out of her stupor just now and taking the passport from Steve's hand to look at it.

"I need you to fly to see me tonight, Steve. Your plane leaves in four hours, which will get you here to the Vatican tomorrow morning our time. I will have the Abbot of the Brown Robes and his companions meet you at the terminal and bring you here to meet with me. Father Rick should have your itinerary in an email that Father Tommaso has sent to him. Included is a picture of the abbot so that you can recognize him when you arrive. Now what questions do you have for us? I hope we can answer them,"

Pope Alexander said to Steve with all of the compassion that a Pope can give to someone in his flock.

"Well, your Holiness, I don't know what to ask. Normally Michele, my wife, would be asking a thousand questions, but she is still looking at the passport. I guess my belief that it is you whom I am talking to is all I need right now. I will save my questions for when I see you tomorrow morning. Just one thing…this ticket is only for me, correct?" Steve asked quickly, hoping that Michele would just nod and agree.

"Unfortunately, Steve, yes it is only for you. Maybe another time you can bring your family to enjoy Italy and the Vatican with me," His Holiness answered.

Steve started to laugh a bit; Michele had not caught on to the last sentence or complained that she was not going to the Vatican with him. Maybe, just maybe, she would let it go. "Your Holiness, is there anything that you or Abbot Giuseppe can tell me about the prophecy, or will that be explained to me tomorrow?" Steve asked.

"Steve, this is Abbot Giuseppe. We do not know much more than what we have told you already. We are reading the instructions from one-hundred-year-old handwritten letters from St. Pius himself. There are two more letters, but both of them are to be opened by you, the first one in the presence of His Holiness per the instructions. So as you can tell, we are in the dark as much as you are!"

"Thank you, Abbot. It doesn't ease my mind, but you cannot answer what you do not know. I guess I need to go and get packed and get to the airport. Until the morning, then, unless your Holiness has any other instructions for me?" Steve asked.

"Just one, Steve. Please keep this between you and your wife for now. May the Lord be with you as you travel, and I will keep you in my prayers. Until tomorrow, then!" Pope Alexander said as the call ended.

"Well, this has really been a very strange week for us, don't you agree, Michele?" Steve asked his still dumbfounded wife.

"That was the Pope speaking to us, speaking to me. Can you believe that the Pope spoke to me?" Michele stammered as she spoke for the first time since the call started.

"Well, honey, he spoke to me. You just sat there with your mouth open wide enough to back the proverbial truck in!"

"Stop it, Steve," Michele said as she nudged him in the ribs. "I heard everything, and thank you for trying to see if I could come with you, by the way!"

Steve was caught by surprise. He had hoped that she hadn't caught that line between him and the Pope, knowing full well that a trip to Rome for

Michele was already in the works. Steve thought to himself that by the time he returned home she would have the dates for the trip figured out and would be looking into what sites she wanted to see. *Well, it could be worse*, he laughed to himself. *She could have told the Pope that if I am going to Rome, she is going also. Maybe, just maybe, divine intervention is a real thing.*

"What are you smiling at, Steve?" Michele asked.

"Oh nothing, nothing at all. Come on. We've got to get the information from Father Rick and get home. I've got to pack and get to the airport for my trip. Don't want to keep the Pope waiting now, do we?" Steve said as he stood up, gathering his ticket and his new passport. Looking at the crossed keys of the Vatican, he wondered what he had just gotten himself into.

Chapter 28

Father Rick gave Steve the information that Father Tommaso had emailed for him and asked that Steve call him upon his return as he did not know anything other than setting up the call from the Pope. Steve grabbed for his hand, shaking it, and told Father Rick, "Once Michele knows, then you will know. I will call you Monday!"

As they pulled out of the church parking lot, Michele looked at her husband with a new and different look upon her face. *How could this man be married to me?* she thought. *He does all of these things yet is still so humble about his achievements and totally devoted to me and Jim.* She smiled and said to herself quietly, *I think I will keep him even if he does do stupid things!* As they pulled into their driveway, she asked Steve, "What do you want to tell Jim about the trip and all?"

"I will tell him the truth and ask him to keep it quiet, which is the best we can do at this point. No reason to lie about it, and since he was there on Sunday, I would like to keep him informed about what is happening. Oh, and one thing Michele: I do not want this publicized. No talking to Elaine and no Facebook about my trip. I still don't understand why the Pope wants to see me and what this prophecy is all about. I mean, a one-hundred-year-old prophecy that no one has heard about and from a Pope who was later canonized as a saint!" Steve said firmly to Michele who understood that he meant no talking about it at all.

"I'll keep it quiet until you get home and we find out about what the outcome is. Now what suit do you want to wear to meet the Pope in? I know just the tie for you to wear!" Michele said and hurried into the house to help pack.

Steve just sat there in the car and began to wonder why indeed the Pope wanted to see him, a man who killed another man. He had been able to keep that part of the equation out of his thoughts since Sunday, but now it was creeping into them, and he was beginning to have doubts about his actions.

Paul from across the street walked up the driveway, calling for Steve, whom he could see sitting in the car. "Steve, you okay? You look a bit lost there, buddy," Paul said in a concerned way.

Coming out of his thoughts, Steve looked in the rear view mirror and waved to Paul. After getting out of the car, he walked up to his friend to shake his hand. "Yes, I'm doing okay. Just having a bit of quiet time," Steve replied, hoping to mask his emotions.

"Well, I can understand the quiet time, but you do look a bit lost, Steve. Is everything okay with the shooting and all that you have been through? You can talk to me, Steve; I've been through it before," Paul simply stated the truth, which caught Steve off guard a bit.

"I had forgotten about that incident, Paul. Plus I didn't want to ever bring that up again. You talked to someone after the shooting that you were involved in. Would you happen to have the number? I have a feeling that no man should be an island with what has happened," Steve told his friend, relieved that he was finally able to look for a resolution about what he did Sunday.

"The guy is still associated with the police force as a consultant; I'll email him tomorrow for you and see what I can work out for you. Actually, I'm happy to help you with this. You and Michele were there for me, and I like the idea of not owing you again!" Paul laughed.

"Well, as far as owing anything to me, that list is long, and I will be calling it in for years, my friend!" Steve laughed back. "But you'll have to take up the score and who owes what with Michele as that's her department!"

Chatting was a relief to Paul, who now realized and understood that Steve was having issues with what happened at the church. It was ten years ago that he shot a man who was lying in ambush to shoot him and his partner; only the training he received in the police department had saved his life. Well, that and his friendship with the Michaelses. They both looked up when Michele called Steve to get in to help her pack.

"Going somewhere, Steve?" Paul asked.

"Paul, you better come in and have a cup of coffee with me. I need a favor while I am gone!" Steve said with a very serious look on his face.

As they walked into the kitchen, Michele turned the corner and was startled to see Paul walking in with Steve. "Hi Paul! Steve you really have to get moving; you have to be there in two hours!" she said bluntly.

"Well, Steve, are you going tell me where you're going or not?" Paul asked again, puzzled that Steve was going and not Michele since they went everywhere together.

"I'm going to Rome to meet the Pope and talk about what I have done," Steve flatly said to his friend whose look of disbelief was precious. *He even has the same open-mouth syndrome that Michele had when the Pope talked to us at the rectory,* Steve thought to himself.

"Rome? Pope? What you have done? Umm, Steve, you have to give me more than just that," Paul joked, but the look on Steve's face was serious. "You do mean the guy with the white hat who talks to God? That guy?" Paul asked again.

"Yep, same guy, and I am under orders to fly there tonight and meet with him. I will be gone — well, let's see when my return flight is...Ah, yes, I will be gone three days, returning on Sunday night at 8:00. Just please keep an eye out for Michele and Jim for the next couple of days? Oh, and one more thing. Please keep this to yourself. No one else," Steve insisted, knowing that Paul was already going to keep it to himself.

"Sure thing, Steve, and thanks for telling me. I'll take care of what we talked about in the garage while you're gone. Michele you have my cell number, right?" Paul inquired.

"Yes, in my phone. Thanks for being there, Paul!" Michele said as she crossed the kitchen floor to give him a hug.

"Okay, got to pack. And thanks, Paul," Steve said, shaking his hand and winking about the other favor he asked about.

Chapter 29

Jim came home from school as Steve was loading his luggage into the car. "Going somewhere, Dad?" Jim asked.

"Umm, yes. Let's go inside so we can talk about it Jim, okay?" Steve answered hesitantly. When they entered the kitchen off the garage, Michele looked at the two of them and motioned for Jim to sit down.

"Okay, you two might want to stop this charade and just tell me what's up. You're scaring me," Jim blurted out. It was not in his parents' natures to make him sit to talk about something.

"Sorry, but I don't know where to begin myself, Jim," Steve answered his son. "So here goes nothing, and no questions until I'm done. Deal? I have been ordered to fly to Rome tonight and meet with Pope Alexander tomorrow morning!" Steve told Jim as flatly as he could. "I don't know what this is all about, but your Mom and I were at the rectory and took a call from the Pope and an Abbot Giuseppe. It concerns a prophecy that is one hundred years old and has just been fulfilled. That's about it."

"Wait, the Pope? He called you? Come on, even you can't pull this joke off, Dad!" Jim said with the same look on his face that Michele had when she saw the passport from the Vatican.

Looking at his son, he realized how much he was like Michele: the facial expression, the non-belief, but, most surprising, the look in his eyes. If he ever wondered why he fell in love with Michele, it was the look in her eyes, the same look that Jim had now. "Umm, well, ask your Mom. She was there," Steve answered his son.

"Mom, is he joking or serious?" Jim asked.

Michele handed him Steve's Vatican passport and the tickets and looked at her son with deadly serious eyes. She stated, "This is serious; for once he's not joking with either of us. He's telling the truth."

"*For once* I'm serious?" Steve exclaimed and began to laugh.

"Well, you do tell some tall tales, Dad!" Jim said while laughing back at his Dad. "So when do you leave?"

"We're leaving for the airport in ten minutes. Would you like to go with us?" Michele answered for Steve.

"Sure, I can ask the rest of my questions while we drive. Let me go put my things away!" Jim told his mom as he got up to go to his room. "The Pope called my dad. Now that is something that doesn't happen every day!

"Jim, would you please download and print out what you can about Pope Saint Pius X so I can read it on the plane? I have a feeling I'm going to need to understand the man and what he's about to do to me!" Steve added.

As they drove, Jim asked his questions without stopping for a breath. Steve tried to keep up but mostly just sat there and smiled. He had let Michele drive since he knew the concentration on driving would help her cope with the anxiety she was having about him going to see the Pope. He continued to wonder about why he was being summoned to have a chat with the Pope. *I mean, I killed a man! No Pope needs to associate himself with a killer.* And the doubt began to set in again about his actions. Steve could not wait until he got back and could go and talk with Paul's associate from the force who had helped him. He came out of his stupor when Jim asked "Are you even listening to me, Dad?"

"Sure, son. I heard every word but have no idea what you said," Steve answered with a laugh, which got him an elbow from Michele and the rolling of eyes from Jim. "So, I don't know why I'm going, but it has something to do with a prophecy and that I fulfilled it, which is all I know."

"Are you going to see the Sistine Chapel while you're there?" Jim asked.

"Umm, no. That's reserved for when I take your mother to Rome, and that trip is being planned by her right now, I would bet," Steve replied as they both laughed at Michele, who was shooting daggers with her eyes at her son in the rearview mirror. "But seriously, please, no talking about this, either of you two, with anyone. Paul across the street knows, and he will help with anything that you need. I'll be home in four days."

"Okay, I have school anyway and will keep it quiet like you asked, but I want to know every detail when you get home. Deal?" Jim said, knowing full well that there was no other answer but *yes* to his father's statement.

As they pulled up to the international terminal at O'Hare Airport, Steve leaned over, kissed Michele, and told her he would text her when he landed. She smiled, not knowing what to say or do. Jim got out of the back and handed Steve his luggage, saying, "See you in a couple of days. I'll make sure mom doesn't call you a thousand times while you're gone!"

"Good luck with that one, son!" Steve laughed back as he grabbed his bag, hugged Jim, and then headed to the door that led to the security line. As he reached the door, Michele called out loudly, "Call me when you get there, Steve Michaels!"

Chapter 30

As they pulled away, Michele looked into the rear view mirror a moment more, wondering what was going to happen to the man that she loved. The past few days had been a blur and now this trip…What was happening? And how could she rewind to Sunday morning and make them go to mass later?

"Mom, kinda quiet there. You okay?" Jim asked as he noticed the worried looked upon his mom's face.

"I'm fine. It's just that this is all happening so quickly, Jim." Michele laughed as she said it, but Jim could see the concern in her eyes.

"So the fact that he is going to Rome without you doesn't have you the least bit upset?" Jim teasingly asked his mom, knowing that this would take her mind off of what was going on.

"You have no idea how upset I am with him, Jim. Why in the hell didn't he just stay in his pew? You had to do what you did, taking care of the Father George, but he did not have to go and play hero! Oh, I could just kick his ass for this one Jim. Oops! Did I just say that out loud?" Michele laughed.

"Umm, yes you did, and it will remain our little secret. It's almost a comic book story: mild mannered engineer takes on the bad guy with a gun, armed only with his beliefs. We could sell a million copies if it went to print, I bet!" Jim said, and they both laughed out loud for the first time since Sunday.

Chapter 31

After passing through the security checkpoint, Steve walked to his terminal, still wondering what was happening to him and why he was going to Rome. As he sat down he noticed that his flight would be boarding in twenty minutes, so he grabbed one of the books he brought for the trip and began reading. When the call was made to board the first class passengers, Steve made his way to the counter and noticed there were only himself and one other person in line. Steve nodded hello to the man, gave his boarding pass to the attendant, and walked down the ramp to the plane. There he was shown to his seat, and his carry-on and garment bag were stowed for him. Smiling as he watched what was going on around him, he thought to himself that he could get used to flying first class but dismissed it, knowing that this was once in a lifetime no matter the outcome of his meeting with the Pope.

As the other passengers took their seats, Steve did not make eye contact with them and continued reading the book he had started in the terminal. As the plane began to back out, Steve put the book away and looked out the window at the tarmac, wondering how in the hell he got there. He wondered why he, a man who killed another man, was being ordered to

Rome; surely this prophecy did not envision that a man would die. As he wrestled with his conscience, he barely realized that the plane had taken off and the flight attendant was asking him his choice for dinner and if he would like a drink. He ordered but asked for just a bottle of water. He knew he'd need a clear head in the next day or so. Just what this prophecy was and how he fit into the grand scheme of things were his only thoughts as he settled into his seat to await the outcome of his journey.

Chapter 32

The Vatican

Abbot Giuseppe looked at his watch, did the mental calculations, and told his fellow brothers that Steve Michaels's plane had lifted off. He got only a nod from each of them in response; even Brother Michael did not respond, which was very unusual for him.

"Michael, are you okay? Normally you would have been telling me about something new that you noticed in the frescos on the ceiling of the Sistine Chapel," Giuseppe told his fellow brother.

"I am fine, your Eminence," Brother Michael responded with a smile since the abbot was still not used to his new title in the church. "But this whole business is beginning to make me have doubts. First the Secretariat of State gets into a shouting match with His Holiness, and now this American is coming to open the other letters in fulfillment of the prophecy. Just a very strange couple of days, and we do not yet know the outcome. You know, I almost wish that it was not fulfilled and that we were arguing over dinner and who was going to do what back at our monastery," Brother Michael said to his fellow brothers in a very somber and almost sad tone.

"I agree," chimed in Brother Angelo. "Strange indeed…who would have thought that I would agree on anything with my dear Brother Michael?"

All three began to laugh out loud, but it was the next voice that made them all sit up and take notice. "I, too, agree with you three as well. We do not know what lies ahead and can only have faith that our dear St. Pius stays true to his calling of being the conservative Pope that he was. I, as Bishop of Rome, do not have any answers and find that I am hoping whatever is in those last two letters makes our faith stronger and that Mr. Michaels is the man who we think and pray he is!" Pope Alexander said to the three. He had slipped into the room next to his outer office and surprised his guests with his unannounced presence.

"Your Holiness," all three exclaimed and began to rise in unison at the sight of their Pope.

"Please, stay seated. I need to talk to all of you. My apologies for overhearing your doubts and your conversation," the Pope said in a very clear but troubled voice. "I have just returned from fully briefing the Secretariat of State on what is happening. He has given me his full support and has asked what he can do. I have asked him to be available when Mr. Michaels meets with us tomorrow. He did agree to be there and with no argument for once. Hmm, wonder how that miracle happened?" the Pope informed the three, and they all shared a laugh together.

"Now, please, let's retire for the evening and be ready to greet Mr. Michaels after you three pick him up from the airport. I am sending with you tomorrow an escort from the Swiss Guard in plain clothes so that you have no problems with customs at the airport. Cardinal Albani does have his uses!" The Pope blessed the three of them as he left the room to retire to his bedroom in the palace.

As the Brothers left the outer office, Abbot Giuseppe just smiled; tomorrow would be a day of fulfillment that had been one hundred years in the making.

Chapter 33

After the flight attendant removed his dinner tray, Steve reached into his carry-on and brought out the downloaded information about St. Pius X that Jim had given him in the car. It was a short bio on him and his time as Pope. Steve was surprised by the fact that St. Pius was labeled one of the most conservative Popes of the twentieth century, yet here he was traveling to Rome by his order. *Okay*, he thought, *orders that are one hundred years old, but still an order is an order*. He read further that St. Pius was devoted to the Blessed Mother and that his manta was "to restore all things to Christ." This made him ponder more as to what prompted him to record this prophecy and to have it guarded by the Brothers of the Brown Robes. Steve noted that St. Pius's death happened just as World War I began, and some claim that it was the war that caused his death. If the war had caused his death, could the prophecy be his way of doing something to help the church that he could not do while alive? As he thought more about it, he realized how little he knew about the church at the time of St. Pius X. To be able to think clearly enough to record a prophecy while he was approaching his death must have been a life force for him to keep going.

As the other passenger in first class snored lightly, Steve turned off the light and settled in to see if he could get some sleep. Tomorrow would be a long day.

Chapter 34

It took an hour to travel the thirty-one kilometers from the Vatican to the Leonardo da Vinci Fiumicino Airport in Rome in the morning rush hour traffic. While they drove, the three Brothers of the Brown Robes were quiet, even Brother Michael, which was very unusual. As they reached the entrance to the airport, Brother Angelo started saying the *Our Father* prayer out loud; his brothers joined in. When they finished, he added, "may God bless us, for we do not know what we are doing!" This brought a laugh from his travel companions as they were greeted outside their van by the guard whom His Holiness had sent them.

"What is so funny, your Eminence?" the guard, Karl, asked.

Abbot Giuseppe answered, looking up at the 6 foot 4 inch member of the Swiss Guard, with a grin, "oh, nothing Karl. Just a little funny thing that Brother Angelo told us in the van. Do you know why you were sent here with us today?"

"No. My Captain did not inform me other than I am to stay close and assist you with the man you are picking up. I have to meet with customs before the plane arrives to make sure that they know that…"

He reached into his coat pocket to refer to his notes, "…that a Mr. Michaels is cleared as an Official Emissary of the Vatican City State," Karl stated in a clear, commanding voice.

"Please lead the way, Karl, and make sure that this is all done with the utmost quiet. We do not want the press asking us questions that we have no idea how to answer," Abbot Giuseppe said as they began walking toward the international terminal.

The press: he totally forgot about how to deal with them, Giuseppe thought to himself. How would they even begin to tell this tall tale with even the College of Cardinals not knowing yet — outside of the Secretariat of State, that is? This was going to make for some very upset Cardinals, but an order from the Pope, even a Pope deceased for one hundred years, he thought, was still a valid order, and he was sworn to follow it. *Funny*, he thought. *I am a Cardinal for only two days, and I am already worried what the other Cardinals think. How quickly the politics of the church begin to creep into one's life once one puts the red hat on.* With the terminal just in front of him, Giuseppe paused a second to take a deep breath and then took a step to see what fate destiny was bringing him that day.

Chapter 35

Steve had asked the flight attendant to make sure that he was awake an hour and a half before the plane landed. As she woke him, he had to remember that he was on a plane and not next to Michele; the thought made him smile and wonder how long it would be until he was bringing her and Jim here to visit Rome. He thought again to himself, *Rome! Who would have thought?* He got his travel kit from his carry-on bag and went to clean up a bit in the not-too-spacious first class lavatory. When he returned, the flight attendant asked him to make sure his seat belt was on and woke the other passenger in first class.

The plane landed without much fanfare and taxied to its gate. Steve stole a quick glance at the picture of Abbot Giuseppe and consigned the image to his memory. As the plane door opened, he was second in line to leave the plane and thanked the flight attendant for her service and attention during the flight. She nodded and then motioned him to bend down a bit. She whispered into his ear, "Not every day that I get to wait on someone famous, Mr. I Believe."

Steve laughed sheepishly and thanked her for keeping it to herself. She smiled, shaking his hand as he left the plane.

As he disembarked, he saw Abbot Giuseppe and Brothers Michael and Angelo standing at the gate with a serious-looking young man beside them.

"Mr. Michaels, I presume?" the abbot asked, his hand outstretched.

"Yes, and please call me Steve, Abbot Giuseppe," he returned.

"Yes, this is our escort Karl, who has been sent by His Holy Father to make sure we have no delays." Abbot Giuseppe motioned to his right as Karl stepped forward.

"Mr. Michaels, may I have your passport and your baggage claim tickets, please?" Karl asked with an outstretched hand.

"Here they are, Karl," Steve replied as he reached into the front zippered part of his carry-on bag. "As I guess I am not in control of this situation, please lead the way," Steve added.

As Karl led them to the VIP customs lounge, he passed the claim ticket to the agent. Abbot Giuseppe made the introductions to Steve of Brothers Michael and Angelo. As his baggage was being brought forth and his passport was being stamped, Steve realized that he was not in Kanas anymore and laughed at himself: Michele would be poking him in the ribs for that attempt at humor. Michele, he thought. He reached for his cell phone to text her that he had arrived safely before the twenty or so texts began to pop up on the phone's display. He asked the Abbot

153

for a minute and walked to the far side of the lounge to text her, asking politely that she not text back since he had no idea what was going on yet. Michele returned agreeing, but it would cost him when he got back. Steve smiled to himself again. *I am so lucky to have this woman in my life; I really do not deserve her.*

"Sorry about that, Abbot. I had to text my wife, Michele. She probably called the airline twice to make sure everything was fine with the flight as well!" Steve exclaimed and was joined in his laughter by Brother Michael.

"My mother is the same way, Mr. Michaels!" Brother Michael said, laughing out loud.

"Please, I don't know why I'm here, but could you three just call me Steve? It will make this less uncomfortable than it already is," Steve asked again. He needed the comfort of his own name to ease his nerves.

"Steve it is, then!" Brother Michael exclaimed as Karl led the way for the five of them to leave the VIP lounge with Steve's luggage.

As they were leaving the airport, Steve noticed that very few people were looking at them as they walked and hoped beyond hope that he would not be noticed as he had been on the plane. That was short-lived. Another passenger on his flight came up outside of customs and asked if he was Mr. I Believe. Steve smiled and nodded and then was hurried along by Karl and the abbot.

"We need to get you out of here quickly. The press has no idea that you are here yet!" Abbot Giuseppe exclaimed as Karl lead the way to the exit.

As they exited the terminal, Karl brought up their SUV and put Steve in it. The three Brothers of the Brown Robes went to their van and got into line to exit the airport behind them. As they got onto the main road, Karl informed him that due to traffic their trip to the Vatican would take about forty-five minutes. Steve settled into the backseat to take in the passing scenery and wondered if this was all of Rome that he would be seeing during his impromptu visit to meet the Pope. He used the time to talk to Karl about the protocol of the Vatican and if he could share any tips.

"Mr. Michaels, the most important thing is to remember to bow and look at his hand. If his thumb's up, that means shake his hand. If the hand is flat, then bow and kiss his ring. Other than that, address him as you would address any other leader of a nation!" Karl said with a slight grin, his first since being given this assignment.

"Thanks, Karl. That's a lot of help. And please, call me Steve when we are alone. I understand that your orders might take precedence when we are in a crowd, but I am just Steve," Steve replied and noticed the smile in the rear view mirror. "Do you know why I'm here, Karl?"

"No Mr. — err, Steve, I do not. My Captain just gave me the orders from His Eminence the Secretariat of State, and I am following them. Do you mind if I ask you a question?" Karl said hesitantly.

"No, please ask away, Karl," Steve replied.

"You are 'Mr. I Believe,' whom I watched on YouTube?"

"Yes, I am; why do you ask?"

"Well, as a professional soldier of the Swiss Guard, it was something to admire. Had you training of any kind, Steve?" Karl asked politely.

"No, none. A little formal boxing training at the YMCA when I was a teenager was all. I have thought about it since and now know how lucky I was in getting out of there without getting myself shot," Steve replied somewhat sheepishly.

"Our training is all about reacting, but what you did was proactive in getting him closer. You should be proud no one got hurt except the priest who was shot!" Karl exclaimed.

"Well, the gunman did die, so someone did get hurt besides Father George. It is something that will haunt me for the rest of my life, me killing someone, and now I am here to meet the Pope because of it," Steve answered in a very serious tone.

"You do have a point there; I am trained to understand that it goes with my duty to protect the Pope at all cost to myself or others.

156

We sometimes forget that someone like you who is not trained acts on his own initiative to protect. Either way, Steve, you should be commended for your actions. It did save lives," Karl said, a note of admiration in his voice.

"Thank you, Karl. My neighbor, who is a police officer, is getting me some help to cope with the aftermath once I get home. He is lining up some professional help to allow me to get over it and stop feeling so guilty about my actions," Steve answered.

"Steve, guilt is not a bad thing as it allows you to accept your actions and not hide from them. If you ever need to talk, please let me know, Steve. We have excellent counselors in the Swiss Guard who specialize in this," Karl answered in the way that he would to a brother in arms.

Chapter 36

As they left the airport, Brother Angelo remarked that Steve looked bigger in real life than on the video, which brought a burst of laughter from Brother Michael.

"Well, of course he is bigger. Or do you mean taller? I mean the iPad is only so big!" Michael answered with a laugh while holding up his hands so show the dimensions of the screen.

"Please, Michael! Stop teasing him," Abbot Giuseppe called out while enjoying a chuckle himself over the statement. "What we need to concentrate on is how he will react once he meets the Pope and reads the next letter from St. Pius X!"

"Good point, my dear Eminence!" Brother Angelo remarked. "And how will this affect him? We really have no idea what he has been though with this ordeal."

"No, we do not. Here he is involved in trying to save people's lives, then a killing, and in the next moment he's on a plane to Rome. It seems almost surreal that this is happening, and we are the ones to blame!" Abbot Giuseppe said in an official-sounding voice. "I just hope that, whatever the next letter reveals, Steve and we ourselves can handle it. So far St. Pius X has been nothing but full of surprises!"

"How do you think His Holiness will handle what the next letter will reveal?" Brother Angelo asked.

"I do not know," Abbot Giuseppe answered truthfully. "He is the Pope, but I think his beliefs are sound enough to trust whatever our good friend Giuseppe Sarto has in mind for us!" As they drove back to the Vatican, they continued to speculate about the next letter and what implication it might have in store for all of them. Abbot Giuseppe became lost in his thoughts as the brothers continued to talk. How would this affect his church, and how would it affect him as well? *Here I am*, he thought, *the one who has unleashed this prophecy onto the world and who will have to live with what is about to transpire because of it.* Could he live up to his new position in the church, and could he help Steve Michaels with what was about to happen to him? So many questions and no way to know what to do…he stopped and cleared his mind and sought the peace of prayer, which he always found solace in as a Brother of the Brown Robes.

Brother Angelo brought him out his stupor by asking him where to take Steve once they got to the Vatican.

"Karl is under orders to take him directly to the Domus Sanctæ Marthæ so that he can freshen up after his flight. A room has been prepared for him by the Secretariat of State, acting upon the Holy Father's order," Giuseppe answered almost robotically; his nerves were beginning to show from this ordeal.

"When does he meet the Holy Father?" Brother Michael asked.

"As soon as possible is all that I was told. Karl will be his chaperon, and all three of us are to be present by the Holy Father's orders as well," Giuseppe replied. As they crossed the Vatican property line, he knew that it would all be answered within the next hour or so.

Chapter 37

Karl parked the car in front of the entrance to Domus Sanctæ Marthæ; he opened the door for Steve and went to the back of the SUV to retrieve his luggage. Karl led the way and was greeted at the front door by another member of the Swiss Guard, but this one was in the blue uniform of the day.

"So, I don't get the royal treatment with the orange uniform and the halberd?" Steve asked.

Karl was somewhat surprised by Steve's reference to the ancient weapon that the Swiss Guard was famous for. "Well, this is supposed to be low-key, Steve. Hardly anyone knows that you are in Italy, let alone at the Vatican!"

"Good point. Low-key it is then!" Steve said with a laugh while looking at St. Peter's Square just a few hundred yards away "Well as low key as anyone can be in front of a Basilica, I guess." This remark got a smile out of Karl and his companion.

"If you will follow me, please, your room has been arranged for you by order of His Holiness," Karl said as he held the door open for Steve to enter. There he was shown to the elevator and escorted to the second floor where another guard held the door open to what looked like a suite. "This is one of the rooms that a Cardinal uses during the Conclave. It is a bit much, but then again so is a Cardinal," Karl told him with just a bit of sarcasm in his voice as his luggage was brought in and laid on the bed for him. "His Holiness would like to see you as soon as you freshen up from your airplane ride. I will be outside to escort you to His Holiness's private office where you will be received," Karl announced as the other Swiss Guardsman left the room.

"Do I tip you now or wait until I check out, Karl?" Steve asked with a grin.

"Umm, later is better as I have no idea what is in store for you, Steve!" Karl answered with a grin as well.

Once Karl left the room and closed the door behind him, Steve was left alone with his thoughts. He said to himself, "What is indeed in store for me…" as he started to unpack the suit and tie that Michele had picked out for him to meet the Pope in. While unpacking, he noticed that there was a universal power adapter in the bathroom and one by the bed. He took advantage and plugged his cell phone in.

After a shower, which helped settle his nerves, Steve took his time getting dressed, knowing that Karl was outside the door waiting to escort him to his destiny. Such a thing would never have gone through his mind a few days ago. *Come on*, he thought. *Snap out of it. You are going to meet the Pope and find out why you're here.* As he finished tying his tie, he made a mental note to thank Michele once he got home. This tie really did look good on him! *Okay, Steve,* he thought, *stop delaying the inevitable.* He looked in the mirror one last time and turned off the light. Opening the door, he said in his loud voice, "Karl, let's go meet the Pope!"

Chapter 38

Karl led the way back to the elevator. While they waited for it to get to their floor, Steve noticed that there was no one else on the floor. "For a VIP boarding house, it seems pretty deserted," Steve mentioned to Karl, whose mood was beginning to take on another form.

"It is deserted; there's no one else on your floor. When we leave this floor, Steve, I will be calling you Mr. Michaels as protocol demands. I am to be your chaperon during your stay here at the Vatican. Remember that the Pope is the elected leader of the Holy Roman Catholic Church and my boss. I do not want to disappoint him or my commander. This is where we get serious; please remain with me at all times while we walk to His Holiness's private study where he will receive you," Karl told Steve in a very serious manner, which only underscored what was about to happen to him.

"So tell me this: is it still okay to address you as Karl in his presence? I have no idea what the protocol is for that," Steve asked without a hint of humor in his voice. He had understood what Karl was telling him. The nerves that he thought he had gotten rid of during the shower had returned, but he was keeping them at bay as they entered the elevator.

"Karl will be fine, Steve. When we get you back to your room, I will then begin to relax a bit. Sorry for making such a rude and demanding statement, but this is serious. No one knows you are here, and the Italian and Vatican presses are famous for their escapades when it comes to the secrets of the Vatican," Karl said in a hushed tone as the elevator door began to open. "I go first, Steve, from this point on. Let me open the doors, and stay on my right at all times. I have other Swiss Guards in the square; just keep walking, and I hope I can take you sightseeing later. Ready? Here we go."

As they left the elevator, Steve noticed that the other plainclothes Swiss Guards were taking up their stations outside, and upon seeing them exit the elevator, they began walking into St. Peter's Square, which would lead them to the Apostolic Palace. As Karl opened the door, Steve began his walk towards his destiny with the first step into St. Peter's Square.

The walk was brisk but not too fast, and the crowds were not particularly interested in them as they walked by. As they walked up to the side entrance, a uniformed Swiss Guard held the door for them, but only Karl and Steve entered while the others took up positions outside the door. He tried not to look around and to keep his focus centered only on what was directly in front of him as he walked with Karl. The grandeur of the building and its famous art was a blur to Steve; neither Karl nor he

165

spoke a word as they made their way to the staircase. As they climbed the stairs, Karl looked at Steve to gauge how he was doing, sure that the anticipation of what was about to happen had to be weighing heavily on him. As he looked at him, Steve just nodded and smiled, and they continued walking in silence with only the sounds of their heels striking the marble floors to be heard. When they reached the entrance to His Holiness's private study, the two posted guards came to attention, catching Steve off guard.

"Professional courtesies, Mr. Michaels, from the Swiss Guard to you!" Karl said as Steve stood up straighter to show respect to the men who guarded the Pope.

Chapter 39

Karl did not enter the room; he just gestured to Steve to enter once the door was completely opened. As he entered the room, only one thought kept coming to his mind: *Bow. See his hand flat, kiss his ring; thumb up, shake his hand. Don't blow it!* He kept his vision straight as he walked forward and then noticed Father Tommaso, who stood up from his desk to greet him.

"Mr. Michaels, welcome to the Vatican. Were your accommodations satisfactory?" Father Tommaso asked.

"Yes, from what Karl has told me, it is one of the rooms that the Cardinals used during the Conclave, so to me it is a bit more than I deserve. Oh, and Father, please call me Steve," Steve answered as he went to shake Father Tommaso's outstretched hand.

"Steve it is, then. If you are ready, His Holiness will see you now," Father Tommaso said and went to open the door leading to the Pope's private study.

"One question, Father: do you know what's going on?" Steve asked very quietly.

"No, but I can tell you that His Holiness is extremely anxious to meet you, and that does not happen to a Pope very often," Father Tommaso said with a hint of a smile on his face. "Just listen to what they say and remember they asked you here, so something is going on."

Father Tommaso opened the door and patted Steve on the shoulder. "Take a deep breath and remember he is just a man," he said softly.

Steve replied, "Yes, but one who speaks with the voice of God on this Earth. Just a regular guy? Right!" He smiled as he shook Father Tommaso hand again, who was chuckling at Steve's last statement.

With a deep breath, he began to move forward to see what mysteries lay beyond this door. Rounding the corner, he was immediately meet by the smiling face of Pope Alexander IX, the Bishop of Rome. Standing to his right was the Abbot of the Brown Robes along with the companions who had picked him up at the airport just a couple of hours ago. *What would have happened,* he thought, *if I had just said no to the Pope and not made the trip? Oh well, here goes nothing…*He moved toward the Pope to see what destiny awaited.

"Mr. Michaels, may I introduce His Holiness, Pope Alexander IX!" Abbot Giuseppe announced formally.

Steve walked forward, urging himself to breathe slowly, and noticed that the Pope's hand was flat out in front of him. He genuflected, kissed the Ring of the Fisherman, and felt the Pope raising him up by his shoulder.

Steve was somewhat surprised by the strength in the Pope's hand as he stood straight and looked into his eyes.

"With what has transpired, Mr. Michaels, it is I who should be kneeling in front of you for your actions for Our Holy Mother Church and those who believe!" His Holiness exclaimed, and in unison all four present knelt in front of Steve, who was completely caught off-guard and embarrassed by what was happening in front of him. Steve offered his hand to the Pope, who took it and rose again, shaking his hand and motioning Steve to sit on his right where a table was set up between them. On the table was an antique wooden box and a metal box that was sealed with red wax and embossed with a crest that he could not make out from where he sat.

"How was your journey, Mr. Michaels? Your accommodations are good?" the Pope asked Steve.

"Yes, very much so. I was informed that the room I have is one that a Cardinal uses during the conclave. Seems to be a bit much for a guy from Illinois, to be honest with you, your Holiness!" Steve said with a bit of a laugh.

"Well, I guess this whole ordeal and why I have brought you here is a bit much as well, so I will let His Eminence Cardinal Giuseppe fill in the missing pieces of why you are here and what we are about to learn," Pope Alexander answered. He motioned to the Abbot of the Brown Robes to take over and tell the tale of St. Pius X and his prophecy.

Chapter 40

Cardinal Giuseppe got up and walked around the table so that he stood directly before the wooden box, opened the lid, and removed the letters from the box. He handed the first letter to Steve and a copy that had been translated into English by Father Tommaso for him to read.

"I am the Fourth Keeper of the Secret that was entrusted to the Brothers of the Brown Robes by Saint Pius X in 1914, a few months before his death. We have had no idea what is in the box that you see here or the contents of the letter like the one you hold in your hand now. The First Keeper was given a letter from St Pius to be opened upon confirmation of his death, and that letter gave the prophecy; this is the letter that was hand written by a saint, telling us what to do and how to do it concerning the prophecy once it had been fulfilled. After looking at the YouTube video of you, we knew that you and you alone had fulfilled the prophecy almost to the letter."

When he finished, he gave the letter to Brother Angelo and motioned for him to read out loud the passage pertaining to Steve from Saint Pius X. Brother Angelo slowly read the words of a Saint,

"There will be a man from the Americas who will display great faith and have the utmost belief in our Lord.

He will withstand a great pressure of faith and will follow his belief in our Lord to do the right thing. He will be faced with death for his beliefs but will not let it sway him, and he will triumph over this, and this will be recorded for the whole world to see. He will win this fight on his beliefs and his beliefs alone.

As Brother Angelo finished reading, the silence in the room was deafening. He handed the letter back to his abbot and noted that his hands were shaking slightly. Once it was finished, Steve could not grasp what had just been read to him: he fulfilled a prophecy that was over one hundred years old. He just sat there, looking at the other four, wondering what was going to happen and staring at the unopened letters that were left in the box. After taking the metal back and putting the letter back into the box, the crest, which he could not identify, came into full view. On it was affixed the seal of office of the Patriarch of Venice. At least, that's what he assumed it was.

He cleared his throat and asked in as strong a voice as he could muster, "Are you sure you got the right guy? I mean, I killed a man. Certainly this must disqualify me from fulfilling the prophecy of a saint." As he looked at the Pope, he continued almost yelling at him, "I'm just a guy from Elgin, Illinois. I might be devoted in my faith, but this is way over my head. I mean, I killed a man! Doesn't anyone realize this? I am not a man to be fulfilling anything!"

Steve rose, looking for the door, but Abbot Giuseppe rose with him and gestured for Steve to sit back down. Brother Michael got up and poured Steve a glass of water; he took it with shaking hands. As he sipped his water and tried to regain his composure, he looked to Abbot Giuseppe for help with a pleading look.

Giuseppe knew the look of despair in a man, and Steve Michaels had that look on his face now. Slowly, the abbot began talking to Steve as if he was the only one in the room.

"When I first heard the calling of God to serve Him, I too was in shock and full of disbelief. Nothing in my life had prepared me for what lay ahead or what I was about to do. I put my faith in Mary and took a step forward. You are at that point now, Steve, and no one will say anything to you if you need to leave now and go home. We here have made the choice to serve him blindly and accept whatever fate brings us."

Giuseppe had his hand on Steve's shoulder now as if he was hearing a confession; this took the Pope back to their days at seminary when Giuseppe was always the one with the most faith and devotion, even then.

As he finished speaking, Steve looked at him like he understood what his concerns were, and a feeling of trust began to fill the room.

Giuseppe continued, "We know that you killed a man, Steve, but you were unarmed and had your faith as your guide. I saw the video; never once did you flinch or shy away from what was in front of you. You knew what needed to be done and only you could have done it. Some say you are a hero, but I believe that you were working under the guidance of a saint, and that is why you are here with us today."

Steve looked at the Cardinal with disbelief but also with a much clearer vision of what was being asked of him. It was not the outcome that had brought him here but the fact that he did something to protect the Church. He and only he acted on that Sunday, and now he must face the consequences of his actions, no matter what they were.

"So you are saying that the outcome is not the reason I am here but the act?" Steve asked, hoping he was right.

"Yes, that is it exactly, Steve!" Giuseppe answered quickly. "You acted and defended the Church and your faith. You are here now as the fulfillment of a prophecy that I never thought would be fulfilled. I am humbled to be here with you Steve as this does not happen in too many men's lives, to be a part of history as it happens and to be the one who started it by holding they sheet of paper in our abbey for over one hundred years!"

When Giuseppe finished answering Steve's question, His Holiness spoke softly, "Steve, please. We do not condone the outcome, but this act of faith of yours is one that should be honored and not swept under a table. Men do things for no other reason than they believe it is right, and your beliefs have led you here to me in this place at this time. I have no idea what is going to happen next as these letters were news to me just a couple of days ago. If you do not think that you can follow whatever is in them, then no matter what, I will absolve you of all responsibilities pertaining to them. Do we have an agreement?"

Steve was taken aback by this statement; he now understood that no one knew what was going to happen next in these letters, quite an uncertain position for him and the Vicar of Christ to find themselves in at this time. Now that he had an out clause, he was more at ease with it.

"Your Holiness, let's open the next letter, and to both of you, thanks for making me feel a bit better about my situation. I am a guest here and am certain of one thing: under normal circumstances, one does not yell at the Pope! I'm sorry about that, your Holiness; please, forgive me," Steve said as his nerves began to wane. He reached for the next envelope.

Chapter 41

The Pope nodded his approval with a smile on his face. He knew that he had just given Steve a ray of hope in what lay ahead. As Steve took the letter, they all noted that it was bound the same way with the wire rope around it and the Ring of the Fisherman seal affixed to it. Steve carefully cut the seal with the knife that Brother Michael produced and handed it back to him; then, he laid the letter on the small table as he unwound the rope. He put the rope back into the wooden box and noticed that the other two ropes had been placed carefully there as well. He opened the letter, which struck him as being in great condition for being over one hundred years old, and carefully unfolded it, placing it on the table for all to see. Inside was another smaller envelope with the notation on the front for this to be read second. Steve looked at the Pope and shrugged his shoulders; nothing was making any sense to him right now.

He looked at the letter and was surprised that it was written in English, which caught everyone in the room off guard. Steve noticed that the two Brothers of the Brown Robes were saying prayers that could barely be heard. He looked at the letter and began reading but stopped and asked if they would like to hear him read it out loud. All four of them nodded as if they all had lost the ability to speak.

Steve cleared his voice and began reading out loud, "*My blessings to you the fulfiller of my prophecy and defender of the faith. I realize that you must be very confused by all of this, so let me start with why you are here.*

I have been unsuccessful in stopping a war that will involve all of mankind as we know it. I, the Bishop of Rome, am powerless to stop what has been happening even though common sense says to stop, but their pride and farfetched sense of superiority has taken them over.

There is never a winner in a war, and no nation can ever recover from the damage and the loved ones that are to be lost. There will be a whole generation of young men destroyed by the whims of older men who think they know better. And yet I cannot get them to stop and work out their differences peacefully; it will boil over and consume everything in its path, and no one will be safe. That includes the one bastion of hope left in this world, our Holy Mother Church, of which I am just a servant.

As there will be no winner or loser, it is up to us, the Holy Roman Catholic Church, to be the ones who begin the healing when the dust finally settles on what is about to begin. With the whole of Europe and Russia up in arms, we will be the only ones whom they can turn to for help and to nurture their faith and trust in the end. We the Church of some 1914 years old will be the only guiding light left in the end, and this is where you will pick up my torch and represent me now as my champion of faith!

In saying this, I hope you now will have a better understanding of why your faith has led you here to Rome to be in the presence of the current Vicar of Christ. I trust that these, my last Pontifical Orders, will be allowed to be carried out. I pray to Mary, His Mother, for guidance in this time of trouble.

"I announce for all that you are to be first invested as a Knight of the Golden Spur, and I proclaim that you are to be granted the title of Colonel of the Noble Guards as one who has protected the faith and, in essence, me, the Vicar of Christ. I also do herby command that the current Bishop of Rome, the Vicar of Christ, lay his hands on you for you to receive the blessings of first tonsure, which is the reason for the second letter. Once first tonsure has been received, you may open the other envelope that was included in this one. This is commanded by me on the Feast of the Epiphany in the year of our Lord 1914.

Pius X pp."

All of them, including Steve, looked at each other in disbelief as the words from the third letter still resounded in their minds. Steve got up and began to speak, but his words left him as quickly as he started. Giuseppe stood alongside of him, not knowing what might happen. All present were in shock upon hearing the words of the saint.

Chapter 42

The only one who could speak was His Holiness, who said in a shaky voice, "Brother Angelo, would you go and ask Father Tommaso to please come in here and bring his notepad?" he asked. As Brother Angelo got up, Steve sat down and looked at the letter again in disbelief.

"What is first tonsure?" he asked to all present as he looked at the order to have him installed as a Knight as well.

"First tonsure is the right of entering the clergy, Steve," His Holiness answered, still in a shaking voice "It had been done away with by Pope Paul VI, and now it is recognized that you enter the clergy when you are ordained a deacon. But is seems, as this letter was written in 1914, it is still in effect, as are his orders pertaining to you as well."

"Holy Father, you asked for me?" Father Tommaso asked as he entered and looked around at what appeared to be a room full of grown men with a look that could only be described as shock on their faces.

"Yes, go fetch a pair of small scissors and bring Cardinal Albani here to meet with our newest Knight of the Golden Spur.

Also please ask the current resident historian on Pontifical Equestrian Orders if he knows if we have any of the presentation medals that go along with the Knight of the Golden Spur. Thank you, Tommaso," His Holiness instructed as Father Tommaso jotted down notes about the Golden Spur.

"Holy Father, did you say scissors?"

"Yes. Now, go and get them, and please bring back Giovanni. I am dying to see the look on his face as well!" His Holiness added, a smile coming to his face as what was read started to sink in.

"Whatever is in the next envelope, I hope it's as good as this one has been," exclaimed Brother Michael, who came alongside Steve to re-read the letter.

"Always the pessimist, aren't you?" Brother Angelo asked Brother Michael in his joking manner.

"Well, it was a lot to take in, but it's beyond our guesses what these letters hold. I remember reading that Pope Pius X had predicted World War I and knew that he would not be alive to see the end. Funny how such a blessed man could predict such a terrible thing and have the presence of mind to record this prophecy for us to read aloud today," Abbot Giuseppe said in his strong but compassionate voice.

"So I am to become part of the clergy? Is that what I'm hearing in this letter?" Steve asked to all present again.

"Yes, so it seems. Once Tommaso and Cardinal Antonelli get here, I will proceed as I have been ordered. It's funny: whoever would have thought that I would be ordered about while I am wearing the Ring of the Fisherman?" His Holiness said and began to laugh out loud. As the others joined in on the laugh, Steve sat there, still looking at the words tonsure and Knight.

"Michele will kill me," he said to no one. "She will skin me alive. Me, part of the clergy! Your Holiness, you will have to sign something for me to show her because she will never believe me in a thousand years!" Steve said as Giuseppe came alongside him and put a hand on his shoulder again.

"I am sure that can be taken care of for the ranking Colonel of the Nobel Guards and a Knight of the Golden Spur. You may not know this, but the Knighthood that you have been granted is the second highest and can be bestowed upon any man only by the Pope. It, if memory serves me right, is granted to someone who performs great deeds for the Church in her defense!" Giuseppe added. He continued, "But Steve, do you wish to have first tonsure as the letter has indicated? Pope Alexander had granted you the right to be dispensed from any responsibilities that are written in these letters."

"I do believe your Eminence that what has been revealed here today is my destiny. I was picked by you as being the one who fulfilled the prophecy,

181

and I could not but accept this fate. This man knew what was coming, and if it is his wish I should carry out his orders, then so be it. But I have to tell you something: this is way harder than facing a man with a gun!" Steve answered. He suddenly knew that whatever was in the next envelope he would be able to do. As he sat there, he picked up the next envelope and felt it for the first time; it had something heavy in it, like a medal, and it was circular in shape. "Cardinal, does this feel like a medal to you?" Steve asked as he handed Giuseppe the next envelope.

Chapter 43

As Giuseppe took the envelope to feel what Steve had asked about, Father Tommaso came into the room with Cardinal Albani following behind.

"Your Holiness," Cardinal Albani announced "You have sent for me. How may I be of service?"

"Giovanni, I am glad you were in your office. Please have a seat. For what I am about to tell you, you will definitely need a chair!" His Holiness said with a very large smile on his face. As he motioned for Cardinal Albani to sit, Father Tommaso brought over another small table and then proceeded to place the scissors and a very formal presentation box on it. He noted the letter but could not read it; he knew that whatever was in it had these men sitting up and taking notice.

"Giovanni, what I am about to tell you does not leave this small circle of friends. Well, at least not until I decide how to make the official announcement of what has transpired so far. Are we clear with that? " His Holiness asked a somewhat confused Cardinal, who just sat there and nodded. "I would like to introduce Mr. Steve Michaels of the United States."

Steve walked over to shake Cardinal Albani's hand, who was still so confused as to why he had been summoned that he did not put his ring out to be kissed.

"Pleasure to meet you, your Eminence," Steve said with a very strong voice.

"Yes, pleasure. Er, Your Holiness, what is happening here? Did you say Steve Michaels?" Cardinal Albani asked as nothing was being processed very quickly. He felt like he was coming in at the end of a football match and had to ask what had happened so far on the pitch.

"Yes, Steve Michaels. You might remember him as 'Mr. I Believe' from the video that is out there now," His Holiness said to one very confused Cardinal.

"I recognize the name, Your Holiness. Is he the one whom the prophecy foretold?" he asked as the pieces were beginning to fit into the puzzle.

"Yes, one and the same, Giovanni!" His Holiness answered. "I have brought you here to be a witness. Steve, please pass me the letter that you just read." As Steve carefully passed the letter to His Holiness, both Brothers of the Brown Robes took up position on either side of Steve. "Please read this to yourself, and no questions until you are finished."

"Yes, Your Holiness," Cardinal Albani answered somewhat sheepishly as he knew that these men owned him and now were exerting their power over him. *Funny,* he thought to himself, *all these years of being a priest, a bishop, and now a Cardinal, and finally*

I understand the power of this office. As he read, His Holiness and Cardinal Giuseppe watched his face for signs of disbelief or of an argument forming as he read. After he finished, he held up the letter. Steve took it and carefully laid it back on the table.

Cardinal Albani stood up, nodded to His Holiness, and spoke to all, "Mr. Michaels, I as Cardinal Secretariat of State, do hereby acknowledge that you are the fulfiller of the prophecy and that you should enter our ranks by receiving first tonsure. A bit outdated way to enter but nonetheless still a viable method. Speaking as one with a doctorate in canon law, I see nothing that would not be true for a letter dating from 1914 written by the hand of a saint!"

Before a somewhat stunned Pope and Cardinal Giuseppe, Cardinal Albani reached out to shake Steve's hand once again and asked, "May I assist His Holiness in granting first tonsure? It seems that we are about to hear more words from St. Pius X, and I would like to be here to hear the Vicar of Christ's last Pontifical Orders."

"You may stay, Giovanni, but this must not leave this room. Are we clear?" His Holiness asked him again.

"Yes, your Holiness is very clear in that sense. If I am to remain in service to you and Mr. Michaels, I shall be silent about this whole affair until given permission to speak," Cardinal Albani responded, clearer now in his resolve to accept what was

185

happening about him. All three of the Brothers of the Brown Robes looked at him with a bit of suspicion, but with this many witnesses they knew that he would be expelled from his post if he broke his word. Trusting a career politician who was also a Cardinal seemed to them to be the letter of the day in the Vatican.

"How do we begin, your Holiness?" Steve asked, hoping to move this along as the suspense was eating him alive. *The quicker I get to the next letter,* he thought, *the quicker I can get home and try to explain everything to Michele. It might take a whole lot of butt kissing to get Michele to go along with what has happened so far,* Steve thought to himself, but he knew that she would accept the orders of a Pope.

"Brother Michael, please move these chairs, and, Tommaso, please bring me the scissors" His Holiness instructed, pointing.

As the chairs were being moved and an opening created amongst them, Cardinal Albani moved to the Pope's side; on the other side was Cardinal Giuseppe, and flanking them were Brothers Michael and Angelo.

"Please kneel here in front of me, Steve," His Holiness pointed to a spot on the marble floor. As Steve knelt he noticed that Father Tommaso was standing with his cell phone out to record what was about to happen. The floor was hard, but Steve knelt like his dad had taught him all those years ago, straight with his hands folded perfectly. His Holiness began by saying "I, Alexander, Bishop of Rome, by the order of one before me, do announce that Steve Michaels shall be granted the rite of first tonsure and placed under the patronage of Saint Pius X and our Holy Mother!" As he spoke he placed his hands on top of Steve's head and then motioned for Cardinal Albani and Cardinal Abbot Giuseppe to place their hands on his shoulders as well. "He will be known as a Brother of the Brown Robes and accepted into their order as only fitting, as they were the keepers of the prophecy all these years. Brother Michael, please, the scissors..." His Holiness asked. As the scissors were being passed, Steve looked up to the Pope, wondering what this was for.

"I shall now take fours tufts of hair in the sign of the cross as a sign of humble obedience to Mary our Mother and to his new position as a member of the Brown Robes." His Holiness took four very small tufts of hair and placed them in Brother Angelo's outstretched hand, who in turn placed them in the box that contained the letters. "By the powers vested in me as Bishop of Rome, and in front of these witnesses, please accept Brother Steve as having received first tonsure today!"

Steve was helped to his feet by Cardinal Giuseppe as the others in the room begin to clap. He had received tonsure and could open the next letter.

Chapter 44

As His Holiness motioned all to sit, Giuseppe handed the smaller envelope back to Steve, who asked for the knife again from Brother Michael. He carefully opened the seal on the back and unfolded the letter, which turned out to be quite a bit larger than it was led on to be. All in the room, except Steve, let out an audible gasp: the circle of metal that Steve had asked about was actually the seal of a Papal Bull. This letter was written in Latin, and since he could not read it, he handed it to Cardinal Abbot Giuseppe to read for him. Giuseppe looked at His Holiness, who nodded.

He began reading, *"Pius, Episcopus, Servus Servorum Dei – "*

"In English please, Giuseppe, as our new Brother of the Brown Robes has not been trained in Latin," His Holiness asked.

"Yes. Sorry your Holiness, but a Papal Bull is not what I was expecting to be reading today," Cardinal Abbot Giuseppe replied.

"Pius, Bishop, Servant of the Servants of God, does hereby decree that having been given the minor order of first tonsure, you the fulfiller of my prophecy and defender of the faith, shall be elevated to the following rank in our Holy Mother Church under the patronage of His Mother Mary.

"You are hereby raised to the level of Cardinal Deacon and with it all honors and privileges that go with this position. You are authorized, by my decree, to wear the Scarlet of the Princes of the Church and ordered to swear obeisance to the current Vicar of Christ.

"Please open the metal box that was brought by the keepers of my prophecy, and in it you shall find a gift from me to you.

"I command this day of the Epiphany in the year of our Lord 1914. Pius X pp."

Steve looked at everyone around him as the table with the box was brought forward by Brother Michael. Steve held the knife with shaking hands. Cardinal Giuseppe took it from Steve, who was grateful, and then cut the seal on the box for Steve. The edges were sealed in wax, and he did not open it. Steve sat in the chair that had been placed for him next to the table and slowly opened the box, looking inside. He removed a scarlet biretta; under it was a scarlet zucchetto. Both were in great condition for being over one hundred years old. The wax had done its job to keep the humidity out.

Next to the biretta was a ring box, which Steve took out and opened for all to see. In it was the ring of a cardinal, a rich-looking gold ring with a red stone that looked to be a very bright and vividly colored ruby. Steve took the ring out of the box and read the inscription inside the ring band out loud for all to hear, *"Giuseppe Cardinal Sarto 12 June 1893."*

"It is the ring from his elevation to Cardinal in 1893!" Cardinal Albani exclaimed as he knelt in front of the ring, now knowing that this was indeed the act of a saint. As Cardinal Albani rose, Steve took a little envelope out of the bottom of the box. He carefully cut the seal and removed the card inside.

He read it and smiled to himself, handing the card to Cardinal Albani, who read out loud, *"These have brought me luck, and I hope there is some left in them to carry out the task that I have assigned for you. Once you are announced, however and whenever you may choose, please open the last letter, my dear Cardinal.*

Pius X pp.

Chapter 45

As Steve held the ring in his hand, His Holiness held his hand out and asked for Steve to kneel again. He put his hand on his head again and blessed him with the Sign of the Cross; he then took Steve's right hand and slid the ring onto it. It was a little loose, but it felt so heavy on his finger, Steve thought. As he looked at it, the weight of the ring reminded him of the new responsibilities that he was facing now that he was a Cardinal. Lost in thought, he did not feel the scarlet zucchetto being placed upon his head. As he rose with help from Brother Michael, his right hand was taken by Brother Angelo, and his ring was kissed.

"My dear Eminence," Cardinal Albani exclaimed "Please let me congratulate you on your selection to join us as a member of the College of Cardinals. I will see to it that you are given all the training that you require for your new role as prelate in our church!"

This caught His Holiness and Giuseppe off guard as they figured that Giovanni Albani would never recognize any honors bestowed upon Steve, no matter who was giving them out.

"Giovanni," His Holiness said. "I thought you would be skeptical of this. I mean, a man who has just received first tonsure and then been given the title of Cardinal Deacon?"

"Your Holiness," Cardinal Albani replied. "I would have been had I not been here to witness the reading and the opening of the box. I know that we have had our differences, but this is different. This is happening before my eyes, and I now know how Thomas felt missing the first visit of our Lord Jesus after he had risen. I have seen, and I believe. There is no doubting that this man is truly the one who has fulfilled this prophecy. Plus one does not doubt a saint if he understands what is good for him!"

This brought a laugh from all except Steve, who was looking at the fourth letter and wondering what Giovanni Sarto had in mind for him and what this task was that he would be given. As he stood there, he did not hear His Holiness asking him if everything was okay. He looked up to see everyone looking at him.

"Did I miss something?" Steve asked.

They all began laughing again as Brother Michael told him that the Holy Father had asked him a question and that he had seemed to look through everyone there, lost in thought.

"Michele will never believe this; she is now married to a Cardinal and a knight. How will I ever tell her? She isn't too good with surprises, and this is one doozy of a surprise," Steve said to all present.

"How about I take care of that for your Eminence," came the voice of Father Tommaso.

Steve looked at him and for the first time understood that this was the fixer of the group: the man who got things done and did them under the radar for the Pope. *Nice to have this guy for a friend,* Steve thought.

"Your Holiness, if I may ask something?"

"Yes, Steve, what is it?" His Holiness answered.

"I feel a bit overwhelmed about all of this. How will the other Cardinals, and for that matter the other clergy, accept me? I've heard stories of the Curia and how vindictive they are..." Steve admitted in a worried state.

Both Cardinal Albani and Cardinal Abbot Giuseppe began to answer, but His Holiness waved them off quickly.

"Steve, I have no control over what men think, and some in this building are petty even after my reforms. The Curia is made up of men much like those in your government: the President changes, but they are the cogs in the wheel, so to speak. Most of the pettiness here stems from being in their jobs too long and feeling entitled to some power that they really do not have. That is a fact of life. As to how the Church will deal with your elevation to a Cardinal Deacon, I cannot predict; but you will have the power of this office behind you and now the power of the Secretariat of State's office as well. Those are two big allies in your corner, so to speak, Steve!" His Holiness replied in a way that made a calm come over a very worried Steve Michaels.

"Your Holiness, if I may," Cardinal Albani interjected.

"Yes please, Giovanni. Please," the Pope answered.

"Steve, how men will react should not worry you. I have seen the letters and now understand what this is all about. St. Pius X was worried what the War would do to his Church. He gave you an order that no one here knows at this time but will have significant measure for the Church as it stood in 1914. The other clergy will abide because you have been given a pontifical order that is valid even to this day. I looked for a way to use my political influence to see what was going to happen to you, but Pius himself saw fit to stop me in my tracks. He ordered me to leave the room before the second letter was opened; he understood and has already protected you by issuing a Papal Bull that decreed you to be a Cardinal Deacon. No one can deny that or argue that point. We have taken a vow of obedience, one that you have been asked to swear to as well. This binds us, Steve, like no other vow could. He was the Vicar of Christ, and I will defend and follow him to my last breath. And so will every other member of the clergy!" Cardinal Albani finished talking and then knelt and kissed the Pope's ring, knowing that this was his revelation, his calling to God to begin anew, which Pius had caused.

Time seemed to stop for a minute or so; no breathing could be heard but for the soft prayer that Cardinal Albani was whispering as he held the hand that bore the Ring of the Fisherman. His Holiness just patted his head and helped him up; then, he gave him a hug and motioned for all to sit. Giuseppe and the other Brothers of the Brown Robes looked upon Cardinal Albani with much more respect and sorrow for the man who had finally come to realize why they all served but had taken this long to see. Giuseppe did not pity him but wished that this had happened much earlier in his time spent as a priest; he had had so much to offer when he was younger as he had seen during their time spent in the seminary. To say that this was another miracle was an understatement; he had not seen Giovanni Albani so humble in a very, very long time!

Chapter 46

Elgin, Illinois

Michele had gotten the text from Steve when he got to the airport but had heard nothing since then. This was a bit of a worry to her, but she knew that he had arrived safely; that she was grateful for. *At least he sent me the text; finally, he is remembering the rules,* she thought as she laughed to herself. With Jim in bed sleeping and Steve gone, she had the time to log onto the Boy Scout website without both of them seeing where she was and begin her research into what Jim might be qualified to receive for his actions at church that Sunday morning. She was still mad at both of them but at the same time so proud of what they had done. *My husband is in Rome because of a prophecy, and my son saved a man's life. Not a bad pair. Now if they could just find the hamper once in a while! Oh well, such is life,* she thought as she laughed out loud to no one. While searching the web page, she came across the page describing what the Honor Medal of the Boy Scouts was and how it was awarded.

"The Honor Medal may be awarded to a youth member or adult leader who has demonstrated unusual heroism and skill in saving or attempting to save a life at considerable risk to self,"

Michele read out loud and then noted to herself that her son's actions fit the bill to a tee. As she downloaded the form, she realized that she could not fill it out but knew the one man who could and whose writings would lend much weight in the deciding committee's decision. She put the forms safely away and went to get a couple hours of sleep before Jim needed to get up and go to school.

Chapter 47

The Vatican

Steve just sat there looking at his surroundings, a bit bewildered, and picked up the case that was on the table.

"Father Tommaso, what is this?" he asked.

"That, your Eminence, is the medallion of the Order of the Golden Spur," Tommaso answered. "I had it in the office safe. This is the second highest ranking Pontifical Equestrian Order, and only the Pope may grant someone to receive it. As you have been granted this honor, I thought it would be a good time to bring it to you. Please open the case, your Eminence, as I for one would like to see what it looks like," Father Tommaso suggested.

Steve looked at the cover of the case. On it was the image of a Golden Spur. As he opened it, Father Tommaso walked behind him to look as well. In the case was an eight pointed star that had a gold spur below it. The ribbon was red silk and came with another, larger medallion that was identical.

"The larger one is to be worn on the right-hand breast pocket of the order's uniform jacket.

As you have received this order in defense of the Church and have been created a Colonel of the Nobel Guards, you are permitted to wear a military uniform for formal presentations. The uniform of the Nobel Guards is quite ornate but they were disbanded in 1967 by Pope Paul VI after the Second Vatican council. I am sure that a suitable uniform could be had," Father Tommaso remarked as all looked on a bit stunned. "It is amazing what one can find on Google, your Holiness," Tommaso said as he sheepishly held up an iPad.

All of them began laughing except Steve, who was looking at the medal. "So, I am a Colonel of a now defunct guard and am authorized to wear a uniform and be a Cardinal at the same time? Sounds like St. Pius must have something in mind for me to do once I am announced. The card did say that I could pick when and how, did it not?" Steve asked.

"Yes, it did, Steve," Giuseppe answered. "Is something coming to mind that you would like to share about that?"

"Ever been to Illinois?" Steve asked.

"No, I have not, but it seems a trip is in my future," Giuseppe answered, laughing out loud.

"Your Holiness, I will need some time to plan everything, but I would like to be announced at my home parish of St. Paul's in St. Charles, Illinois. Since that is where this all started, what better place is there to stage this event?" Steve asked hesitantly but with a strong conviction to his voice.

"Your Holiness," Cardinal Albani interrupted. "That would be an excellent idea. We could still control the event, as Steve is calling it, but not have to worry about the immediate implications of his being announced as a Cardinal! This is something that I know I can help with, your Holiness, and make sure that it is done in a way to shed a positive image for the Church and for you as well!"

His Holiness thought for a moment and began to weigh the consequences of such an act. The Curia would find out at the same time as the rest of the world; the American press would treat this positively as having one of their own citizens honored for his actions. He could from afar bless the event but not be there, creating the distance needed to protect him and a buffer for the fallout here at the Vatican if there was any. He was beginning to like Cardinal Albani a bit more now.

"I agree, but the one thing is there must be no word of this to anyone. Steve, you can't tell anyone, and we will not be involved in the planning. I will let you and Cardinal Giuseppe take care of that; Father Tommaso can help with funding as he will know what to do. But first, Steve, I need to do what St. Pius X has asked me to do. Please kneel in front of these witnesses and repeat after me."

Steve knelt in front of Pope Alexander and repeated, "I, Steve Cardinal Michaels, do hereby solemnly swear obeisance to the Bishop of Rome and will subject myself to the rules and observance of Our Holy Mother Church." His Holy Father blessed him, and Steve kissed the Ring of the Fisherman to seal his allegiance to Alexander, the Bishop of Rome. As he rose again, he placed the scarlet zucchetto back into the metal box and put the ring back in it as well. No one but Michele would know what was in that box, and he could cover this all up by telling folks that he was knighted for his actions. The plan was beginning to take shape, and he knew that with Cardinal Giuseppe's help he could and would carry it off.

"Your Holiness, the only person that should know outside the six of us should be Karl, my duly appointed Swiss Guard bodyguard. I would like to use him here to help myself and Cardinal Giuseppe brainstorm how I should be announced. He can also help with getting my new wardrobe shipped back to Elgin. Seems if I am to be an officer, I might need to look the part; plus, his help will be huge in getting me to notice the things around me and what to look out for moving forward. I have a lot to learn and only a couple of months to get ready," Steve said to His Holiness with a certain calm about himself now.

"A couple of months, Steve? What do you have planned? Or better yet, when are you thinking about being announced?" asked Cardinal Albani.

"Well, if my cell phone calendar is correct, December 6 will be the date. It is the Sunday before the Feast Day of the Immaculate Conception. As I have been pledged to Mary our Mother, and as she is the Queen of the Men's Club, there is no better date. It will give me time to prepare correctly and to have Cardinal Giuseppe be in Chicago to give me the fourth letter once I have been announced as a Knight of the Golden Spur and as a Cardinal," Steve said with the gears already turning.

"Well, Steve, it sounds like a plan, but isn't Chicago a bit cold in December?" Giuseppe asked laughing. "Couldn't we make it sometime warmer or maybe somewhere warmer, like Florida? I hear it is nice in December."

"I do have a request, your Holiness," Steve remarked.

"Yes, what is it? And please don't ask if you can take Father Tommaso away from me," His Holiness answered with a laugh.

"Your Holiness, to look the part I will need to dress the part. Do you have a private tailor that can help me design my uniform? As you will have my measurements from the fitting, I am sure that Father Tommaso can acquire the correct sizes and dress robes for me to be presented as a Cardinal," Steve asked as the plan was beginning to take shape.

"I do like how your plan is shaping up. It allows us here at the Vatican not to be involved, yet I can still help you and advise you through Father Tommaso and my dear friend Cardinal Giuseppe," His Holiness replied to Steve. With a nod to all, His Holiness asked Tommaso if they he might be able to get some food as everyone had skipped their morning meal. As they were talking, Cardinal Albani cautioned everyone again about keeping this quiet. He now knew that whatever St. Pius X had in store was going to be big. This had already been the most exciting thing to happen in the Vatican since the last conclave.

As Father Tommaso opened the door, he was greeted by Karl, standing at attention, and motioned for him to enter the room. As he entered the room, he bowed in front of the Holy Father and approached him to kiss the Ring of the Fisherman.

"Karl," His Holiness began. "You need to have a seat as you are not going to believe what has just happened here!"

Chapter 48

As Karl took his seat, the Pope and Cardinal Albani sitting with him as well, the others, including Steve, stood behind His Holiness. Karl looked a bit stunned to be sitting with the two most powerful men in the Vatican, and he had no idea what was going on.

"Your Holiness," Karl began very formally. "Is there something wrong or something that you need done? I am at your service."

"Well, Karl," His Holiness began. "There has been a turn of events here today, and I need you to be brought up to speed so to say. First I must ask you to vow that what is about to be revealed to you will be kept in the strictest of confidences, and you may not speak to anyone but to myself and the other five in this room. Is that clear?"

"Yes, your Holiness," Karl said, sitting up even straighter. "I will take a solemn vow if need be!"

"No, your word is good enough for me. How about you, Cardinal Albani?" His Holiness asked.

"I have known Karl for two years, and his word will suffice for me, Holiness!" Cardinal Albani answered with a smile.

"Karl," the Pope began. "Steve has fulfilled a prophecy that was foretold by St. Pius X some one hundred years ago. Our friends, the Brothers of the

Brown Robes, were entrusted with this prophecy and concluded that Steve did fulfill it one hundred percent, and I have agreed with them on that fact. St. Pius X left four letters with instructions in them, and we have just opened the third one today. Steve, by the Grace of God, has received first tonsure and has been confirmed and appointed as a Cardinal Deacon by St. Pius via a Papal Bull. I and Cardinals Albani and Giuseppe administered it to Steve a short time ago, and then he swore obedience to me as Bishop of Rome.

"What we are going to ask you to do, Karl, is to be his bodyguard moving forward. He is going to go back to the United States and prepare to be announced on December 6th at his home parish of St. Paul's. I want you to be there with him until he is announced, not only as a bodyguard but to teach him military protocol and how to walk and act like a military officer. You will be compensated for your travels, and you shall by my command be made a Sergeant Major of the Swiss Guards for your duty and this act. Steve will fill you in on the rest of the details. So, Sergeant Major, do you accept your assignment and vow to keep all of this quiet?"

Karl looked at the Pope, then at Steve, and tried to focus and take it all in. "Um, well, your Holiness, yes I do accept. It is going to take some time for all of this to sink in. I can be packed and ready to leave in an hour if need be!" Karl answered, knowing that his life would never be the same again.

Steve walked forward to Karl with an outstretched hand, and while shaking his hand continued, "Thanks, Karl. What I will need you to do first is get with Father Tommaso about what the uniform of a Knight of the Golden Spur is; then, you can begin helping to get me ready for whatever St. Pius X has in store for me with the last letter. As far as being ready to travel, I believe that I will need some time at home to arrange for a place for you to stay and so that certain articles can be sent to me. We will talk as Cardinal Giuseppe and I, along with my Brothers of the Brown Robes, are going to start the planning for it. I will need you to come with us today after a bit and will bring you up to speed. Oh, and Karl…thanks for your help," Steve said as he continued to shake his hand.

Karl looked at Steve and then at the others in shock. The man he had picked up from the airport a couple of hours ago had just been made a Cardinal Deacon. He looked and did not see a ring on Steve's hand but believed that it had happened.

"Your Holiness," Karl asked, a bit shaky. "I understand that this needs to be kept quiet, but what did you say about a uniform?"

"Steve has been made a Knight of the Golden Spur and a Colonel of the Nobel Guards. As such, he is authorized to wear a military uniform by the grace of St. Pius X. I do not know what he has in store for his being announced, but under the guise of a Knight of the Golden Spur, I am sure he can make it happen. He will need to learn how to walk and salute as an Officer, and you will be his teacher and his protector!" His Holiness answered in a very clear manner that Karl understood without question.

"From what I saw on the video, Your Holiness, I do not think that His Eminence needs me to be his protector!" Karl said with a slight laugh.

The rest of the room started to laugh as well, but Steve did not. His mind was racing and not just about being presented and having the world find out. How was he going to break this all to Michele? *Me, a Cardinal and a knight! She will skin me alive and never let me live this down. I can just begin to hear the one-liners that she is going to use on me,* Steve thought. *'My husband, the Cardinal, went to Rome, and all I got was a metal box to show for his visit!' She is going to have a field day with me. I wonder if Karl can bring his gun with him? He might need it!*

Father Tommaso came back in the room and announced to all that a light breakfast would be served in the dining room next door and should be there in a few minutes.

207

"Karl, I do believe that we need to sit and talk, and then once the plan is laid out, we can begin my training. Welcome aboard!" Steve said and patted him on the back as they all left to get a bite to eat. Karl just looked on in amazement as what he had just agreed to started to sink in.

Chapter 49

As they retired to the Pope's private dining room, Father Tommaso asked Steve if he had a tailor at home in the USA. Steve replied that he did not. He bought his suits at the local store that did alterations but was not a real tailor shop.

Cardinal Albani looked at both of them and said just one word, "Gammarelli's!"

"What is Gammarelli's?" Steve asked.

"They are the ones who outfit the Popes and the Cardinals here in Rome, Steve. They hand make everything and can get your uniform and the other articles of clothing for you so that you can be presented in December!" Cardinal Albani answered. "If they cannot make it, then no one can, Steve. Karl can take you there to help you with your uniform and to get your measurements for your robes as well. As we have some time, no one will notice a request for a new set of Cardinal's robes. So how does that sound to you, Steve?"

"Sounds great. Do they take Visa?" Steve asked with a laugh.

"Steve," Father Tommaso interjected. "You will not need your credit card as this will fall under the same household account as the Cardinals who are being presented at their Consistory. The first set of robes is…how do you Americans say it? Oh yes! 'On the house!'" They all had a laugh at Father Tommaso's usage of American slang for who would pay for the robes. "Your uniform will also be covered by the same account that covers a Cardinal's first choir dress."

"Well, that takes care of that. Now all I have to do is decide what my uniform will look like and how to get it back to Elgin. Seems our work is not done, Father Tommaso, but I am looking forward to this new challenge in my life. Now my next problem will be how to convince Michele, which will be the real chore!" Steve said with a hint of seriousness to his voice.

"I am sure you will think of something, Steve. I can have a letter drafted and signed by His Holiness, explaining what has happened if you wish," Father Tommaso answered.

"No, the only way to convince my wife is to tell her straight forward and then get ready for the barrage that comes after I'm done. We dated for three years, and we have been married for eighteen years. If I have learned anything, it is to give it to her straight and then try to ride out the storm after!" Steve said, knowing full well that these men had never had to talk to their wives before and explain anything. Speaking of Michele…he looked at his watch and did the mental time zone calculations. It was almost 1:00 p.m. in Rome, which meant it was 7 a.m. in Elgin; he set a reminder on his cell phone to give her a call at 8 a.m. her time. Lost in thought, he did not notice Father Tommaso laying a couple of sheets of paper at his side.

"Steve, here is what I could find on the uniform of a Knight of the Golden Spur, but you can make your own changes as long as it doesn't end up looking like your football jerseys in America!"

Steve laughed and looked over the pages. It sounded quite plain but very formal, a black velvet coat with red piping and more red piping down the sides of the pants. *Nicely understated*, he thought. Not too gaudy and definitely something that he could wear with confidence.

Karl asked for the printout to get an idea and then asked, "Will you wear your rank or just the insignia for the Knight of the Golden Spur?

"I believe that to wear the insignia of a Colonel would be wrong, Karl. I am not a military officer, no matter what our friend St. Pius X has decreed. I respect those who serve too much ever to wear the eagles of a Colonel on my collar. The insignia will be just that of the Knight of the Golden Spur and that alone!" Steve answered strongly, and those at the table took note of his conviction for the rank and the respect that he had for it.

"I agree with Steve, Karl," Cardinal Albani said. "He is already the highest ranking Cardinal in the Sacred College as of now. No other Cardinal has been granted a Pontifical Equestrian Knighthood since the mid-1800s, much less the Order of the Golden Spur in defense of the Church."

"Highest ranking Cardinal? Are you sure?" Steve asked.

"Yes, Steve. Since you were awarded your knighthood before you read the Papal Bull, your knighthood cannot be taken away once you received your appointment as a Cardinal. As a Cardinal Deacon, normally you would not be able to be presented with any honors except those that are honorary, such as some of the present members of the Sacred College who have received honorary Doctor of Letters degrees from various universities for the work that they have done in their homelands. But you received this before you were announced; in ranking your position, you would be the highest ranked Cardinal for your defense of the Church."

Steve just looked at Cardinal Albani, a bit dumfounded as all of this new information slowly sank in, but to hear this made him cringe. He did not want to be the highest rank of anything.

"Your Holiness, is there anything that you can do so that I will not be ranked like Cardinal Albani has informed me?" Steve asked, almost pleading.

"Steve, please do not worry yourself about rankings and such," His Holiness answered. "It only will matter when you are present in a consistory or a conclave. There you will take the position of First

Cardinal as your rank will outweigh seniority. Some might be jealous, but then again those men are already too consumed with themselves even to want to understand why you are there with them. You will be fine, and once they get used to you being there no one will bother you. Oh, yes, maybe rumors, but then again it is the way of the Vatican!"

Cardinal Giuseppe added, "I can help you with that more than the others, Steve, as I will be treated the same way the first time I take a seat in the College of Cardinals. We were appointed to wear the scarlet as a Prince of Church by St. Pius X himself, and there is no denying that fact. You will be greeted with open arms once they realize that you have earned your way there with acts in defense of our Holy Mother Church!"

Steve looked a bit more relieved but still uneasy about the whole situation. If only he had gone to a later Mass! But not to worry about that now as he finished his meal…what he really needed to do was get a couple of hours by himself to think this through and maybe get an hour of sleep to help him through this. He stood and thanked everyone there for their kindness that morning and asked permission to be shown back to his room as he needed to think and relax from his flight. He had not had a chance to unpack or even sit once he landed. The Holy Father asked Karl to show him back to his room, and Father Tommaso informed all there that the letters and the

box containing his gifts from St. Pius X would be kept
in the Pope's private meeting room until they could
talk more about his plans. His Holiness nodded his
approval, and Steve and Karl left the room quietly,
both walking a bit straighter since both of their lives
had certainly changed over the course of the last few
hours.

Chapter 50

Elgin, Illinois

After she had gotten up and gotten Jim off to school, she knew what she needed to. As it was now 7:00 a.m., she took the chance that someone was up already. She picked up the phone and dialed the rectory for St. Paul's.

"Hello, this is Michele Michaels; may I speak to Father George, please?"

"Father George here, Michele. How are you doing?" Father George asked while adjusting the sling for his arm.

"Doing good, Father, but more importantly how are you feeling?" Michele asked like a mother hen.

"I'm getting better; the surgery went well, and I'm convalescing the best I can do here. I had to plead with my doctor to get out of the hospital early as I was going crazy in there. Now all I can do is sit and read or watch some TV. No masses for a little while. Father Rick's orders!" Father George said with the customary lighthearted laugh to his voice.

"Well, that's good and sorry about the boredom. So really, do you need anything, Father?" Michele asked, trying to mask the concern in her voice.

"Oh, no, Michele. I'm fine. Father Rick is my personal servant, and I'm going to take full advantage of it! But on a serious note, I'm getting better from the gun shot. The surgery went well, and I will get to begin physical therapy to regain my range of motion in about a month. I'll call if I need anything, but what I have not done is talk to Jim yet about what he did for me after I took that tumble. Is he home? Can I speak to him?" Father George asked her.

"He's in school right now, but I have a favor that I need to ask of you, Father. This is one that you can do to help stem the boredom that you are facing while you recover," Michele said in such a way that Father George did not realize that he had just been a bit manipulated. "I need you to write a report on how Jim helped you and what the doctors said about the first aid that he gave you after you were shot. I'm going to be using your report and the police report to nominate Jim for the Boy Scout Honor Medal, but I need your help to do it!"

Father George was smiling on the other end of the phone, hearing what a mother was going to do for her son. "Now this is something that I can do for you, Michele, and it will give me something to focus on besides my injured wing! Let me give you my email

216

address, and you can send me the info on the medal that you have so I can review it and write up the nomination accordingly. This would be my pleasure, Michele, and the least I could do for him."

"Oh, just one other thing, Father George: let's just keep this to ourselves, okay? No telling Jim or anyone else. I don't want the troop getting wind of this until it has been decided by the national office of the Scouts. I've downloaded the nomination form and will attach it to the email. Father, I know that this has been crazy, but what Jim did is beyond belief. To do what he did, and all because of the training he received from the Boy Scouts!" Michele said, trying to keep her personal pride and emotions out of it.

"Michele, he was trained by his father. Never forget that. His father put himself in front of a gun that a madman was holding and then disarmed him and stopped anyone else from getting hurt. You should be proud of both of them. And I did hear from Father Rick about the little scene you caused at the church, trying to get to them after they had taken me away. Father Rick is still laughing at when you told the police to move or so help you, which was way too funny, Michele!" Father George said, laughing at the last line.

"Well, what did you want me to do, kindly ask them to step aside so I could go tend to my family? That idiot put himself in front of a gun, and I will never forgive him for that. He could have been shot! Or worse!" Michele almost yelled into the phone and then started laughing as Father George was laughing even louder at her now.

"You know, Michele, you might want to cut him some slack. He did save people's lives, and your son saved mine! And please keep reminding me never to get on your bad side; you really can get carried away a bit!" Father George said through his laughter.

"Ok, Father, I will lay off him for now, but if he ever does something as lame-brained as this again, I will kill him!" Michele answered, and they both continued laughing as they hung up.

As she sent the email to Father George, she looked at the form and then decided who else she could ask to be a witness who could keep this quiet.

Chapter 51

The Vatican

As they walked, neither of them spoke; Steve was keeping himself in step with Karl and noticed that he was a bit more relaxed but still very alert to his surroundings. *Funny*, Steve thought. *A week ago I was a nobody, and now I am a Cardinal. Who would have thought it was ever possible?* They made it to the side door they had come in through earlier to exit the palace, and Steve made a motion to Karl to have a seat over near the door. As they sat there was still no talking between them; neither knew what to say at that moment.

Steve broke the ice, "So, nice weather you are having here this Fall!"

Karl began laughing out loud at the remark, "The weather? You want to talk about the weather? You are funny, Steve, very funny. Nice to know you can still keep your wits about you after what you have been through today. I mean you have been knighted and have been made a Cardinal, and you want to talk about the weather!"

"Well, I didn't know where to begin; plus, you looked like you needed to laugh a bit after all that

219

stuffiness in the office. It's funny: he lives here in a palace but has no central air. I think he needs a brother-in-law who does HVAC, to be honest," Steve was on a roll. He knew humor would be the one thing to get through this, and Karl did need a laugh right now.

"Stop it, Steve, I cannot take much more. Are you always like this?" Karl asked.

"When I get nervous, yes. I let my humor take over, as bad as it is," Steve answered with a grin. "I know that once I am announced, things will change, Karl, but until that time please just let me be me. I just hope that you can put up with my wit. I know my wife thinks it's a bit too much at times."

"Well, if she is married to you, I am sure that she can put up with anything!" Karl laughed, letting his guard down for a quick minute.

"Good come back; wait until I tell her that one!" Steve joked back as Karl mimed mock horror at the thought. "Oh, you just wait. Michele will turn you inside out, Karl. Speaking of her, we need to get back to my room so that I can call her. I have no idea what I am going to tell her!"

"Word of advice, Steve. Do not tell her over the phone about the red hat thing. Keep that for when you are there with her back in the States. Tell her you have been knighted, and leave it at that.

I am sure there will be questions coming from her just about that," Karl consoled Steve, who understood and nodded.

"Well, let's go and tell Michele that her husband is a knight and see what trouble this will cause!" Steve said as they got up and headed back to his room across the square. Steve did not notice that the Swiss Guards were stationed at either side of Steve just within arm's reach as they walked. When he did notice, Karl just smiled and said, "You are correct. Your life has changed!"

Chapter 52

As the door to his room closed, Steve took off his suit coat and tie and then hung them up in the closet. He looked at his cell phone, knowing that he needed to make the call. He did not want to lie to Michele but knew that he needed to tell her in person about being elevated to a Cardinal. As he dialed, he took a deep breath and hoped that she would be in a good mood this morning.

"Hi, you. About time you called me. What did I tell you when you left the car? Call me when you get there! How many times do I have to tell you that, Steve Michaels?" Michele started on him without taking a breath but smiled, knowing he would never change.

"I'm fine, thanks for asking! How are you and Jim doing?" Steve asked, hoping that she would take the bait he put out there by changing the subject quickly.

"Don't you be asking how we are. My god, Steve! Just call next time, okay? Is it that hard to just call?" Michele yelled into phone.

"Michele, the Pope says *hi* and is praying that you don't have a coronary over me not calling when I landed!" Steve answered her, knowing that this tack might get her to stop for a minute so they could talk.

"Oh sure, Mr. I Believe, bring the Pope into it. I'm sure that he will fix everything!" Michele laughed back at him, knowing that she had won the battle but not the war with him over not calling.

"He did say *hi* by the way. So did Cardinal Giuseppe and Cardinal Albani and Father Tommaso!" Steve said, not stopping. "They all said *hi* and wished that you were here to share with me what has happened to me today!"

In a split second, Michele's tone went from sarcasm to serious. "What happened, Steve? Can you tell me what has happened?" she asked, knowing that he had something to say but did not know how to say it to her.

"Everything is fine, Michele. It's just that I was knighted by St. Pius X, nothing too earth-shattering. Just a regular knighthood!" Steve answered, waiting for the onslaught of questions to begin.

"Did you say knighted, as in Sir Steve? Or is it different at the Vatican? Am I to be known as Dame Michaels now? Do I get to wear a tiara? Come on, Steve, tell me what the hell do you mean, knighted?" Michele almost yelled through the cell phone.

"Well, to answer your questions, no and no and no. I am a Knight of the Golden Spur because my actions were deemed to be in defense of the Church," Steve answered her calmly.

"So, no tiara? What a gyp, Steve. You get a medal, and I get to hold your bag. You are so going to owe me when you get home, and speaking of that, I am not going to call you sir, and you are not wearing any spurs…no matter how attracted to them I am!" Michele laughed back at him, knowing there was more to the story he did not want to tell her over the phone.

Throughout their marriage, he had always preferred to talk to her in person and as an equal. It was one of his most endearing qualities that she admired about him. He never once treated her as not part of his life; well, if he knew what was good for him, he never would start either. Michele was smiling now; she knew there would be no more exchange of what had happened until he got home. "So have you seen any of Rome since you have been there?" she asked, which gave Steve the signal that she understood.

"Nope, not a thing yet! They picked me up from the airport and drove me directly to the Domas something or other where the Cardinals stay during the conclave. Nice place but a bit too plain for me, no mini bar or cable!" He was trying hard not to laugh as he talked, but he knew it was a losing battle.

"Steve, please be serious!" Michele pleaded with him. "You haven't seen anything?"

"No, I might go out later with Karl, my duly appointed bodyguard from the Swiss Guard. I met the Pope and then came back to my room. I'm exhausted. I slept on the plane, but with what has

224

transpired in the last couple of hours, I feel totally spent right now," Steve replied in a voice that Michele knew was truthful.

"So, a Knight of the Golden Spur. I am looking at it on my iPad right now. Quite an impressive honor to be given, Steve; I mean for a guy from Illinois!" Michele exclaimed.

"Geez, thanks Michele. Thanks for the support there," Steve laughed back at her. "I'm going to get an hour of sleep or so; then, I'm going to go out with Karl for a bit. I have to go get fitted for a uniform to be presented in as a knight. Not bad for a guy from Illinois, is it now?"

"No, I guess not," Michele replied. "Get some sleep and call or text me later. Okay, Steve?"

"I will, and thanks, Michele; we'll talk when I get home," Steve answered, knowing that the next round would not go as well as this one had.

Chapter 53

He tried to sleep but to no avail as his mind was working overtime with what had transpired in the last couple of hours. He needed to start making plans but first decided that another hot shower would refresh him; then, maybe he'd go and see some of the sights of the city, that is if he could get Karl to be his chaperon. After the shower, he changed into much more comfortable clothes and wondered how many more days of dressing like a regular guy he had left in him now. He kept wondering since he had no idea what the protocol was for being a Cardinal or for that matter what St. Pius X had planned for him with the next letter.

As he tied his shoes, there was a knock at his door, and Karl announced that he had a visitor. Steve opened the door to find a smartly dressed older man with a perpetual smile upon his face, holding a small black bag.

"Steve," Karl began. "Let me introduce to you Anthony Alberici from Gammerelli's."

"Mr. Michaels, pleasure to meet you. Karl here has been telling me that you are in need of a uniform suit that we have not made for a hundred years at Gammerelli's," Anthony said as he shook his hand and sized him up for his suit size.

"5'8"? 170 pounds, I would guess…am I close, Mr. Michaels?

"Yes!" Steve responded, impressed by Aberici's accuracy. "Well, what Karl has said is true. I am in need of a new uniform or suit or whatever you call it over here," Steve answered, still in shock over a tailor coming to him instead of the other way around. *Well,* he thought to himself. *When in Rome!* As Steve stood there smiling at Anthony, he noticed that Karl was just barely laughing at him as the introductions were going on.

"What's so funny, Karl?" Steve asked, still trying to figure out how Anthony knew he needed to be sized for a uniform.

"Well, Steve," Karl said with just the slightest of grins. "It seems a certain Cardinal acquaintance of yours made the call, and then Anthony was at the main entrance within twenty minutes. For a guy who has been in Rome for hardly a day, you do seem to have made yourself quite at home!"

"Knock it off, Karl," Steve said back, laughing as he just now understood the joke that must be going around the Swiss Guards who had been assigned to him.

"Yes, Steve, I will leave you in Anthony's hands, and he will take your measurements. You have a fitting at 4 p.m. this afternoon as well," Karl answered, looking at Steve's face for a reaction as his schedule was slowly not becoming his own.

227

"Thanks, Karl. A fitting, did you say?" Steve asked, now completely lost.

"Umm…Karl, if I may?" Anthony interjected. "We received a call from Cardinal Albani to come and measure you for the uniform of a Knight of the Golden Spur. This is quite an honor, Mr. Michaels! We have not made this uniform for quite a long time."

"Oh, so I have the Secretariat of State to thank for arranging this fitting?" Steve said as the pieces were beginning to fall into place. "Please remind me to thank His Eminence later, will you, Karl?"

"Yes, Steve," Karl replied, laughing again. "I will be right outside if you need anything else!"

Anthony set his bag on the bed and took out a tape measure and a file folder, which he opened, laying out the designs for the uniform of the Knight of the Golden Spur. Once they were laid out, he motioned for Steve to come over. "These are the designs for the uniform that we have on file for your dress uniform, Mr. Michaels."

"Well, first things first, Anthony. Please call me Steve, no matter what my laughing bodyguard has informed you to call me!" Steve said just loud enough so that Karl could hear from the other side of the closed door to his room.

"Well then, Steve it is. Now please let's look since you do have some say in the design. It can be changed; there is no precedent in how the uniform is to look in modern times!" Anthony said, businesslike.

Steve now knew what Cardinal Albani was referring to when he said Gammerelli's was the very best at what they did and that if they could not make it, no one could. As he looked at the uniform design, he knew that he wanted to keep it as simple as possible and that whatever they were going to add, there would be no plumes on it at all. He joined the St. Paul's Men's Club 4th Degree but never wore the regalia of the degree because he was just not a plume kind of guy. Smiling to himself, he got an idea and began to explain it to Anthony, who nodded his approval and then set about measuring him for the uniform that he would wear to be announced in. When Anthony left with the measurements and Steve's idea for the uniform, he handed his card to Steve and shook his hand again.

"See you at 4 p.m. Please come in the side door; Karl will know what I am talking about!" Anthony said as he reached for the door to leave. Opening the door, he was greeted by Karl, who smiled. Anthony continued on his way.

Karl entered the room and went directly to the designs that were left behind by Anthony on the bed. He looked over them and some of the notations that had been made in the margins and nodded his approval.

"So, it will be a very modest uniform that you have decided on, then?" Karl asked.

"Yes, it will be," Steve answered. "It will be formal but not gaudy with just the slightest of a military look to it. I do believe it will do justice to honor the Golden Spur insignia medallion that I will wear with it."

"Steve, as this is a military honor, you will need to wear a sword with it as well. I believe that Father Tommaso can help you with one from the private collection that they have in the Vatican!" Karl informed him.

"Yes, Anthony informed me of that as well. The coat will have the slit needed to handle the sword belt as he called it. Who knew when I stepped off the plane that we would be discussing me wearing a military uniform and a sword?" Steve said to Karl as he was just beginning to understand all of the details that he needed to learn in order to be presented in December. "Karl let's go and see if there are any books on protocol that I can borrow so that I can begin to study up on what I am going to have to learn!" Steve suggested as he headed to the door with Karl tagging behind.

Chapter 54

Karl pulled out his cell phone and made a quick call to Father Tommaso, asking if he could bring Steve by to look at a sword for his dress uniform and also to see what books on protocol that he might have. Father Tommaso agreed to have some swords brought up for Steve's review and some books as requested.

Karl looked at Steve and grinned, "Father Tommaso will have everything for you shortly. I mean, the private secretary to the Pope running errands for you is really quite amusing, Steve!"

"Karl, again, knock it off! I am never going to get used to this treatment, Cardinal or not. Do you think even for a minute that Michele will let me get away with anything? Oh no...she'll be saying *Your Eminence, take out the trash* and *Your Eminence, go cut the lawn.* I would not be surprised once I tell her if she doesn't punch me in the gut and then start yelling at me again!" Steve answered as they both laughed at what Michele would do to him.

"You know Steve, I have not met her, but I like her already!" Karl said in between laughs.

As they exited the hotel, they walked briskly to the Palace and entered through another door that was also guarded by two Swiss Guards who came to attention when they recognized Steve.

"They only know that you are a guest of His Holiness, Steve, and that you are 'Mr. I Believe'," Karl said softly. "And please understand again how proud we are to have you here with us as one who has served and put his life on the line for the Church!" Steve nodded to Karl as they walked but was silently thinking again that he did not deserve such an honor as he was just himself.

When they came to the outer office door, Father Tommaso was there to greet them and took both of them to another office down the hall.

"I have had some very fine presentation swords brought up for your review, Steve. His Holiness has given me the approval to loan you a sword from the collection to wear on the condition that it will be returned to the Vatican once you have passed," Father Tommaso said as he opened the door to another room.

"Pleasant thought, Father. They are already talking of my demise here at the Vatican?" Steve asked as Karl tried extremely hard, almost too hard, to stifle a laugh.

"Umm, that did not come out as I had planned it, Steve. Sorry," Father Tommaso answered as he too began to laugh, which was the cue for Karl to laugh out loud with both of them.

As Steve walked into the room, there were six swords all laid out on a velvet cloth in their presentation boxes, looking like they belonged in a museum. Each of them was encrusted with jewels and fine engravings but for one of them. This sword was extremely plain next to the others with a hilt that formed a cross with one red ruby in the center. It looked like no more than just a presentation sword, and the scabbard was not engraved but of a plain golden color. Steve picked it up out of the presentation box and felt the weight and how it felt in his hand, almost like it belonged to him.

He slowly removed it for the scabbard and looked at the blade and the etching that was near the hilt. It was written in Latin, and he asked Father Tommaso to read it for him: "'This is the sword of a Templar, and it shall save the world.'" As the words flowed from Father Tommaso's mouth, a strange feeling came over the three of them. Steve took the sword back from Father Tommaso.

"This one will do just fine!" Steve exclaimed as he put it back into the scabbard slowly. "Does anyone know which Templar this belonged to?" Steve asked.

"The information on whom this sword belonged to is a bit sketchy, Steve, but it has been authenticated to have been made in Toledo, Spain, in the year 1200 by a family of sword makers that are still in existence today. I did not know that they would bring this sword when I asked for some presentation swords for your review," Father Tommaso said almost reverently to Steve and Karl.

"Well, thank whoever had a hand in bringing this one as it is just the right one for what I need to be presented with. But who would have thought that I would have picked a Templar sword to wear as a Knight of the Golden Spur when I am presented? Maybe St. Pius X is still working his miracles even to this day!" Steve remarked to both men as he put the sword back into the presentation box that it was displayed upon.

Father Tommaso picked up the presentation box and told them that he would put it with the other items that were in the Pope's private study for him. He also informed him that Cardinal Albani was putting together some reading material for him as he had requested. As they left, Karl just looked at Steve again but with a much more proud feeling, knowing that he had been a part of all that had happened that day. Steve picking the simplest of the swords but one that had the greatest historical significance was beyond words for him to explain how it could happen right before his eyes.

Chapter 55

Elgin, Illinois

Michele was still reading about the Knight of the Golden Spur when Elaine called to chat about the article from the interview that Steve had given.

"Michele, how are you doing? Is Steve doing better?" Elaine asked in her usual fast-paced interviewing manner.

"Yes, we are both doing good. Thank you for asking. So this is an unexpected call. What's going on, Elaine?" Michele asked, knowing that getting to the point with Elaine was not always the easiest thing to achieve.

"Well, I wanted to talk to Steve about the interview and what my editors would like to do. He did insist on the final say, and I'm not going to cross him on that even if my editors told me I was crazy," Elaine answered quickly.

Knowing that she could not tell her where Steve was, Michele needed to make sure that the next question was not *where is he?* Michele answered carefully, "Steve is out right now; he needed to get some air. What does your editor need to ask him?"

"They would like to air the interview as it was given in the video that I recorded. It is a much more powerful piece than what I could have written. To do this, I need Steve's approval. I don't want a lawsuit over this. He was pretty adamant about the final control over the piece," Elaine said in one breath, hoping that Michele would agree with her.

"Well, he did give quite the interview and made it very clear why he did what he did. He even got a bit emotional about it, which is totally out of character for my husband. I have never seen him get that way before," Michele answered with pride for Steve beaming through. "So I take it that you want to air the video? And when do you want to release it?"

"We have a deal in place to release it on Channel 5 News tonight and our website simultaneously, but to do this we need his release. So can you call him and get him to give us the permission? This is big, and we have not even edited the interview. It is the best one I have ever seen, and I have been doing this for quite a while, Michele!" Elaine said breathlessly.

"Channel 5 and show it tonight…can you send me the interview, and I will have Steve review it and then give his approval? That's the best I can give you right now, Elaine," Michele said with almost no emotion showing through her voice.

"That seems fair, but we need to know by 10 a.m. so that they can start promoting it on their noon

broadcast. This is big, Michele. For me and for Steve.
It's in his own words with no one trying to make it
sound any different than the way he wants it shown
to the world," Elaine said in an almost begging voice.

"Send me the video, and I will get back to you
in twenty minutes," Michele said, masking her
emotions even more. "That is the best I can do right
now!"

"I'm sending the link to you now; this is
exactly what will be shown. No final editing or
making it into a sound bite. I fought hard for that, and
they agreed after viewing it themselves at our office.
Please call me back on my cell as soon as you can,
Michele," and with that Elaine hit send on the email
and said good bye.

The email was received in her email file just as
Michele had put the phone down. With a slight
tremble to her hand she dragged the mouse over it
and hesitated for a second before opening it. Without
Steve here she wanted to do the right thing and as she
had witnessed the whole interview she knew how
powerful and emotional it was. She took a deep
breath and clicked on the file to begin viewing it.

As the video began, it showed the two of them
sitting at the table, holding hands and looking like
every other middle class American family. She was
glad she had taken the time to do her hair in the
morning. Steve looked confident and quite assured of
himself; this was right after he had told them all to sit

and be quiet. As it continued, Michele noticed that it was not edited, and the raw emotional power of the event was pouring out of Steve as he talked. As he talked about the other family and asked for their forgiveness, she began to cry. She knew that this was her husband talking and trying to make right what he had done. She immediately thought about calling Steve or sending him a text but knew that it would take more than twenty minutes to be able to get his approval. Since they did not change anything and it would be shown complete, Michele took it upon herself to get the video out there for the world to see what this act of bravery cost her husband and how it affected him. As she typed the approval back to Elaine, she knew that this was the right decision and that Steve would understand that what she was doing was the right thing.

Chapter 56

The Vatican

It was close to 2:00 p.m. when Steve finally got back to his room after a little tour of Saint Peter's Basilica, courtesy of Brothers Michael and Angelo. As he was shown to the door, Karl reminded him that the car would pick him up at 3:45 p.m. to go to his fitting at Gammarelli's. *So a whole hour and half to relax and maybe just maybe close my eyes for a bit.* He plugged his cell phone in to charge. Before he laid on the bed, he texted Jim and sent him a picture he had snapped in Saint Peter's. He was really wishing both he and Michele were there now with all that had happened that day.

As he closed his eyes, he could not believe the knock at his door that startled him from his nap. Karl was there asking if he was ready to leave for his fitting. He sat up in the bed, realizing that he had slept the whole hour and a half like it was just a second. *So this I what jet lag is all about*, he said to himself.

"Come on, sleepy head. Let's go get your uniform," Karl said as a little smile and a laugh came to his face. "Not every day that you get to be fitted at Gammarelli's!"

"Really? Come on, Karl. Do you have to go with the laughter again?" Steve asked as he got off the bed. "You would think you'd have had your fill of that by now."

"Just getting started, to be honest. Well, until you put that red hat on, of course. Then everything changes for both of us," Karl replied very seriously with no hint of a smile.

"I understand and hope that we can still carry on like this during my training leading up to the big day," Steve answered. "It will be nice to have one person in my corner who is not afraid to make fun of me!"

"You do mean besides your wife, don't you?" Karl asked as the smile came back to his face.

"Dirty pool, Karl! And who ever said she was on my side, anyway?" Steve joked back as they both headed to the door.

They took a car that was provided for them and headed off to get the fitting for his uniform. As they drove, Steve looked out onto Rome as it passed by him, still in shock over his day. As he looked at the scenery, he could see some of the sights that he so wanted to show Michele and Jim and share in that adventure as a family, which he missed so much right now. As melancholy as he was feeling, he was still excited about the events, though he still did not understand how they could be happening to him. Lost in his thoughts, he did not hear his cell phone text message alert going off until Karl asked him what the noise was.

"Oops, sorry. Michele is sending me a text. She knows I don't answer them unless it makes a racket and I have to do something about it!" Steve replied as he tried to get his phone to quiet down. As he read the message, he said to no one there, "No way. You got to be kidding me!"

"Kidding you about what?" Karl asked in a startled manner.

"I was interviewed back home by one of my wife's friends from the local paper, and it seems that they are going to show the whole interview today. She sent me a copy of the final version, and according to Michele, they did not alter anything," Steve answered, a bit worried about how this might play out in the press.

"Well, I would not be too worried about it. So far the whole world has seen the video, Steve," Karl added, trying not to sound too worried about it as well.

"When we get to Gammarelli's, how about we take a few minutes to watch and see exactly how bad I did in the interview?" Steve suggested as the worry began to creep back into him.

As they pulled up to the side door as requested, Steve laid his cell phone on the dash of the car and turned the volume up to its highest setting. As he hit the start button for the video that Michele had sent him, he said, "Well, here goes nothing!"

As the video began, Steve could not look at the small screen, but his voice could be heard quite clearly, beginning to describe what had transpired. As the interview continued, he noticed that Karl was watching intensely while the story of what happened unfolded. When the interview was over, Karl got out the car without saying a word and got his cell phone out to make a quick call. As Steve got of the car, he noticed that Karl's face was very stern, and he was talking in a professional manner to whoever was on the other end. Karl opened the door and motioned for Steve to enter quickly. As the door closed, he noticed that Karl did not say anything and that the smile on his face had not returned.

They were both greeted by a smiling Anthony Alberici, who gestured for them to come into the private fitting area. As they walked in, Steve noticed the uniform was beginning to take shape as it hung over a mannequin. Alberici had chosen a rich-looking black fabric that allowed the red accent piping to show even more. The epaulets on the shoulders were plain as he had requested, but the buttons were of a rich-looking gold and seemed to be emblazoned with the crossed keys emblem of Vatican City. It was then that Steve noticed that Karl was standing at attention and showing no emotions, which seemed totally out of character based upon their chats from just a few minutes ago. Anthony was describing the coat when Steve could no longer stand it.

"Excuse me, Anthony. Karl, can I see you a minute over there?" Steve asked, pointing to the opposite corner of the room. "After you saw the interview, you began acting like you were at the airport terminal this morning. What is going on?"

"Steve, that video is going to be shown in a very few hours, correct? You are here in Rome with only a handful of people who know what is going on. With this type of press, someone will notice you here, and we cannot let that happen until you are ready to be announced. Your stay in Rome will be short this time, Steve, as we have to get you back to the USA today so that you will not be missed. More press will be calling, and you are going to be a very public person in just a matter of hours. Let's make this quick and then get back to the room to pack and fly back on the next plane out. I called Cardinal Albani, and he is organizing everything right now with Father Tommaso's help, no doubt," Karl answered professionally as only a trained bodyguard could think.

"I see your point clearly. Let me see what Anthony needs to finish; then, we can have everything shipped to me. I only need the silver box to go back to the States with me as that is what I need to explain to Michele. Can you make a call and have it ready for me to take with me?" Steve answered as Karl dialed his cell phone to make it happen.

"Anthony, we must unfortunately rush this fitting as something has come up. What more do you need while you have me here?" Steve asked, masking his emotions the best that he could.

"Try on the coat and the pants. I can make the clothes for the final fitting, and you can be on your way. I also have been asked to have your hat ready to ship as well for the uniform. We have chosen a Navy officer's dress hat for you to wear. It is very modest in style, and we can have it matched in color as well. I will be done in twenty minutes tops, if that is okay, Steve?" Alberici asked as though this seemed like no inconvenience to him at all.

As Steve stood there in his partially fitted uniform, he looked at Karl, who nodded his approval of the choice they had made together back at the room. *Amazing how these private tailors can do their work so quickly, like it is no problem. This might be something that I could get used to,* Steve thought to himself and then laughed out loud at the very thought.

"What is so funny, Steve?" Alberici asked.

"I just bought a new suit coat from Kohl's two weeks ago for work and was complaining about how expensive it was. Now I'm being fitted for a one-of-a-kind suit in Rome by the famous Gammarelli's tailors. No one is going to believe this!" Steve said with a grin that made even Karl laugh as he worked hard to get him on a plane and back home.

After Alberici was done, he brought out a cassock for Steve to try on for size. Steve looked at Karl, wondering how Albert knew, and just got a shrug in return.

"Steve, by order of his Eminence Cardinal Albani, I have been asked that we have you fitted for this as well. I just need to measure the hem and the shoulders for you while I have you here. I have also been placed under the strictest confidence not to say anything about this as well. I hope that whatever is going on that you will always think of Gammarelli's as your personnel tailor for all of your future needs," Alberici said with a grin that told the whole story.

"Nice to have the Secretariat of State working you for, eh, Steve?" was all that Karl could say.

Chapter 57

On the ride back to the Vatican, neither Karl nor Steve said a word as the implications of the interview going public were now just starting to sink in. As they pulled in front, Karl just nodded to Steve, who understood the meaning and closed the car door. As Steve walked to the door, it was opened by another Swiss Guard member, and another one was waiting for him inside the door with a package from Father Tommaso.

"I have been instructed to give this to you and to take you directly to your room. Father Tommaso will be by in about thirty minutes with your tickets, and we have to get you packed," the Guardsmen said in a very professional manner. "Karl will be taking you to the airport and is making arrangements for you to be escorted through security here and back in Chicago."

As Steve got onto the elevator carrying what he could only surmise was the box containing the biretta and the Ring of Pope Pius X, he held it with the reverence that it deserved. As he entered his room, he was startled to find Cardinal Albani and Abbot Giuseppe there waiting for him.

"Sorry for the surprise, Steve, but we wanted to talk to you privately before you go back to Chicago about what has happened today," Giuseppe said in a very respectable way. "You will need to move up the date for being presented as you probably can understand."

"I can, your Eminence. Does his Holy Father agree with this as well?" Steve asked, already knowing the answer.

"Yes, Karl contacted Cardinal Albani right after you showed him the interview," Giuseppe said with a renewed belief in what had happened that day. "He agreed with Karl that you need to get back to Chicago now. Too many folks have seen you here in Rome but with a bit of luck will not be able to put two and two together."

"How soon should I be presented under the current situation?" Steve asked the both of them.

"Steve," Cardinal Albani said, speaking first. "His Holy Father believes that you should be presented within two or three weeks. Albert at Gammarelli's has informed me that your uniform and cassocks for you new position will be ready within in a week. We are going to have the Brothers of the Brown Robe bring these to you along with the letters from St. Pius X. As they have been the Keepers of the Secret, they should be there to hear the last letter read out loud by you after you have been presented."

"Steve, Brothers Michael and Angelo are looking forward to helping you in any way possible, as am I," Abbot Giuseppe said in the same manner that he spoke to Steve in before the letters were read. "His Holiness is arranging lodging for us now, and we will be ready to help you in any way."

"I am having some books on Vatican protocol and on the duties of a Cardinal and a Priest sent to you. This will be best as then no one will see them but your family back in Chicago. I am giving you this book to read on the plane; it is the book I found on St. Pius X. You should understand who the man was and what he did as Pope," Cardinal Albani said as he handed the book to Steve.

"Thank you both for all you have done for me today, for trying to help me understand what has happen to me and preparing me for my future!" Steve said to both of his brother Cardinals. "Please thank His Holiness for me as well. This certainly has been quite a full day for all of us!"

As he finished talking, there was a loud rap at the door; figuring that it was the same member of the Swiss Guard to inform him that Karl was ready to leave, he opened the door quickly. To his surprise, standing there was Father Tommaso and His Holiness, Pope Alexander IX. As surprised as he was, Steve moved out of the door and motioned for both of them to enter the room. As they entered, both of the Cardinals bowed to His Holiness while Steve, dumbstruck, just stood there holding the handle to the door. Only then did he notice that the hall was filled with Swiss Guards and Karl, standing there at attention and on guard.

"Your Holiness, please. You did not have to come to see me off. I know how busy you must be," Steve said as he knelt to kiss the Ring of the Fisherman again.

"Nonsense, Steve," His Holiness said as he again helped Steve to his feet with his surprising strength. "I wanted you to know that you go with my blessing, and those of all of us here; this journey is going to be quite an unusual one for you and your family, and we want you to know that we are here to help you in any way!"

"Your Holiness, I am so grateful for that. This day was not what I expected it would be after taking your call. I hope that the interview did not cause problems for you. I did not know about my trip or what was in store for me before I gave it," Steve replied to His Holiness.

"Well, Steve, I have seen the interview. Cardinal Albani shared it with me, and I was quite moved. The idea of doing what you did because of your service as a member of the St. Paul's Men's Club in protection of your priests and church is quite admirable. Please remember that we are with you, and no matter what happens with the last letter of St. Pius X, we will support you. Please go with God, Steve, as you have been truly blessed by Mary, his Mother!"

"Steve, if you have any problem with telling your wife what has happened, please have her read this letter. I am sure it will help you out!" Father Tommaso said as he handed Steve a letter.

"If this doesn't work, you will get a call from me in a few hours," Steve said with a smile as he shook Father Tommaso's hand again.

As Steve looked at the letter, His Holiness made the sign of the cross, and Steve bowed and kissed the Ring of the Fisherman again. As His Holiness left the room, Karl entered, looking very serious and ready to react to anything.

Steve said goodbye to Cardinal Albani and to Abbot Giuseppe as he began to pack his belongings for his trip back home. As he packed, Karl spoke for the first time to Steve since their visit to Gammarelli's.

"I hope you are not upset with me, Steve, but that interview is going to bring you more attention than the video of you standing up to the gunman did. I need you to be ready to handle yourself and to take your security very seriously. I will be there to help you, but you need to remember that everything has changed for you. You are a Cardinal now, and your time will not be yours once you are presented. I cannot tell you how proud I am to serve you and to be granted the opportunity to help you during this time!"

Steve was taken aback by Karl's speech. He knew that his hardest task was still to come: telling

Michele what had happened to him that day. As he continued to pack quickly, Karl was again on his cell phone making more arrangements for his departure to the airport. Steve looked at the package that Father Tommaso had packed up for him and wondered what the fourth letter might have in store for him from St. Pius X.

The ride to the airport was quicker this time as they had a police escort, and they entered through the VIP entrance to the international terminal. There Steve was whisked through the security check point and showed to a private lounge.

"Your flight leaves in thirty minutes, Steve. I will be in Chicago in two days. I need to have some things taken care of before I can travel," Karl informed Steve as he handed him his first class ticket for the return trip to Chicago. "Please take care, and please watch your surroundings. If it looks bad, it probably is. Just keep your guard up!" And with that, Karl shook his hand and left the lounge.

The flight boarded, and Steve was the last to be seated so that the other passengers did not see him in first class while they passed through to their seats. The flight was half-full, and Steve was able to get comfortable quickly. He opened the book that Cardinal Albani had given him before he left and began to read. As he read, he started to drift off. The day was beginning to catch up with him all at once.

Chapter 58

Chicago, Illinois

He awoke, startled, as the plane touched down at O'Hare International Airport in Chicago; he had slept the whole way and still felt a bit out of touch. Beginning to wake up, he noticed that there was a blanket on him and that his book was in the seat next him. The first class flight attendant just smiled as Steve mouthed *thanks* to her for the blanket. She came over to collect it and added, "You might want to wait to disembark. There are reporters in the terminal waiting for you; your friend in Rome asked us to check when we landed." Steve nodded again and wondered which friend, laughing a bit to himself.

"Thanks. Umm…is there another way out of here?" Steve asked.

"Yes, there is. Customs is coming on board and will take you out though their VIP section. I don't know who you know, Mr. Michaels, but someone up there likes you!" she said. Steve noticed her nametag.

"Thanks again, Mary. I sure hope someone is looking out for me today. I have to go and face my wife, Michele. Wish me luck!" Steve said with a grin, noticing that he was the only one left on the plane.

The customs agent came on board and asked for Steve's passport, which he had out and ready for him. As the agent gave it his once over, he asked Steve if he had anything to declare. Steve held out the wrapped present offering to have it passed through the screening device. Looking at his passport again, the customs agent just smiled and left the airplane. *Hmm,* Steve thought to himself. *I wonder how much this red hat will help me at Starbucks in the morning?*

Steve gathered his belongings and thanked Mary again, who just smiled and said very softly to him, "Anything for 'Mr. I Believe'!" Steve returned her smile and left, wondering how long that line was going to follow him around. He started laughing at himself; he now finally understood the look Jimmy Stewart gave the conductor of the train at the end of *The Man Who Shot Liberty Valence*. He wondered if Michele would cut him the same slack once she found out what had happened.

As he walked through the terminal, he remembered Karl's words about security and started to look around instead of just aimlessly walking about. He got to the baggage claim area and stood to the back, waiting almost until the end to grab his luggage, and then headed up to flag a cab to take him home. Karl had told him not to make a call and not to hang around waiting for Michele to get to O'Hare. *Just take a cab home,* he said; *no one will be the wiser.* As he got into the cab, he pulled out his phone and called

Michele but only got her voicemail. He hung up, not wanting to have her call right back upset that he was on his way home without telling her. He settled into the seat for the hour drive back to Elgin and just looked out the window as the road passed by, wondering how he was going to tell the love of his life that she was married to a Cardinal.

Elgin, Illinois

Michele looked at her phone, did the math, and knew that it was 3 a.m. in Rome. She wondered why Steve would call that early. She decided not to call and went back to filling out the online form to have Jim nominated for the Boy Scout Medal of Honor while enjoying her once-a-week coffee at Starbucks. Jim played on his phone. They had enjoyed a dinner at their favorite Mexican restaurant. Steve was not too keen on that cuisine, so they could enjoy it together. These times were becoming less and less frequent as Jim got older. *Funny,* she thought to herself. *Just a couple of days ago, her son had helped saved a man's life and here he was playing on a game on his phone. So much like his Dad: not caring, just doing.* She was so proud of them both but would never tell them.

As she finished her coffee, Michele finished the form and sent it to the Scout Office along with Father Rick's account of what had happened. This would take only a week to be approved; she had already talked to the committee, who would recommend it to the next level without delay. As they pulled out of the parking lot, she looked at her son and wondered where her little boy went to. When they pulled into the drive at home, she noticed that the lights were on in the den and that the front door was open, although she knew that she had locked the door before she left. She left her car in the drive and carefully approached the front door only to be surprised to find her husband standing there, smiling and opening the door as she walked up the steps.

Chapter 59

"Steve Michaels! What are you doing here? How did get here? Why are you not in Rome? Did you get kicked out of Italy? What are you doing here?" Michele exclaimed as her husband helped her into their front room.

"Hi, Michele. How are you? I'm fine, by the way. Thanks for asking," Steve said with his trademark smirk, grabbing his wife in a bear hug and giving her a kiss before she could say anything else or give him a quick elbow. "Seems that someone gave the folks at the paper approval to air a video of which I was the star attraction! I had to come home quickly. You will not believe what has happened to me!"

"Dad!" Jim yelled as he rounded the corner, oblivious a minute before to the fact that his dad was home as he was still playing the game on his phone "When did you get back?"

"I came back tonight. There is some news that I have to share with both of you, and I needed to make sure that people saw me here and not in Rome! Did either of you two leak where I was to anyone?" Steve asked, already knowing the answer but just making sure.

"No Dad, I told no one, and no one asked either. So what is this big news that made you fly back so quickly?" Jim asked, not waiting for his mother to answer.

"Yes, what is this big news, Steve, that you had to leave Rome so quickly?" Michele asked carefully, trying to get a read on the situation that was starting to unfold in front of her now.

"Well, first, Jim, would you go across the street and ask Mr. Roberts to come over, please?" Steve asked, knowing that he would need Paul's help in case anything did happen before Karl got there.

"Sure, Dad," Jim said as he walked out the door and headed over to the Roberts's house across the street.

"Why do you need Paul over, Steve? Are you in trouble? Or did something else happen beside you being knighted?" Michele asked as only she could ask.

"Something else has happened, Michele," Steve said as he jerked his thumb over to the metal box sitting on the table. "What is in there is has changed all of our lives, and we will never be the same again. Never!"

"Stop it, Steve. You're scaring me, and you know I'm no good at being scared!" Michele said in a very serious voice as she knew her husband was not joking around. She figured this must have been what he had alluded to on the phone when he called to tell her he had been knighted. "What is it, Steve? What has happened?"

As he looked at her and was about to say something when the front door opened and Jim and their neighbor Paul came into the room.

"Paul, thanks for coming over. I hope I didn't interrupt anything important?" Steve asked his friend.

"Oh, no. Was just reading. So what's up that you need me here? Why are you home from Rome so soon?" Paul asked.

"Well, let's just start at the beginning shall we? Please everyone have a seat as I have a hell of story to tell you!" Steve said with just a glint of smile coming to his face.

As they took their seats, Steve stood. The jet lag from being in Rome would not let him relax. He started with landing and being met at the airport by the Brothers of the Brown Robes. He went on to explain that he now had a personal bodyguard named Karl, who would be there in a couple of days to help in the preparations that were going to come.

"Preparations, Steve? What are you talking about?" Michele asked, impatient.

"I'm getting to that, Michele. Please, there is a lot to tell all of you, and I have to do it in order or I will mess something up," Steve pleaded with his wife, knowing it was not going to stop the questions.

"Well then, could you give us the CliffsNotes version? The suspense is killing me," Michele answered with a smile that she used to get her way with her men.

"Sure. Jim can you pass me the metal box at the end of table, please?" Steve asked.

As Jim passed the box to his Dad, Michele noticed the red wax seal that was on the top but could not make out the design in the wax. She took out her phone, took a quick picture, and then began typing away to see what it was. As she searched, Steve looked at all three of them and slowly lifted the lid. Then he reached in and took out the ring box and handed it to Michele.

"Steve, really? A present for me? I thought you didn't have enough time to go shopping," Michele exclaimed as she opened the box with the excitement of a child on Christmas morning. As she looked at the ring of St. Pius X, she realized all at once that it was not for her, and a puzzled look came over her face. "Steve, what is this?"

"That was the ring of Giuseppe Sarto when he was installed as a Cardinal in 1893; you may know him by his other name, Michele," Steve answered with the same little grin on his face.

"What other name?" Michele asked, still not sure of what she was hearing from her husband.

259

"His other name is St. Pius X, and he is the one who wrote this prophesy that I fulfilled. That is his ring, which he has given to me," Steve answered.

"Given to you? Isn't he dead, Steve? I mean, what is going on?" Michele said, knowing that this CliffsNotes version was not what she expected.

"As I was saying, my dear wife, let me start at the beginning because the short version will only get you more confused," Steve said. The look on Michele's face was the same as at the rectory when Pope Alexander had talked to both of them just a couple of days ago. "Um, Michele, you might want to close your mouth as those little guys with the red cones are directing traffic again!" Steve teased her as he got out of the way of her elbow, which was being directed at him. Michele kept the ring, just looking at it in its box as Steve started at the beginning again.

"I was not told anything by the Brothers of the Brown Robes at the airport or by Karl on the way to the Vatican. They were in the dark as much as I was, Karl even more so since he had been ordered to be there. When we arrived at the Vatican, I was taken by Karl to the Domus Sanctæ Marthæ. I hope I have pronounced that correctly; I had to write it down," Steve said, looking at the scrap of paper that he had written it down on. "This is the hotel that the Cardinals stay at during the Conclave, and I was shown to one of their rooms for my visit. I was taken immediately to His Holiness's private office in the

Apostolic Palace. By the way, Michele, that tie you picked for me looked really nice," Steve mentioned, which got her out of the stupor that she was in looking at the ring.

"Thanks, Steve. This ring…is it real?" Michele asked, still not following what was being said.

"Yes, Michele, it is real. Like you never saw the ring of a saint before!" Steve said to her in his teasing way.

"Oh, you will pay for that one, Steve Michaels!" Michele exclaimed, which brought a laugh from Jim and Paul.

"So you were shown to the Pope's private office?" Paul asked, hoping the question would help Steve in moving his story along.

"Yes, I was introduced to Father Tommaso Antonelli, who is His Holiness's private secretary, and he showed me into meet the Pope," Steve said, continuing the story.

"Were you nervous, Dad?" Jim asked.

"You have no idea, Jim. Father Tommaso reminded me to kneel and kiss his ring. It all happened so fast that I was glad for Father Tommaso's help!" Steve said as he took a deep breath and a sip of water; his mouth had suddenly gone dry.

"They read St. Pius's prophesy and allowed me a minute to let it sink in. I was then handed the third letter of St. Pius, which was bound with wire and a wax seal that was the crest of the Ring of the

261

Fisherman. Your phone didn't find it, Michele? The same crest is in the wax on this box, as well.

"I opened the letter and began to read it; it was written in English, much to everyone's surprise. The letter informed me why I was there, and the reason will surprise you, Michele. You pointed out the reason at the Church when you showed us the video. I was there due to being 'Mr. I Believe' and because of my actions at church on Sunday, and it was foretold over one hundred years ago by a man who became a saint! I didn't know until yesterday — well, today — that it even existed and neither did Pope Alexander. This is the most amazing thing that has ever happened to me. Well...since meeting you of course, Michele," Steve said quickly, hoping against hope that it would soften what he knew was coming from her shortly. "As I read the letter, it announced that I was to be knighted as a Knight of the Golden Spur for my actions and that I would be named a Colonel of the Nobel Guard," Steve said, pausing as he let that sink in to the three of them.

"Did you say *knighted*?" Paul asked. "Like a real knight? Like in England?"

"Yes, but this is a Pontifical Equestrian Knight. I won't be addressed as 'Sir' or Michele as 'Dame.' It's a real knighthood but one that does not bestow any honors outside of the Vatican or a Church function!" Steve answered his friend.

262

"So I don't have to bow or anything?" Paul asked jokingly.

"Um, well…we'll get to that, Paul," was all that Steve replied, which got a quizzical look from Paul.

"What do you mean, Dad?" Jim asked softly.

"Steve, just tell us, would you? The suspense is driving me — er, us crazy!" Michele added.

"Well, after I was granted my knighthood and made a Colonel, I was given, by His Holiness, the rite of first tonsure," Steve added meekly.

"First what, Steve? Tonsure?" Paul asked.

"Yes, it is the giving of minor orders, and then you are considered entered into the ranks of the clergy. Today you must be ordained a Deacon, but in 1914, it was the rite of first tonsure," Steve said trying to make the suspense last a bit longer than necessary.

"Clergy? Did you say clergy?" Michele blurted out. "Steve Michaels, you had better tell me that you are not an ordained priest; I did not sign up to be the wife of a priest."

"I'm not an ordained priest, Michele, but I am a Cardinal Deacon!" Steve said as he lifted out the biretta of Giuseppe Sarto very carefully.

All three of them just looked at the scarlet-colored, watered silk biretta that signified the rank of a Cardinal of the Holy Roman Catholic Church. After setting it on the table carefully, he took the ring box back from Michele and took the ring out; then, he slid it on his right ring finger. There was not a sound in the room as they all looked at Steve in total disbelief. Michele stared at her husband, not knowing what to believe at this point, while Paul and Jim exchanged glances, almost wanting to pinch themselves to make sure that what they were seeing was real. Steve then took the zucchetto out of the box and placed it on his head slowly and with much reverence.

Michele was the first to speak, "Umm...Steve, did you say *Cardinal Deacon*?"

"Yes. By order of a Papal Bull, I have been proclaimed as a Cardinal Deacon with all rights and honors that go with the position," Steve answered in a sure voice.

"Steve Michaels, this is a nice charade, but how can you ask us to take you seriously? Really? A Cardinal?" Michele asked in her typical skeptical voice when she thought that her husband was trying to put something over on her.

"Michele, please read this out loud, will you?" Steve asked somberly as he handed her the envelope that Father Tommaso had given him before he left.

"Really, Steve? Who did you have write this one up? Come on, Steve, the jig is up. Ha ha, nice laugh!" Michele said to him in a mocking fashion. Jim took the envelope from his mother and looked at the seal on the flap; it was embossed with the seal of the Vatican. He then opened it and began to read it to himself; he dropped the letter on the table after the first paragraph.

"Um, Dad…this really happened, didn't it?" Jim asked, still looking down at the letter.

"Yes, Jim, it really did," Steve answered. "What's in the letter? And why did you drop it so quickly?"

"Well, it's a letter from the Pope addressed to Mom. Methinks you owe Dad an apology there, Mom!" Jim said as he handed the letter back to her. Michele took the letter with a non-believing look and then began to read it out loud for all to hear.

"*Dear Michele, I hope this finds you well and that you are happy that we got your husband back to you in one piece and so quickly. I am sure that Steve has informed you of the prophecy and that he has been knighted and made a Colonel of the Nobel Guards. If he told you about the rite of first tonsure and about being named a Cardinal Deacon, he is telling you the truth. I was with him when he found out and am as surprised as you are. You might want to believe him as I believe in him!*

Signed, Pope Alexander IX."

When Michele finished, she just looked at her husband as the pieces of what he alluded to on the phone started to fall into place.

Paul and Jim regarded Steve, who was still wearing the zucchetto on his head. Steve noticed them staring at it and smiled. He took the letter from Michele, who looked like she was not breathing, and put it carefully back into the envelope. "I have to keep this one handy; I wonder what else I can use it for with you, Michele," Steve said with a smile. Michele just nodded, not saying anything.

"So, a real Cardinal. Do you get to attend the next time they vote for a Pope?" Paul asked, not fully understanding the scope of what he had just been told.

"Yes, I will get to attend the next conclave, but I would prefer just to worry about tomorrow to be honest, Paul," Steve answered seriously.

"Steve, I guess I owe you an apology," Michele stated in a meek voice that took Jim and Paul by surprise.

"No need, dear. I know it's a lot to take in. So that's it in a nutshell. I'm going to be presented at St. Paul's Madison Street Church in two or three weeks, and then I get to read the last letter!"

Chapter 60

"Umm, Dad…did you say 'the last letter'?" Jim asked.

"Yes, His Eminence Abbot Giuseppe along with Brothers Michael and Angelo of the Brown Robes will be here to give me the last letter once I have been announced," Steve said to Jim, matter-of-factly.

"So, wait a minute. Another Cardinal is coming to witness you being presented — announced — whatever, and then you will be given the last letter?" Michele asked as everything was fitting together a bit better for her now.

"Yes, and then I will know what my orders are from St. Pius X. It's kind of exciting, wouldn't you say, Michele?" Steve asked without his customary smile, giving everyone a clue that he was serious.

"It does sound quite exciting, Steve," Paul said. "So why am I here?"

"Until Karl from the Swiss Guard gets here, I need you to help with my security, my first responsibility now that I am back here," Steve answered. "I would like to see if you could have a squad car visit the neighborhood just to check. With the interview video out there and my visit to Rome, I need to be extra cautious. I was able to get back only with the help of the Swiss Guards and the Pope's office!"

"Why are they worried about the interview video?" Paul asked.

"Well, being in Rome when the video was released might have raised more questions than I'm prepared to answer. I know I could convince you, but if this is not done right, it could blow up in everyone's faces, and that would not be too good. No one knows what is in the last letter, and everyone involved is taking this quite seriously. So that's why I need your help in keeping the press and the gawkers away from the house," Steve told his friend who sat there taking it all in and beginning to see the reason for the concern.

"I can have an extra squad come and visit on each shift; do you need anyone here at the house until this Swiss Guard—what's his name? Karl?—gets here?" Paul asked.

"No, I think we will be okay. Plus, you're just across the street if anything seems out of place. Michele and Jim, please keep your eyes open, and please be careful answering the phone or the door until Karl gets here," Steve said to his family.

"No problem, Dad. Can I see your ring?" Jim asked before his mom could start in with her twenty questions, which he and Steve knew were coming.

"Sure," Steve said as he took the ring off and put it back in the ring box, handing both to Jim. He then took off the zucchetto as well and carefully placed in back into the box. He put the biretta over it. "Well, that's about all. Not bad from a guy from Illinois!"

Paul stood first, went over to his friend, and shook his hand, looking at the hats in the box and just shaking his head. "I will take care of everything until Karl gets here. Just make sure that you keep the doors locked, and try not to put yourself in a situation that you cannot get yourself out of."

As he was getting ready to leave, he motioned for Steve to follow him to the door. There he took a business card out of wallet and gave it to Steve. "This is the guy I talked to after my incident. He would be glad to talk to you, Steve, whenever you need to. Just call him anytime; he can meet you here at the house or at my house, for that matter, to keep it even quieter," Paul said as he put his hand on his friend's shoulder and smiled. "A Cardinal...you sure know how to light up Michele. Good luck with that!" Steve stood there smirking and closed the door as Paul left.

"Well, I think it has been a long day; at least for me it has. I think I am going to try to get some sleep," Steve said hoping against hope that Michele would not start peppering him with questions.

"Bed? Did you say bed?" Michele said as she jumped up. "Jim, why don't you go to your room. Me and your dad need to talk."

"Well, Mom, for what you need to ask him, I think I need to be here as well. This does concern me as well unless you're shipping me off to military school in the morning…" Jim said to his mom, who was caught off guard by her son's frankness. Steve moved quickly to get between the two of them before Michele could react.

"Did you hear me, young man? I said go to your room now!" Michele yelled while pointing to the stairs. Steve smiled at his wife who was red in the face from her son talking back to her. Jim looked at his dad for help, but all Steve did was mouth to him, "stand firm."

"Mom, this is my business as well. What Dad did was to help me. I know how upset you are with the two of us still, but did you hear him a minute ago?" Jim pleaded with his mom. "He is a Cardinal of the Holy Roman Catholic Church, and I am his son. Do you know the implications that this will have for all of us? Do you not see what is going to happen once he is announced? Our lives are going to change, and I am going to be smack dab in the middle of it! I love you, Mom, but we have to accept it and be ready to help him!"

Michele just stood there, not knowing what to do as her little boy became a man in front of her eyes. As she started to speak, her vision clouded; then, she felt the tears rolling down her cheeks. Steve put his arms around her gently as Michele buried her head in his shoulder, sobbing.

"Mom, are you okay?" Jim asked, not used to seeing his mom showing this side of her emotions in front of him.

"I'm fine," Michele stammered as Steve held her tight. She calmed herself down a bit, realizing that her life with her son had just changed.

Michele let go of Steve. "When did you grow up?" was all she said to Jim as she turned to face him again. She reached out and hugged him like she did in church after she knew that he was okay. Jim, feeling her tears still on her cheek, felt a bit uncomfortable but hugged her back as his dad gave him the thumbs up. As Michele let go of her son, she hit Jim in the chest with a soft punch. She began to smile at the two men in her life, knowing that she had nothing else to say about what had just happened.

"Well, since there is nothing to discuss, I'm going to bed," Steve announced, taking the box containing the ring and the two hats of St. Pius X and putting them safely in the closet.

Chapter 61

The Vatican

Karl was placing his last call to the Secretariat of State's office to get clearance to carry his sidearm in the United States while he was there providing protection to Steve. Father Alphonse, the private secretary to Cardinal Albani, had been instrumental in getting the red tape cleared for him before his flight to the U.S. His superiors in the Swiss Guard had welcomed his appointment as Sergeant Major and were now clearing his schedule for his trip to Chicago. As he was going over in his mind what to bring and what needed to be done in such a short time, there was a knock at the door of the office he was in. "Come in" was all that Karl said in a clear, professional voice.

"Karl, they told me that I could find you here. How is the planning going for the trip?" Abbot Giuseppe asked.

"Your Eminence, how did you find me here?" Karl asked while he stood up to greet Giuseppe.

"Well, when the Secretariat of State is your new best friend, it's not much of a stretch to find out!" Abbot Giuseppe answered, laughing at Karl.

"Well, I guess that should not surprise me after what has transpired lately around here. To answer your question, yes, I am ready to leave tomorrow. I am waiting for my permit to carry a sidearm from the FBI and their state department office here in Rome. It seems we both have friends in high places, my dear Cardinal!" Karl answered, returning the laugh.

"Yes, so it seems," was all that Giuseppe could say in return. "Are you bringing any items that Steve will need to be presented?"

"Yes, I am having them loaded on the plane with me in an oversized hard case. I wanted to keep things as inconspicuous as possible for the trip there. It is being sent as an official Vatican shipment, which can clear customs without being opened. The sword will be in there, as well as the books that Cardinal Albani has picked out for Steve. His uniform and cassocks will not be done until a bit later. We are going to have to ship those to Steve's house," Karl answered in a very professional manner.

"I am sure that everything will be fine, Karl, and I am extremely grateful that you are handling all of this for him. He is going to need the help once everything is known to all. I should be arriving next week as I have some things to clear up at my abbey and need to have the next abbot installed. Would you like me to bring his uniform and cassocks? It will not look out of place for me to have them," Abbot Giuseppe said to Karl.

"That would be a huge help, Your Eminence," Karl answered with a smile.

"I am glad to help, Karl," Giuseppe said. "Brothers Michael and Angelo have both decided to stay with me here at the Vatican in my new position once Steve has been presented," Giuseppe said, waiting to see if Karl had taken the bait of his hint at a new position.

"New position? What did His Holiness ask you to do, Your Eminence?" Karl asked, surprised at the news.

"Well, I am going to be working for His Holiness as his 'Special Assistant.' Since we don't know what the last letter will bring, he wants to be ready. I might be going to the U.S. for a while, and while you are there, I might be needing your services, so to speak," Abbot Giuseppe said with just a hint of a smile.

Karl picked up on the subtlety. "I will do what I am asked, but you already know that, Your Eminence. Is this all going to be going through proper channels?" Karl asked, trying not to laugh.

"Well, what do you think, Karl?" Giuseppe answered as he too was trying hard not to laugh.

"I guess not, then. Nice to know that the politics of the Vatican are alive and well, my good Cardinal!" Karl answered as they both shared a laugh.

Becoming serious, Giuseppe said, "Karl, your presence and your professionalism have been instrumental in getting all of this done in such a short time, I know that His Holiness greatly appreciates it's as much as I do!"

Chapter 62

Elgin, Illinois

Steve slept soundly for the first night since the shooting and did not get up until well after eight the next morning. As he brushed his teeth, he looked out the window facing the front of the house; there, he noticed a news van parked down the street with two people milling around the side of it. He quickly finished, threw some water on his face, changed into some clothes, and ran down the stairs. There in the kitchen, he found Michele having a cup of coffee and looking at her laptop screen.

"Good morning, sleepy head!" she said without even looking up from her screen as she read another email.

"Did you know there's a news van down the street?" he asked as he went to get a cup of coffee.

"Yes, they got here at about six this morning. Should I offer them some coffee?" Michele asked.

"Coffee? Are you serious? I don't even want them near our sub-division," Steve said loudly.

Michele just smiled back at her husband. He realized he'd taken the bait and began laughing.

"Good one, Michele. I'm sure I have quite a few more of those coming my way with what I sprang on you last night. Oh, and thank you as well," Steve said as he walked up behind her to give her a hug.

"Thank you for what? Not strangling you in your sleep last night after telling me that you're a Cardinal?" she asked, not letting Steve know that she was already on board with everything that had transpired over the last few hours.

"Well, I didn't want to tell you over the phone, and the look on your face was worth it," Steve said as he hugged her tight.

"You do have me on that fact, Steve. I'm sure the look of disbelief was quite funny," Michele answered smiling, knowing that her husband could not see.

"You know what I love the best about you? Your smile, Michele, which I can see very clearly in the reflection on your laptop screen," Steve laughed as his wife now struggled to get out of his grasp.

"Oh, I will get you for that one, Steve Michaels!" she yelled, knowing that the she never would.

"So, have they approached the house at all? Or rung the bell? Do you know what channel they are from? Did they bother you or Jim when he left for school?" Steve asked very quickly, not waiting for any answers in return.

"Um, well, no, no, and no!" Michele answered as she went back to her screen.

"*No, no, and no?* What kind of answer is that?" Steve asked as he took a sip of his coffee.

"You asked three questions, and I answered them: no, no, and no," Michele answered, laughing at her husband, who was definitely suffering from jet lag.

"Oh, yeah. Sorry, still a bit foggy this morning from all the time changes. Are they the only ones who have shown up since the interview?" Steve asked.

"Yes. They're from Channel 5. They've kept their distance, but I don't think that they will too much longer," Michele answered.

"Why do you say that? You going there dressed like that to scare them away?" Steve asked as he quickly put distance between himself and his wife.

"Funny there, Steve! Really, really funny! No, but they should be gone within ten minutes. I've already texted Paul and asked for some help," Michele answered, looking for something close by that would not break if she threw it at him.

Steve laughed, holding the plastic salt and pepper shakers that normally sat on the table in front of her laptop. "Looking for these?" he asked, showing her what was in his hands.

"How did you get those off the table without me seeing? And yes, I was looking to throw one of those at you," Michele laughed at her husband, who always seemed to be one step in front of her.

"Well, Michele, just a bit of self-preservation after all these years," Steve laughed, knowing he would pay for it later. "So you texted Paul. Did he reply?"

"Yes, he's just sending a car by to get them to move along. Should be no problem but nice to have a friend like him," Michele added. "So you haven't said anything about the interview video being released. Are you okay with me giving them the approval for you?"

"Michele, you did what you thought was right on our behalf. They didn't edit anything from the interview, and it was in my own words, so no, I don't have a problem with it being released. Of course, the timing was a bit strange since I was in Rome. How has the response been to the interview? I haven't read or heard anything about it," Steve answered his wife.

"Well, surprisingly, it has been extremely favorable. And even the major networks are giving it its due. I received a couple of calls right after for further interviews and have their information if you wish to see it. The best have been the blogs written about you and what happened, Steve, about your account of what you did, how you care for the man who died and his family, and the reason you did it. I've been having a hard time keeping up, but Elaine is keeping a list and will send it to us for review," Michele said without looking up from her laptop.

"A list? She's keeping a list?" Steve asked looking a bit amazed.

"So far, there are requests for interviews and to go on talk shows, and of course the Bishop of Rockford has called asking about you as well," Michele answered while typing.

"The Bishop? Hmm, wonder what he will say when he finds out I technically outrank him now," Steve replied laughingly.

"You outrank him?"

"Yes, as a Cardinal I do outrank a Bishop but not in his Dioceses. In the Dioceses of Rockford, he is leader, and I am part of his flock. At least that's what the research I've done shows," Steve answered her, knowing that this was all still too new and had not completely sunk in yet for the both of them. "Remind me to send an email to Abbot Giuseppe today asking what I should or should not do concerning the interviews; it would be nice to have his advice on this."

"Did he make that much of an impression on you, Steve?" Michele asked as she looked up from her computer screen for the first time.

"Yes, he did," Steve answered as he sat next his wife. "It was like he had this way about him. Even the Pope looked at him when he spoke almost with reverence."

"Reverence?" Michele asked, looking surprised.

"Yes. He made me feel like what I had done, though tragic, was okay. It was the reason I opened the letter and accepted my fate," he answered somberly.

"So he's the person that I get to blame for all of this?" Michele joked.

"Well, no. The person to blame is still me for doing what I did. He just made me understand that it was my actions, not the outcome, that brought me to them," Steve said seriously. "When Abbot Cardinal Giuseppe read the Papal Bull announcing that I had been elevated to a Cardinal, no one was more surprised than he."

"So no one knew anything: no hunches, no guesses, or anything? The Pope just accepted this as it was written? No one questioned the outcome, that you were now a Cardinal?" Michele asked in her famous thousand-questions statement.

"Um, well, to answer you, no, yes, maybe, and yes!" Steve answered, smiling, knowing how much she hated it when he answered her question that way.

"Steve Michaels, I hate it when you do that!" Michele said, looking for something to hit her husband with, but he had moved everything out of her way when he sat down. "Oh, you make me so mad when you act so quickly to move everything away from me!" Michele said, laughing at her husband, knowing that there was more he wanted to discuss.

"Paul has given me the name of a counselor to help me cope with what's happened. It's the same person who helped him after the shooting he was in. I need to know, Michele, if you think it's a good idea to reach out one-on-one or should I keep trying to do this on my own?" Steve finally asked with a look of relief.

"Are you having nightmares? Is it more of shame or guilt over what you did?" Michele asked seriously, understanding now almost fully the magnitude of the pressure upon her husband.

"No nightmares, and the correct phrase might be *why me*? I've been given a fantastic honor by the Roman Catholic Church because of what I did. Cardinal Abbot Giuseppe broke it down simply that I was being honored for my actions and not the outcome that day. I had no intent of killing that man just to save others who were in danger. I read an article once in which the author said it would be prudent to kill someone to save a village, even if it was one of the villagers. That's what I did: to save the parishioners, I killed one of them," Steve said, letting go of what had been bottled up inside of him since the shooting. "Michele, the funny part is I feel no guilt over what I did but rather concern as to how is will affect you and Jim moving forward, not by being named a Cardinal but by being a killer."

"Well, for me, Steve, I'm more worried about you wearing a red hat than knowing I sleep next to a killer!" Michele said. She moved from the table quickly, knowing Steve was going to get her for that one. As she positioned herself between the table and Steve, there was a knock at the door.

"This is not over; I'll get you for that line, Mrs. Michaels!" Steve said, laughing, as he went to get the door.

Chapter 63

Before Steve opened the door, he peered through the window to see who was there, and with much relief he saw standing there on the front porch Paul in uniform.

"Paul, come on in. How did it go with the folks down the block?"

"Well, they gave me the usual about freedom of the press, but I gave them the usual about trespassing and being a nuisance. I asked for their registration and license for the van and gave them a ticket for having an expired plate. That should keep them away for a while or until they get another van or a new license plate sticker," Paul answered with only the slightest of grins on his face.

"Well, glad that you are fulfilling your quota, my good friend! Can I get you a cup of coffee or anything?" Steve asked and noticed that Michele had moved to the back of the table, looking a bit apprehensive.

"Oh, no, I'm good. Have to go and protect the good citizens of Elgin," Paul answered quickly and then noted, "Michele, I don't know what you said to him, but that table will not protect you too much; might want to figure out another line of defense!" As

he shook Steve's outreached hand, he was laughing at
Michele, who had a guilty look upon her face.

"Thanks again, Paul. Maybe dinner one night
this week? Cook something on the grill?" Steve asked.

"Thanks, that sounds good, Steve, and good
luck, Michele!" Paul laughed as he went back to his
squad car.

As Steve closed the door, he turned to face his
wife, who by now was holding a rubber spatula that
she got from the kitchen drawer while his back was
turned. "I am warning you, Steve Michaels. If you so
much as take one step closer, I will whack you with
this!" Michele said to him while laughing.

Steve just looked at her grinning and burst out
laughing, which signaled that this round was over. As
he moved toward her, his cell phone rang, and he
looked at the incoming number, a bit puzzled.

"Who is it?" Michele asked, coming from
behind the table to look at the screen.

"Don't know. Might as well answer it," Steve
said as he pressed the button to accept the call, using
the speakerphone so that Michele could hear as well.

"Steve, this is Karl. Sorry for the call. I forgot to
give you my cell number. I am calling to tell you that I
will be there in two days, as they have your uniforms
completed, and all of the other items that we talked
about are packed and ready to ship to you as well.
How are you doing?" Karl asked.

"Doing good, thanks. Things here didn't go as badly as I expected, but I will go into detail later with you about it. My family is anxious to meet you. They don't believe about me having my own personal bodyguard!" Steve answered, knowing that Karl would be grinning a bit over that remark.

"Well, I hope you downplayed that, Steve. And please remember what I told you here in Rome about watching everything until I get there," Karl answered briskly and to the point.

"I have, Karl. I have my neighbor watching the house, and we're able to call him anytime to handle any suspicious actively or bother from the press or the news crews here at home," Steve answered, knowing that this was what Karl needed to hear.

"Good to hear. Remind me to buy him dinner for the help, Steve. Call me anytime you have a question or need something, and I will see you in two days. I am renting a car, so no need to pick me up from the airport. I have to get used to my surroundings there. I will call when I land to let you know about what time I will be at your house. I have to go. Both of the Cardinals asked me to send their greetings and tell you that you are in their prayers!" Karl said and then hung up on his end.

As Steve hung up the phone, Michele asked, "Who are both of the Cardinals that he referred to?"

"Cardinal Albani, the Vatican Secretariat of State, and Cardinal Abbot Giuseppe of the Brown

Robes were whom Karl was referring to. Cardinal Giuseppe will be here when I am presented for the first time and will be introducing me," Steve replied.

"Wow, so you have the second top man at the Vatican in your corner. Nice to know in case I need an annulment!" Michele said as she moved quickly to dodge her husband.

Steve left to talk to his boss at work about a short term leave of absence. He didn't know what the fourth letter of St. Pius X might hold and wanted to be ready just in case. Michele took the time alone, while Jim was in school, to call about the progress of her Honor Medal recommendation to the Boy Scouts for Jim.

Chapter 64

The next two days went by without any trouble from the press. The Channel 5 crew had stopped camping out down the block, much to the neighbors' relief. Steve had gone back to work after a heartfelt talk with his boss; things were starting to fall back into a somewhat normal routine. Steve was at his desk at work when his cell phone began to ring.

"Hello," he answered.

"Steve, it is Karl. I have landed and will be at your house in about two hours. I have your address, and the GPS on my phone will get me there."

"Great, I will let Michele know. Do you need anything?" Steve asked.

"Oh no, Steve, I am fine. Please do not trouble yourself with anything," Karl answered.

"Well, I'm sure that Michele will be the judge of that, Karl. You don't know my wife. I'll let her know and meet you in a couple of hours. Glad you're here, Karl!"

"See you soon. Any issues that I need to worry about when I get there?" Karl asked in his usual professional voice.

"Oh no, no issues. Everything has been quiet here the last two days," Steve answered.

"Great. See you shortly."

As Karl hung up, he exited his rental car onto I-90 west towards Rockford to begin the next stage of this incredible journey that he had gotten himself into. As he took in the scenery, he began mentally to organize everything that needed to be done to get Steve ready to open the next letter. He started to chuckle to no one as he thought that just a couple of days previously he was assigned to bring some American to the Vatican. Fate must have brought him here, he thought. Now he was driving in the United States to help a Cardinal get his orders from a saint.

His phone gave him the roundabout directions so that he could take in the lay of the land if he was going to protect Steve and his family for the next couple of weeks.

After an hour and a half of driving, he came upon the subdivision where Steve lived, all the while noting the exits and hiding areas around it. He pulled over about a block away and called Steve's cell phone once again. He answered on the second ring.

"Hi, Karl. Find your way okay?" Steve asked.

"Yes, I am near your house. Just checking to make sure you are home. Did not want to meet Michele without you there," Karl answered.

"What are you, chicken, Karl? Scared of a 5'2" woman?" Steve asked, laughing. Karl noted there was a bit of commotion in the background.

"Not scared, Steve. Just know better. See you in a minute," Karl answered, hearing Michele's voice in the background.

As he pulled in front of the house, he saw Steve standing in the front door, being jabbed in the back by a woman whom he assumed was Michele. He got out of the car, grabbed his carryon bag, and made his way up the walk. Steve opened the screen door, smiling at him.

"Karl! Glad you made it in one piece. Hope you didn't get lost or anything from the airport. Please, come on in," Steve said with an outstretched hand. "Karl, this is my wife, Michele, whom you have heard all about." As Steve finished speaking, Michele jabbed him in the ribs and walked up to Karl.

Karl, who had his hand outstretched to shake hers, was totally surprised when she walked right by it to give him a hug. Steve stood there grinning; the look on Karl's face was priceless. Michele finished hugging him and took a step back to gauge her husband's bodyguard; it was then she realized he was armed.

"Nice to meet you, Karl. I'm a bit of a hugger," Michele said with a sheepish grin on her face.

"No problem there, Mrs. Michaels. Very nice to meet you indeed," Karl answered professionally.

"Mrs. Michaels? You have to learn something right now, Karl. It's Michele as long as you're in my house. Got it?" Michele said firmly but politely. "I am not that old to be called Mrs. in my house. Did you not tell him anything Steve? You are useless!" Michele teased as she jabbed Steve in the ribs again.

"Michele it is, then. And please stop hitting him; I am here to protect him!" Karl said, holding in a laugh and figuring out everything that Steve had tried to tell him about his wife.

"Protect him? You were lucky I wasn't there the day this happened; I would have killed him for doing what he did! 'Mr. I Believe!' More like 'Mr. Stupid' if you ask me!" Michele exclaimed almost breathlessly.

Both Karl and Steve looked uncomfortably at the floor as Michelle's anxiety poured from her.

Finally, Karl broke the tension. "Steve, you had everything right about her except that she is a bit younger-looking than you said!" Karl stepped in front of Steve to protect him from her.

"Oh, getting in front of me will not help him, Karl. Believe me, he has to sleep sometime," Michele said as all of them began laughing. Steve led the way to the kitchen table so that they could talk about the plans that Karl had brought with him from the Vatican.

Chapter 65

Karl reached into his carryon bag, took out two file folders, and handed one to Steve. "This is from Cardinal Giuseppe; he has taken the liberty to come up with some ideas to help you with planning being announced," Karl said while he opened the folder up.

"Steve, give me yours and let me make a copy before you start scribbling all over it," Michele said with her hand open, waiting for it.

"No need, Mrs. Mic—umm, Michele. I made you a copy as well. Here you go," Karl said, fighting back a smile.

"Steve, you could learn a few things from Karl here, like how to be prepared," Michele said as she sat back smiling at the two of them; Steve just rolled his eyes at her.

"Thanks, Karl. You really know how to score points with her," Steve said as he fended off another poke in the ribs. "So is there anything from Cardinal Albani in there?"

"Cardinal Albani just sends his well wishes and has informed me that he is ready to help. All we have to do is ask," Karl replied. "It is nice to have the Secretariat of State in our corner. Just saying, of course!"

"Please tell me, Karl, who is involved in all of this from the church's side of things?" Michele asked, marveling again at the mention of the Secretariat of State.

"Well, the Pope, of course, his private secretary Father Tommaso Antonelli, Cardinal Albani, Cardinal Giuseppe, and Brothers Michael and Angelo of the Brown Robes. So with you, Steve, your son, and myself, this brings the total to nine at this time," Karl answered like he had practiced the answer.

"You forgot Paul, our neighbor across the street," Michele said.

"You informed him, Steve?" Karl asked.

"Yes, I needed him to understand why he was looking out for me. Plus if he knows the reason, he just might be a little more attentive to why I was asking for his help!" Steve said, a measured response.

"Not a bad idea. It is easier to help if you know what you are helping with, so that makes ten to answer your question correctly, Michele," Karl said with just the slightest of smiles on his face.

"So let's see what Cardinal Giuseppe has laid out for us, shall we?" Steve suggested.

"The plan is pretty simple, really. Steve, you will be presented at the last Sunday mass of the day at St. Paul's, which is 11:45 a.m., correct?" Karl asked.

"Yes. How did you know that?" Michele asked.

"Their website," Karl answered sheepishly. "The plan is to get with the pastors of St. Paul's, Father Rick and Father George, and have them announce you as a Knight of the Golden Spur to the parish. Then Cardinal Giuseppe will take the podium and announce your elevation to Cardinal. It should be pretty plain and simple, really."

"Sure, Karl. Plain and simple!" Michele exclaimed. "Just get up and announce it, and everyone will believe it. I'm having a hard time believing it, and I have a letter from the Pope telling me what happened!"

"You have a letter from the Pope, Michele?" Karl asked.

"Yes, Karl. I asked Father Tommaso for a little help since I knew she would not believe me, my little doubting Thomas here!" Steve said laughing as Michele turned a bright shade of red.

"Good idea. And red really is your color, Michele!" Karl said, now understanding more of their relationship and the love they had for each other.

"Karl, is that gun loaded on your left hip?" Michele asked. "And can I borrow it for a minute?"

"Umm, yes, it is, Michele," Karl answered, trying to hide the shock of not noticing that she felt it when she hugged him. "And no, you may not borrow it!"

"Damn. Oh well. I will go with plan B while he is sleeping," Michele replied, laughing out loud at both of them.

"Well, I am no help to you, Steve. You are on your own after I leave tonight. Sorry about that," Karl said while laughing himself.

"Ha ha to both of you. Can we get back to the plans, please?" Steve said, knowing that this round went to Michele and Karl and thinking to himself, *I have to keep these two apart, or I will be sorry for sure*.

"Sure, my darling husband. Whatever you want," Michele responded, but Steve was not buying it at all.

"There is nothing about the reading of the last letter, Karl? Did Cardinal Giuseppe say anything about that?" Steve asked.

"Well, my Dear Eminence, that is your privilege; once you are announced, you get to make that decision. I would imagine that you could have Cardinal Giuseppe read it from the pulpit after you are announced," Karl answered.

"Might not be a bad idea. You know, in case it is written in Latin like the Papal Bull was," Steve said seriously. He stopped to think that if it was another Papal Bull, how would the world react? This was not going to be a *go forth and preach the gospel* order. *Oh well*, he thought. *Cross that bridge when I get there*.

"I had not considered that, Steve. That might be a very good idea. You could be standing at attention in front of the altar receiving your order from Pope Pius X. Might make it even more dramatic for those viewing it," Karl replied.

"Viewing it? You mean those at the mass, Karl?" Michele asked.

"Well, we are going to have to record this for prosperity, Michele. The presentation and the reading of the last letter. This is going to be one of those once in a lifetime events. Cardinal Giuseppe suggested it to me, being here to help organize everything before they arrived next week," Karl answered.

"So saying it should be recorded...how about having the press there? Say as a follow up to the interview?" Michele asked Karl.

"That is one of the ideas that Cardinal Albani had for me to explore. You do have a friend who works for the news, do you not, Michele?" Karl asked, seeing the opportunity presenting itself to him very clearly now.

"I do. Elaine works for the *Daily Herald*. She did the interview and would be champing at the bit to have another exclusive with Steve," Michele said laughing as she knew how much Steve liked Elaine.

"Please, Michele, anyone but her!" Steve said with a laugh.

"Ok, then," Karl said. "We can have Elaine and her camera crews at the church to record it and conduct the first interview with your Eminence once you are announced!"

"Sounds like a plan, Karl; I like how you think. Do you have a list of what else we need to decide or do before this great event?" Michele asked, tongue in cheek.

"I have some other things, Michele, but mostly it will be to teach Steve how walk and act like a knight. As he has no military training, it will be a very condensed course to get him ready. I have taken the liberty of calling the Great Lakes Naval training center in Waukegan and speaking with a friend who is stationed there presently. He is getting us clearance so that we can practice drilling there with a drill instructor," Karl answered precisely.

"Wait, Steve on a military base to practice? Oh, you have got to take me with you, Karl. Please? You have no idea how much fun this will be," Michele exclaimed as Steve just rolled his eyes at her.

"Well, Michele, I would love to, but I did not include your name on the list that I have turned in already. I am very sorry about that!" Karl answered while laughing at Steve.

"Who is your friend, Karl, who is stationed at Great Lakes?" Steve asked, ignoring the laughter coming from Michele.

"Well, the friend is the Chief Chaplin of the Navy, Captain Mahoney, who is personal friends with Cardinal Albani, whom he meet during his time here in the United States as a Diplomat for the Holy See," Karl answered.

"Wow, talk about friends in high places!" Michele exclaimed.

"Indeed. Michele, I am still amazed as to who knows whom in the church!" Karl responded.

"So back to what we need to do…when do we travel to Great Lakes Naval Base?" Steve asked.

"We start tomorrow; we have an 11:00 a.m. appointment with Captain Mahoney, who is by chance stationed there right now," Karl answered looking at the notes in front of him. "As you have been named a Colonel of the Nobel Guard, Steve, His Holiness has amended that and has named you as an officer of the Swiss Guards as well so that you will be able to be addressed by anyone in the military as Colonel," Karl said as a matter of fact.

"This is only to allow me on base as a cover, correct?" Steve asked.

"No, Steve," Karl answered as he took a small box out of his carryon and slid it across the table to Steve "From His Holiness."

Steve paused, not wanting to open the box, which was quickly snatched up by Michele when he hesitated. She opened it to reveal a pair of silver eagles representing his rank as a Colonel. She carefully put the box back in front of Steve with trembling hands. All of this was happening so quickly that she was not really registering it all.

"Are those what I think they are?" was all Michele could ask.

"Yes, you have been given the rank of Oberst—er, Colonel by Pontifical order, and your commission is a lifetime commission," Steve answered as he handed a file folder to Michele, which contained the orders.

"I really need to talk to His Holiness, Karl. I am not a military officer, and I do not like parading around as one. You have earned the right to be addressed as Sergeant Major, but this is preposterous to say the least," Steve said in a huff.

"Steve, you are going to yell at the Pope again? Not a wise choice for a man who has sworn his obedience," Karl said quickly, trying to end this discussion.

"You yelled at the Pope, Steve? My God, what were you thinking?" Michele asked before he could answer Karl.

"Yes, I did yell at him. Should have walked out of there while I had the chance!" Steve answered petulantly.

"Well, you didn't, Steve, so we have to deal with this. Whether you wear these or not is your choice, but you will be addressed as Colonel while on the base, so get used to it!" Karl said sternly. He had been warned by Cardinal Giuseppe about how Steve would react to this news.

"Yes, Sergeant Major!" Steve responded, embarrassed by his recalcitrance. As he looked at the eagles, he made a mental note not to lose his temper again. All of this was out his hands and a consequence of his own actions. "How about something to eat? You must be famished from your travels," Steve suggested, hoping to change the subject quickly.

"I'm fine, Steve. Thank you. I am going to go and check into my room as I have some things to get ready before tomorrow. I will pick you up at 9:30 a.m. sharp for the trip to the naval base. Michele, it was very nice meeting you finally, and you have a very nice home!" Karl said as he stood and put his folders into his carryon bag. He took Steve's outstretched hand, shook it, and nodded to Michele as he headed to the door. As he left, he looked left and right, slowly noting that there was no one outside, and walked to his car.

"Well, that didn't go so bad," Steve said to no one as he watched Karl pull away from the curb. Lost in his thoughts, he could only imagine what an idiot he must have looked like in front of Karl and Michele concerning the Colonel insignia. *All of this is moving so fast*, he thought. *How am I ever going to live up to all of this hype and these honors?* He still did not understand why he needed to be a Colonel or a Cardinal. What in the world did Giovanni Sarto have in store for him with the last letter? As he stared into space, looking out the front door, Michele came up behind him and put her arms around his waist, lightly hugging him.

"Penny for your thoughts," Michele said softly.

"Well, right now, my dear wife, I could give you change from that penny," Steve said as he turned to kiss her and hug her tighter.

Chapter 66

The night passed quickly, and the silver eagles still bothered him as he held the case in his hand, not wanting to open it. As he waited for Karl to get to the house for the trip to Great Lakes, Steve was just lost.

Seeing her husband this concerned gave Michele a bit of worry, but he was sleeping the whole night through now, and there had been no word of the shooting or the fallout from it in the past three days. Maybe, just maybe, she thought, this was what Steve needed to get him over it and moved on. She looked at him just standing while she held her coffee cup.

She smiled and said in her best Victor McLaglen voice, "Aye, something troubling you there, Colonel darling?"

Steve turned around, laughing out loud. "Michele, that was the worst Victor McLaglen impression I have ever heard! How in the hell did you come up with that one?"

Michele replied through her own laughter, "Well, he said something like that at the end of *She Wore a Yellow Ribbon*, which you have only made Jim and me watch a couple dozen times.

Thought it might lighten up the mood since you still look upset about the whole silver eagle thing!"

"Couldn't hide that from you, could I? Well, let's just say I have come to terms with this silver eagle thing and moved on," Steve said as he walked over to sit next to her at the table.

"Come to terms?" Michele asked.

"This whole thing is bigger than me and my petty concerns over not being worthy," Steve said, taking her hand in his. "This is all moving too fast, but the end game is what is so damn important and so un-nerving to me: the fourth letter. What is in the last letter that Saint Pius X would do all of this before it was revealed? I've done some research on the man, and he was one of the most conservative Popes ever. His motto was 'restore all things in Christ.' He opposed modernization of the Church and was devoted to our Mother Mary. How could this man come up with this for me? This is so out of character according to everything I have read about him."

Michele looked at him, talking about Pius so seriously, and knew then that everything was getting better. He was doing research, and his mind was tackling a bigger problem. "What else did you find in your research about St. Pius X, Steve?"

"I was told back at the Vatican that he actually predicted World War I, and he referenced it in the third letter. Funny, a man like him, so devoted to Mary and so against the violence around him, blames himself for not being able to stop a bunch of egotistic maniacs from going to war," Steve said to her, still holding her hand. "I'm scared that the last letter will order me to do something I don't know that I can carry out or that the conservatives will like. This might be St. Pius's revelation of his conscience, and he will want me to change something that he himself could not change while serving as Pope!"

"Do you think it will be something that radical, Steve?" Michele asked. "I mean, if he was that conservative?"

"I don't know, Michele. But whatever it is, we are signed up for the long run now," Steve said as he leaned over to give her a kiss. There was a knock at the door, which startled both of them. They had forgotten about Karl coming to get him. Steve got up to go to the door and noticed that Karl was in the uniform of a Sergeant Major of the Swiss Guards. He was holding a garment bag.

"Karl, come on in," Steve said as he opened the door.

"Good morning, Michele," Karl said as he entered, looking very professional in his uniform.

"Morning, Karl. Don't you look all soldier today. Careful, I have a thing for a man in uniform," Michele said as she came over to hug him again, which made Karl blush. "You know I might just trade him in for a new model if he comes with a uniform like this!"

Karl just stood there blushing, not knowing what to say.

"Thank you, but I might be able to help you with that," Karl finally replied as he handed the garment bag to Steve. "Please go change," he said.

"What's in the bag, Karl?" Steve asked.

"Just go change and quickly. We need to get going!" Karl answered shortly and sternly; Steve remembered the tone from the walk from the hotel to the Vatican Palace and understood without asking again.

"Karl, what's in the garment bag?" Michele asked in her own stern voice.

"You will see, Michele, if someone would move!" Karl answered, pointing his thumb for Steve to move towards the stairs.

"You heard the man. Move it, Mr. I Believe!" Michele said in a voice that made them both understand who really was in charge here. "What did you give him to wear, Karl?"

"Let just wait and see, shall we?" Karl answered with a grin.

After he entered the bedroom, Steve opened the garment bag. He saw a navy blue suit jacket and pants. On the epaulets were the pinned insignia of the Swiss Guards and the silver eagles of a Colonel. He laid them on the bed, not sure if he should even put them on or just call the whole thing off right now; Pontifical order or not, he was not a military man and would not disgrace the uniform. He picked up the coat again and noticed a letter in the inside coat pocket. He unfolded it and started to smile instantly. He read the letter to himself:

"Steve, please do not have second thoughts about this! I have been waiting too long to find out what was in this box. Please just put this on and get on with your training. If you look carefully at the Pontifical Crest on the epaulets, it is the personal crest of St. Pius X. Wear it proudly! Your fellow Brown Robe and your friend, Giuseppe"

Steve took off his belt and was glad that he had put on blue dress socks that morning. As he finished dressing, he tied the tie that was included and then slipped the coat on. He took the officer's hat with the gold braid on the brim and put in on, looking into the mirror again. Looking back was an officer of the Swiss Guards in full uniform. He saluted the best he could, took a deep breath, and yelled down the stairs, "Michele, you are not going to believe this!" He took the letter to show Karl and headed down the stairs. As he turned the corner to the living room, Michele saw him first and just stared at her husband.

"Oh my God. You really think I'm going to let you out of this house dressed like that? What was the saying from *Top Gun?* 'Hey, Goose, you big stud! Take me to bed or lose me forever!' Michele walked over to her husband with a look in her eye but was put off by Karl politely clearing his voice off to the side.

"Michele, we really need to get going. Steve, you will need your Vatican passport with you today," Karl said, trying not to laugh. Steve just looked at him smiling as Michele realized what she had said out loud and started to blush in front of both of them. All three started to laugh out loud as Steve gave Michele a hug, turned to get the passport, and then headed toward the door.

Chapter 67

As they pulled out of the drive way, Steve noticed the large suitcase on the back seat of the rental car. He decided not to ask since, with any luck, Karl would tell him in due time. As they made their way on I-90 east to pick up I-294 north to get to Great Lakes Naval Station, neither of them spoke while the scenery passed them by.

Finally Steve could not take it any longer and said to Karl, "Out with it. What do you want to say?"

"I silently agreed with you at the Vatican when you said that you would not wear the silver eagles of a Colonel, but seeing you here today, I am so honored to have given them to you, Steve. I have been in the military for a total of eight years now, the last four as a Swiss Guard, and never have seen an officer look like one until today. You earned those eagles and now are wearing them so honorably. What made you do it?" Karl asked, almost out of breath.

"Cardinal Giuseppe wrote me a letter; he kind of made it a bit easier for me to be here in this today. Funny how a man who has such a way with words wanted to go into a monastery and pray when he could have been so much more," Steve answered, knowing that he was gushing emotion for a man that he had known only a few days.

"He does seem to be more than just an abbot, doesn't he?" Karl said reverently.

"Yes, he does!" Steve said. "So, what is my training going to consist of, Karl?"

"You will be given a crash course in acting like an officer: how to stand at attention and how to salute. I have a feeling you will get plenty of practice doing that shortly," Karl said smiling. "Just one thing: you will be one of the highest ranking officers on base, so everyone will be saluting you. Return the salute smartly and do not linger. Remember you are a Colonel and have no time for privates," Karl said with that slight laugh of his.

"What about Sergeant Majors? Do I have time for them?" Steve asked, knowing that this banter is what he needed to make it through the day.

"Well, let's hope so!" Karl answered quickly as they both shared a laugh.

The drive was shorter than he expected once they were outside of Chicago's famous traffic mess. As they pulled into the base, Karl looked at Steve saying, "Follow my lead. You will be addressed as Colonel by me, and you will reply by calling me Sergeant Major. This is not an option once we get out of this car; you will be saluted at the gate by the guard. Return it, and then we will drive on; we are meeting Captain Mahoney at his office. When we walk inside, take off your cover—err, your hat and hold it in your hand."

"Sure, Karl. I've seen enough of *NCIS* to remember that. What about my status in the Church? Does Captain Mahoney know about that?" Steve inquired, not knowing how big the circle of who knew was getting at this stage.

"He does not know; he just knows about you being a new officer, but we are going to invite him when you are presented as it should be an honor for him. You never know who can help you once the fourth letter is read, Steve!" Karl said as he pulled up to the gate.

The sentry at the gate saluted sharply upon noticing the eagles on Steve's epaulets and asked for their IDs; they both passed over their passports. Steve noticed that Karl passed a set of secondary IDs to him as well. After they were checked, the sentry handed them back and directed them to the main building for their meeting, saluting Steve again, who returned it as best he could while sitting in the car. As they drove, Karl handed the secondary ID card to Steve, who looked at it in disbelief. It was a formal ID card of the Swiss Guards, showing his rank and service number, his picture was one taken at the Vatican upon his arrival, he guessed. He didn't actually remember.

"Put that in this," Karl said, handing him a small leather ID case. "This is what you show at any military base that you enter moving forward from today!"

"Nice picture. Almost as good as a mug shot after a three day bender," Steve replied, laughing. He got a smile even from Karl with that line.

As they pulled up to the main administration building and parked the car, Steve could not but help notice the silence there. This was a city-sized complex after all, but there was no noise whatever: no cars or trucks running and even the birds were silent. Steve felt the hairs on the back of his neck begin to rise as they walked towards the main entrance. As Steve turned to mention this to Karl, he noticed that he was getting the case out of the back seat of the car. At the door was another sentry who smartly saluted; Steve returned the salute, which brought a nod from Karl. As they entered the building, they were met with a main hall lined by seamen recruits, all standing at parade rest. As they began to walk forward, a command was given to come to attention from Captain Mahoney, who stood at the end of the hall with his hand raised in a perfect salute from one officer to another. Steve stiffened at the command while both he and Karl saluted the Captain. As they passed, all eyes were front and center, not looking but seeing everything. Steve kept his emotion in check, taking his clue from Karl, who wore a face of masked emotions himself. Steve was conscious of the fact that every one of the recruits were seeing the silver eagles of his rank and wondering who he and Karl were. They finally made their way to the end of the hall and into Captain Mahoney's office as the recruits remained at attention. Once inside, Karl set the case down and pulled from his inside pocket a letter that Steve surmised was from the Secretariat of State himself.

"Captain, this is for you with our orders," Karl announced while standing at attention himself.

"At ease, Sergeant Major," was the only reply from Captain Mahoney.

Karl stood with his hands behind his back and his legs slightly apart, looking forward. Captain Mahoney opened the letter, noticing the seal and the signature, and immediately stood at attention in front of Steve without saying anything.

Steve guessed that the letter was from Pope Alexander since Captain Mahoney had the same look that Michele had had upon reading the letter from him.

"Please, Captain. I am the one here for training, not you!" Steve said, trying some humor to lighten the mood in the room.

"Colonel, do you know who this letter is from? Do you have any idea what this means to me? I mean as an Officer in the United States Navy and as a Roman Catholic priest!" Captain Mahoney blurted out in reply.

Steve smiled, having guessed right about whom the letter was from, and said, "He has that effect on everyone who gets a letter from me lately!" He motioned for Karl and the Captain to have a seat. Captain Mahoney took his seat behind a very simple desk while he and Karl took the chairs in front of it. The Captain just stared at the seal of the Pope on the letter made out to him.

Karl looked at Steve, winked, and said, "Captain Mahoney, thank you for the very professional greeting today for Colonel Michaels. Your recruits are very impressive."

Captain Mahoney came out of his stupor, which made Steve wonder if he himself had had the same bewildered look on his face after meeting the Pope for the first time. "I have never been given a request from the Pope himself in my twenty years of being an Officer and a priest. Exactly who are you, Colonel?" the Captain asked.

Karl answered quickly for Steve, "Captain, please, with all due respect, who he is is not important. But what he is doing here is very important to his mission. I have been asked by His Eminence, the Secretariat of State, to have Colonel Michaels taught the proper way to walk and act like an officer and to be given a crash course in sword presentation from your best drill instructor. We have all day if you have the right man on base that could help us!"

"Sergeant Major, I take it you are a bit more than a case-carrying aide. Can you tell me anything about this since I'm going to be letting you and the Colonel here loose on a Navy base? I do have to answer to higher ups, and this is definitely one of those things that will have to be included in my report to them," Captain Mahoney asked in a way that made it clear it was really an order.

Karl removed another letter from his inside pocket and gave it to the Captain, who took it and said with amusement, "You seem to have more letters than the alphabet there, Sergeant Major!" As he read the letter, his mouth opened, and Steve knew that this letter told the good Captain that he was a Cardinal and that this was now an order from the Pope. "Your Eminence, I did not know. Let me get you the best drill instructor here. Please give me ten minutes," Captain Mahoney gushed as he stood up.

Both Steve and Karl rose with him as he moved from behind his desk and took Steve's right hand, bending down to kiss it. Steve patted his back and helped him stand upright again, like he had witnessed the Pope do for Cardinal Albani. Karl witnessed this kind act of Steve's and knew that he was beginning to act like a Cardinal. This was all beginning to fall into place in front of his eyes. As the Captain composed himself, he picked up the phone, called the duty office, and asked where Chief

MacGregor was. He got a reply and then called his aide from his office to take them to the Chief.

"Captain, no need to ask you to keep this to yourself, is there?" Karl asked in a serious tone.

"No, Sergeant Major, this will not be leaked. I can refer to the letters you have given me; knowing who sent them will ensure my silence. I don't know what's going on, but can you make sure I'm there when it does?" Captain Mahoney replied.

"Captain, I will call you personally and invite you myself," Steve answered. He shook his hand once again as the aide knock on the door.

"Please take the Colonel and the Sergeant Major here to see Chief MacGregor. Presently, she is in class at the main lecture hall," Captain Mahoney ordered the aide, who turned to carry out the order without speaking. He left the office with Steve and Karl in tow.

Chapter 68

There was no small talk as the three of them walked toward the main lecture hall. Karl was impressed with the sheer size of the base and the fact that this was a naval base located on the shores of Lake Michigan. As they entered the building, Karl took his cover off, and Steve followed suit as the aide walked briskly to the main lecture hall. Waiting outside the entrance door at attention was Chief MacGregor.

"Colonel, Chief MacGregor here will take over. Chief, please let me know if you need anything signed from the Captain pertaining to this request," the aide said as he came to attention and turned and left the hallway.

"Colonel, I am Chief Ellen MacGregor. What can I do for you?" she asked as the fact that she was a very good-looking woman began to resonate with Karl.

"Well, Captain Mahoney informs us that you are the best drill instructor on the base. Is that true?" Steve asked as he noticed Karl looking a bit uncomfortable standing there.

"Well, sir, the Captain might be a bit biased as I am a regular at his services every Sunday and enjoy his Bible study group as well. So, really, what can I do for you?" Chief MacGregor asked again, all business.

"We would like to have you instruct the Colonel here in basic duties of being an officer and how to handle a presentation sword," Karl blurted out. Steve noticed the hesitation in his voice and knew to take over quickly. This was a side of Karl he had never seen, not even with Michele.

"Chief, I really need to be a bit more polished. I have a very important presentation coming up shortly. I need some pointers and a basic kick in the pants to get me though this. Care to kick a Colonel's butt for a couple of off hours today? I'll make sure that the Sergeant Major here buys you a nice dinner for your trouble!" Steve said and elbowed Karl in his side.

The Chief just stood there, not knowing what to say, as Karl tried his best not to blush. He was failing miserably at it.

"Sounds like a deal, Colonel. And just so you know, Sergeant Major, I am not a cheap date," Chief MacGregor replied, noticing that Karl was indeed blushing just a bit. "You would think a Sergeant Major would know how to control his emotions. Don't you agree, Colonel?"

"I do wholeheartedly, Chief; I might have to ask for another one. Or should I just keep him around?" Steve asked, knowing full well that Karl was no match for her.

"Well, he is kind of tall, and that does come in handy to get things off the top shelf. Let's see how he stacks up during your polishing, as you call it. Colonel, Sergeant Major, please follow me," Chief MacGregor said in a tone more command than request.

"Colonel, remind me to have a short word with you once we are done here," Karl said as he began to breathe again.

"Certainly, Sergeant Major. Right after I tell Michele about you blushing in front of the Chief here!" Steve said laughing as he walked.

"Begging the Colonel's pardon, but do I get to know why you need polishing or is this some kind of a secret?" Chief MacGregor asked in a formal manner.

"For now, Chief, let's just call it a secret, but I will invite you to the presentation if you care to join Karl and my family?" Steve asked, knowing that Karl was beginning to blush again.

"You have a deal, Colonel. What do you say Sergeant Major? Is it a date, then?" Chief asked, picking up on the ribbing that Karl was enduring at Steve's hands.

"Umm, yes. Sure. That will be fine. Whatever," Karl blurted out as Steve and now Chief MacGregor laughed out loud.

They came to an open classroom and entered, careful not to disturb the class that was in session next door. Karl laid the case on its side and opened it to reveal the Templar's sword that Steve chose back at the Vatican. He removed it and the belt and handed them to Chief MacGregor, who took it reverently from his hands. As she held the sword, still in its scabbard, she noticed the fine detail about the hilt. Then she looked to Karl, asking "May I remove it, please?"

"Please do, but be careful. This is not a presentation sword," Karl answered.

As Chief MacGregor carefully removed it from its scabbard, she looked at the etching in Latin and then at Steve, eyeing him. This was not the sword of a Colonel, no matter what they were going to say next.

"This looks to be quite old, but it bears no damage. And it is really a thing of beauty. Is it Spanish?" Chief MacGregor asked while holding the exposed sword and looking at Steve.

"From what I have been told, this sword was made in Toledo, Spain in 1200," Steve answered quickly, hoping against hope that Chief MacGregor would not question the age of the sword.

"Colonel, I beg your pardon, but did you say 1200? As in an 800 year old sword?" Chief MacGregor asked as she looked at the sword again, this time with much more admiration.

"Yes, he did say 1200. And the engraving simply states the following," Karl said, not waiting for the next question. *"This is the Sword of a Templar, and it shall save the world."*

Chief MacGregor just stood there looking at the sword. Karl walked up to her; he looked into her eyes when she looked up at him.

"We need your help, and I will get the permission needed to tell you what is going on, but until that time, you need to trust me. Deal?" Karl asked.

"Earth to Chief! Earth to Chief!" Steve was almost snapping his fingers to get Chief MacGregor to come back to reality.

"Yes, Colonel? Were you saying something, Sergeant Major?" Chief MacGregor asked.

"Yes, I was. I will get the permission to tell you what is going on, but right now we need your help. Even though I am a Sergeant Major in the Swiss Guard, please call me Karl," he said as he took the sword and put it back into its scabbard.

"Sure, Karl. I hope you'll call me Ellen. I'm sure it's a doozy of a story as well!" Ellen said still looking at the sword. "Colonel, no matter what your real name is, I will have to address you as sir or Colonel while you are on this base, so please don't ask me otherwise. Now, let's begin. Can you please put your cover back on and walk over here in front of me? Please, stand here at attention."

As Steve did as ordered, Karl moved off to the side and got his phone out to record this so that Steve could review it later. He stood at attention in from of Ellen, looking forward at a spot on the wall behind her. "You have had no formal military training on how to stand at attention, have you, Colonel?" she asked bluntly.

"No, none. Why do you ask, Chief?" Steve asked.

"Your posture is correct, and I noticed that you looked behind me and not at me. Most folks need to be trained to do that. You also knew to have your fingers clasped with your thumb pointed downward, not clenched tight, another mistake that rookies make," Ellen said as Karl nodded approval.

"I am a trainer for the Color Guard of the Boy Scouts. We practice monthly how to stand and present our swords. I'll let the Color Guard Commander know that he has done a good job of training us," Steve said proudly. Now he knew why everything had to be so precise with their practices.

"Well, he must have had a hell of a drill instructor. We don't have to spend much time on this formation. Now Karl, would you show the Colonel here the proper way to come to *at ease* from standing *at attention*, please?" Ellen asked.

Karl walked over, stood an arm's length away from Steve, and came to attention; then, he waited for the order from Ellen. She barked "at ease," and Karl, in one swift motion, spread his legs apart and put his hands behind his back, all the while not looking anywhere but forward. Ellen walked behind Karl and noticed that his hands were not touching and that his elbows were both at the same degree.

"Seems all of your training has been done at a bit of a higher level than ours, Karl. Very nicely done," Ellen said with the slightest hint of smile on her face. "Colonel, please mimic what Karl has done for me."

As they practiced, Steve noticed how Ellen was helping him with ease and all the while looking at Karl with a bit of interest. *I hope,* he thought to himself, *that maybe Karl might enjoy his time here now that he has a very cute Chief looking at him. The ride home will be interesting when he starts to tell me how inappropriate it was for me to mention dinner to her. Oh well, sometimes you have to stir the pot."* He smiled again at himself, knowing that this was all Michele's doing. She was famous for stirring the pot, so to speak.

"Something funny, Colonel?" Ellen said, catching Steve by surprise.

"Oh, no Chief, just thinking. Colonels are allowed to think, aren't they?" Steve answered, which brought a smile to both Karl's and her face.

322

"Just as long as they don't think too much. It usually means we worker bees have to do something after you are done thinking!" Ellen replied as she and Karl both started laughing out loud.

"Attention!" Steve yelled, and both Karl and Ellen stopped laughing and came to rigid attention with a surprised look on their faces. "Well, I guess I don't have to work on how to give an order, then," he said with a smile. As both of them realized that he had gotten their goat, they all chuckled. They went back to practicing; Captain Mahoney had cleared Ellen's scheduled for the day.

Chapter 69

Back at the house, Michele took this time alone with Jim in school and Steve gone to check on the progress of the Scout Honor Medal that she had recommend Jim for. As she waited on hold for the clerk to get her to the right person, she made a note to call Elaine after to set up what Karl talked about. She finally got to the person who had the recommendation and got the news that it had been approved and would be announced at the next board meeting, two days hence. She thanked him and asked that they not mention this to anyone since no one knew what she had done for her son. When she hung up, she was all smiles and said aloud to herself, "The heck with a call. I think I deserve to go on a lunch date!" As she called Elaine on her cell phone, she noticed in the hall mirror that she was still smiling.

"Hello, Michele. How are you?" Elaine asked when she answered the call.

"Doing good. Say, are you free for lunch today? I think I have the follow up to Steve's interview all lined up for you," Michele answered.

"Really? I didn't think after the first one that he ever wanted me to come over again," Elaine replied, a bit startled.

"I don't think I suggested coming over here, Elaine. Did I?" Michele answered with only the slightest hint of laughter in her voice.

"No, you did not; meet you in an hour at Steve's Diner on Route 64. See you then!" Elaine said and then hung up.

Michele changed her clothes and began to formulate her plan to have the medal presented to Jim right before Steve's announcement. As she got ready, the pieces started to fall into place, and even Karl and his gun could not stop her.

Chapter 70

At the restaurant, Elaine was running a bit late, which was her usual way. Knowing this, Elaine ordered a glass of house Merlot to enjoy before she got there. As she looked up, she heard the front door open, and Elaine hustled in. Michele waved her hand to indicate where she was. As she greeted Michele, Elaine noticed the glass of wine and asked, "Celebrating something, missy?"

"As a matter of fact, I am. Care to join me?" Michele answered with a smile. She motioned for the waitress to bring another glass of wine along with their menus. As the wine was served, Michele could imagine the look in Steve's eyes when the medal was pinned onto Jim's shirt.

"So what is this news about a follow up interview? Is this your idea or Steve's?" Elaine asked without a blink.

"Well, this is going to be an exclusive for you and your paper because Steve is going to be presented with an honor from the Vatican. I cannot tell you what the honor is, so don't ask. But let's just say that this offer does not come along very often!" Michele gave just enough information to Elaine.

"Oh, come on, Michele! You can't ask me not to ask any more questions. Really?" Elaine said as she grabbed her notebook and pen. "So he is to be given an honor from the Vatican?"

"Yes," Michele said with just a very sly grin on her face. "The honor is from the Pope himself, and I want you and your camera person there to record it. You would have an exclusive because I'm not inviting any other newspapers or TV stations. Just you, Elaine, but with a couple of rules, of course, since we are dealing with Steve."

"Oh, I'm sure there are more than just a couple of rules that your husband has, Michele!" Elaine replied with a laugh as they clinked wine glasses in a mock toast. "So, can you give me anything at all to go on so that I can sell this to the higher ups?"

"You already have a Pulitzer-worthy video in your bag from Steve. Do you really need to sell anything at all, Elaine?" Michele asked in a way that put an end to that line of questioning.

"Well put, Michele. Okay, so when is this all going to take place and where?" Elaine asked, knowing that the information was going to be sketchy at best, but anything at this point was better than nothing.

"It's going to happen at St. Paul's Church on Madison Street in St. Charles. When? I'm still working that out but more than likely in two weeks. Steve will be presented for the first time and the announcement of his honor will be disclosed. Unfortunately I have been sworn to secrecy on any further information," Michele said, trying to mask the fact that she wanted to blurt everything out.

"Steve made you promise not to tell anything? Come on, Michele. I know you better than that. Since when do you ever promise not to tell anything?" Elaine asked, knowing that something big was up.

"Well, it wasn't Steve that I had to promise, Elaine. It was Karl, his bodyguard from the Vatican!" Michele said with a serious look about her.

"A bodyguard? From the Vatican? Here in Illinois? Really, Michele? What exactly is going on here?" Elaine asked in an excited voice.

"Well, his name is Karl, and he is quite tall and good-looking and carries a gun. That is all I can tell you," Michele answered her without breaking a smile.

"Umm, how good-looking is he, Michele?" Elaine asked, and they both started to giggle.

Chapter 71

The three of them worked until almost 5 p.m., not even taking a break for lunch, to polish Steve as much as he could be in such a short amount of time. His training in the Color Guard of the Boy Scouts had paid off immensely; all he had to work on was positioning rather than how to stand or how to walk.

All of this surprised Karl, who took notice of how serious Steve was through all of this and did not complain as Chief MacGregor made him repeat her instructions over and over and over. He looked at Steve being transformed before him, acting like an officer but more importantly gaining the confidence that he belonged there, wearing those silver eagles. As he went through the command of attention, at ease, parade rest, and then attention again, Karl just smiled, knowing that Michele would be smiling when she saw her husband that night. Karl started to chuckle to himself that he might just drop Steve off at the corner so that he was not in her way when she saw him again in his uniform. Steve caught the smirk on Karl's face and asked quickly, "Something funny there, Sergeant Major?"

"Oh, no, Colonel. I was just thinking of how you are going to make it back into your house when I drop you off tonight!" Karl said, smiling.

"Why would you say that? Is there a problem there, Karl?" Ellen asked.

"Yes, Chief, a one hundred and fifteen pound problem: my wife, Michele! I almost didn't make it out of there this morning when she saw me in my uniform!" Steve answered her quickly as Karl attempted not to laugh at his answer.

"I take it your wife has a thing for a man in uniform then, sir?" Ellen asked and, noticing Karl biting his lip, tried not to laugh again.

"Well, Chief, I didn't know it until this morning, and I am sure hoping that Karl stays close in case it gets out of hand once I get home," Steve said. Karl could not contain it anymore and burst out laughing, which left Ellen just standing there. "Ok, Karl, that's enough. It wasn't really that funny," Steve said pleadingly, begging for Karl to stop.

"What is going on here, sir? Karl really can't contain himself over there," Ellen observed, knowing she was missing something.

"Michele quoted the line from the movie *Top Gun* to him when she saw him. I was standing there and thought he was never going to make it out of there alive!' Karl said between fits of laughter.

"Not the 'take me to bed' line. Is that what she said to you, sir?" Ellen asked as she moved behind Karl's 6′4″ frame to hide.

"Yes!" Steve answered almost blushing. "Now can we continue, please? And hiding is not going to help you there, Chief, no matter how much bigger he is than I am!"

"Yes, sir!" Ellen answered as she pushed Karl in front of her anyways. "We are done here anyway. You have most of the basics down, and Karl took enough video to help you practice. So when is this *thing* you have coming up going to happen?"

"It looks like two weeks from this past Sunday. It'll be held in St. Charles at St. Paul's Church. I'm hoping that you can make it, Chief. It's the best payment I can offer you at this time!" Steve said as he extended his hand toward her.

"Well, sir," Ellen said while shaking his hand. "I'm getting a dinner out it with from your bodyguard here. That will be payment enough! I expect that you are a man of honor, Sergeant Major, and will not renege on your payment," Ellen suggested in a way that was more of an order.

"No, I will not…whatever that word means, Chief. I will gladly take you to dinner, and I will have permission by then to tell what you have helped with," Karl said as he offered his hand to her as well. Ellen took his hand and then got onto her tiptoes to give him a peck on the cheek. As she did, she miscalculated his height and fell off balance into his arms. Karl caught her; Steve just smiled off to the side.

"You two might want to get a room or something!" Steve said, repeating the same phrase that Jim had said to him and Michele on occasion.

"Sorry, sir! Oh, sorry Karl! Oh my God, that did not work out as it should have," Ellen said, blushing as she regained her footing. Karl just smiled and then properly leaned over and gave her a quick kiss on the lips, which made her blush even more. He handed her his card, which had his cell number on it, as he turned back to the case.

"Looking forward to having that dinner, Chief; let's hope you do not fall then!" Karl said with a huge smile upon his face as he put the sword back into the case. Steve just stood there holding his cover, wondering if this was how Michele felt when she stirred the pot with her friends.

As they finished packing up, Steve asked Ellen to thank the Captain for her time. She came to attention and snapped off a very crisp salute to Steve, who returned it just as crisply, which made her smile again. As she left the room, she looked at Karl, who made the international *call me* sign of the thumb and pinky finger in the form of a phone.

As they exited the building to walk back to the car, Steve noticed that the parade ground was full of recruits in formation being drilled. Upon seeing him and Karl, the closest drill instructor, a Senior Chief, called out, "Attention! There is an officer on deck!" and came to attention. At that moment, all of the recruits and other drill instructors on the parade ground came to attention as well and in one uniform act saluted Steve. Karl came to attention and saluted as well. Steve came to attention and snapped off a crisp salute to all present. Steve gave the order to carry on and proceeded to walk to Karl's rental car.

"Nicely done, Steve," Karl said in a stage whisper. "Very nicely done."

"Thank you. Now let's get home and see if I can sneak in without Michele making me pay for leaving this morning," Steve said, and they both chuckled as Karl started the car.

The ride home went by quickly, and neither of them mentioned the kiss or the dinner date. Steve thought there would be hell to pay later for what he did, but maybe it might turn into something else besides dinner. Michele really was rubbing off on him, he thought to himself as they turned off of I-90 and onto Randall Road, heading back to his house.

Chapter 72

When they pulled into the drive, Karl got out of the car and got the case out of the back seat. Steve made his way to the door in the garage, hoping against hope that Michele was not in the kitchen when he walked in. As he walked in, Michele was standing there laughing.

"Still trying to sneak in your own house after all these years? Really, Steve!" she said as she moved toward him to give him a kiss. Their embrace was cut short when Karl knocked on the door, carrying the case with the Templar's sword in it. As he walked in, he pretended not to notice Michele hugging her husband and proceeded directly into the living room, carrying the case. Once there, he laid it on the table and opened it carefully.

"What do you have in the case, Karl?" Michele asked as she let go of Steve and walked toward him.

"This is the sword that Steve is going to wear when he is presented as a Knight of the Golden Spur. It is quite a sword, don't you think?" Karl answered her as he took it out of the case.

Michele stood there, looking at it as he laid it on the table so that he could wipe it down with a cloth that was in the case.

"Would you mind taking it out of its sleeve or whatever it's called, please?" she asked.

"It's called a scabbard, and of course I will, but please, be careful. This is not a presentation sword, Michele," Karl warned her the same way he had warned Chief MacGregor just a couple of hours earlier. As Michele took it in her hands, she could feel the weight and noticed how richly it was engraved in Latin.

"*Hic est gladius, ut salvet mundum Templarii*," Michele read out loud. "Loosely translated, I believe it says, *This is the sword of a Templar, and it shall save the world*." Both Karl and Steve looked at her with amazement at how quickly she translated the Latin to English. "What, the two of you never took Latin in high school?" she asked as she laughed at both of them. Still looking at the sword, she looked up at Karl and asked softly "Who gave him this sword? And why?"

"Pope Alexander gave it to Steve personally. It is from his private collection in the Vatican; it was made in Spain in 1200. It is quite an exquisite piece, don't you agree, Michele?" Karl asked her.

Michele just looked at it again and handed it very gingerly back to Karl. "You did you say 1200? I did not misunderstand you, did I?" she asked.

"Why is it every time we say 1200, everyone looks at us funny, Karl? Even Ellen said the same thing," Steve said.

"Ellen? Who's Ellen, Steve?" Michele asked quickly before he realized what he had said.

"Ellen is Chief Ellen MacGregor, who was my drill instructor at Great Lakes Naval Base, Michelle. If you play your cards right, you could be meeting her soon. Isn't that right, Karl?' Steve answered.

"Karl, why might I get to meet this Ellen?" Michele asked as she threw a jab at Steve's exposed stomach.

Grunting from the punch, Steve said to Karl "Please, tell us how, Karl!"

Karl looked at Steve with a glare, and Michele started to laugh but walked over to him and just looked at him in a motherly way. She said, "Don't listen to him, the man who yells at Popes! So, who is she, Karl?"

"She is the best drill instructor at the base, and she drilled Steve for over five hours today. Here, let me show you a video I took so that Steve can practice at home," Karl answered, realizing that Michele was not teasing him but actually interested in who she was. As he got the video queued up on his phone, Steve walked over to them and was greeted with another punch to his stomach and a stern look from Michele.

"Ouch! What was that for?" Steve exclaimed.

"Picking on Karl, that's what. Don't do it again, Colonel or no Colonel," Michele said to him not very subtly.

"Okay, geez. I was just having a little fun, that's all," Steve said sheepishly. "I mean now he has to take her to dinner for helping us!"

"Steve Michaels, did you do this? Tease Karl into asking her for a date?" Michele asked looking at the sword a bit closer.

"Just a little. I mean she is quite attractive for a Chief. Don't you agree, Karl?" Steve answered.

"Karl, you do not have to answer that!"

"Please, Michele, she is quite attractive, and I have no problem telling you that. If you are going to throw an elbow at him, I can help with where to aim. I would be more than happy to show you," Karl said. They both looked in Steve's direction as he backed away.

"Karl, please remember that I outrank you. It's against all that is holy to hit a Cardinal," Steve said, backing into the wall behind him, which brought a laugh from both Karl and Michele.

"Thank you for the support, Michele, but I will be fine; plus, it will be nice to have dinner with another soldier," Karl said.

"Well, if you wish, I'll make you dinner here at the house, and all three of us can gang up on Steve together," Michele said, which brought a snicker from Karl.

"You know that might be the best. I do not know too many restaurants here, and then I can tell her why we were there. She might even be helpful in getting this all set up," Karl answered with a smile. "You would not mind? I can pay for the food if you wish?"

Michele looked at Karl and just started to laugh, "Oh Karl, you do not have to pay for anything. You buy the wine, and dinner is on me for all the help you are giving him." She jerked her thumb over at Steve who was still looking for a way to get out of the room without being noticed.

"Do I get a vote? I mean it is my house after all," Steve joked.

Both Michele and Karl turned towards him and at the same time said, "No!" They laughed out loud.

"Geez, in my own house I get no respect. What is this world coming to?" Steve exclaimed in a self-mocking way.

"So, let's see if she will call me, and when she does, Michele, we can set up this dinner date," Karl said with a sheepish smile upon his face.

Chapter 73

The next week went by very quickly with Steve practicing the drill movements that Ellen had shown him so that they happened without him thinking about it. Karl had downloaded the video so that he could practice at home and began wearing the sword to get used to its weight as he walked with it on. He had been reading and studying everything that Cardinal Albani had sent him pertaining to being a Cardinal and the Vatican and how it worked. Karl had been insightful in that sense as well, giving him tips on the political make up that only one who had witnessed it at his level could know.

As he was having his coffee and enjoying the peace and quiet of a Saturday morning with no one up but him, the phone rang. He answered it quickly so as not to wake Michele.

"Steve, Abbot Giuseppe here. Good morning. I hope I have not caught you at a bad time?" Giuseppe asked.

"Oh no, your Eminence, just having a cup of coffee. It's nice to hear your voice. Everything okay there at the Vatican?" Steve asked, not knowing what else to ask him.

"Yes, Steve, everything is good here. You know, politics as usual," Giuseppe began to laugh a bit at his reply.

"So, what can I do for you this morning?" Steve asked, sensing that this was not a *how are you doing* call.

"I wanted to give you my arrival information; we will be landing at Chicago O'Hare on Tuesday at 4:00 p.m. I have made arrangements for us to stay at the rectory at St. Paul's parish. Father Rick has been very accommodating."

"I'm sure he has been. He probably dropped the phone when you told him who you were! Do you need anything?" Steve asked.

"Yes. Can you pick us up? You have a van, I hope? We will be bringing some items for you," Giuseppe asked without going into detail. "Also, please bring your Vatican passport; the items are in a sealed diplomatic case."

"Yes, of course I can pick you up. The three of you, correct?" Steve asked.

"Yes, Brothers Michael and Angelo are quite excited about coming to see Chicago and get something they are calling deep dish pizza, whatever that is," Giuseppe said as he heard Steve stifle a laugh on the other end of the phone. "Something funny there, Steve?"

"They are coming from Italy to have pizza? Just something ironic about that. Wait until I tell Michele that one," Steve said through his laugh.

"I understand what you mean, Steve. You should try being with these two as long as I have. Funny how God's plan works for each of us," Giuseppe replied, smiling through the phone.

"I will bring Karl with me. He can help in case there are any problems with customs, and then we have someone to lug around whatever you're bringing over. Nice to have a bodyguard, isn't it, my dear Cardinal?" Steve said jokingly.

"You will not use Karl as your manservant, Steve Michaels. You will lug it yourself, whatever it is you're talking about," Michele said loudly to her surprised husband.

"Cardinal, I have to go before my lovely wife hits me again. I will see you at 4:00 p.m. on Tuesday." Steve said, getting out of the way of Michele.

"Really, you wake me up and then plan to use him as your luggage boy? Seriously, Steve, you really need to change your way of thinking. I will not let you use that poor man that way! So who was on the phone at this hour anyway?" Michele asked as she looked at him sternly.

"That was Cardinal Giuseppe. He and his fellow Brothers of the Brown Robes, Michael and Angelo, will be here on Tuesday. I'm going to pick them if I can use your van?" Steve answered her quickly.

"Well, yes, you can use the van, silly. But you will not use Karl that way. By the way, he got a call from Ellen last night, and we're having dinner here tonight. You're grilling steaks for us, and you better not burn them," Michele said to him in a not so pleasant manner, still angry with the unkind thing he had said about Karl.

"Really, here tonight? Well, that sounds like fun. I can't wait for you to meet her; she is very cute and very good at her job," Steve replied.

"Well, whether she is cute or not is immaterial, Steve. She's coming here as our guest and to see Karl. You will be on your best behavior or so help me!" Michele glared at him as she spoke.

"Yes, ma'am. Best behavior, no jokes, and don't burn the steaks. Will there be anything else, ma'am?" Steve said with his best pouty face.

"*Ma'am*? Did you just call me *ma'am*? Steve, can't you be serious for once?" she asked. Steve, realizing he had perhaps pushed his wife farther than he should have with his attempts at humor, moved closer and hugged her tightly as she squirmed to get away. He planted a kiss on her forehead when she calmed down a bit. "Really, Steve, somedays I wonder what I see in you," she said, and he smiled, wondering the same thing.

Chapter 74

Karl came over at 4:00 p.m. promptly, carrying a bag with him; he knocked on the door and was greeted by Michele, who opened the door for him.

"Karl, me making dinner means I make everything. You didn't have to do this," Michele said as she took the bag and led him into the kitchen. "Now, let's see what you brought us." Michele removed two bottles of red wine and two bottle of white. She recognized the label on the red and knew that he had good taste in wine. "Karl, this is a very good bottle of wine. You shouldn't have!"

"Michele, I am from Switzerland. You have no idea what we pay for this wine over there. Remember here it is domestic; there it is imported, a huge difference in cost. Plus, I can't let you pay for everything. It would be impolite," Karl said as he took the last item out of the bag and handed it to Michele.

"What's in the box? Not another surprise from the Vatican, I hope. I've had my fill of those kinds of boxes lately," Michele said with a serious look.

"No, this is not from the Vatican, Michele. Just open it, please," Karl said grinning.

Michele opened the box slowly to see fresh cannoli for dessert in the box. "Karl, you certainly know the way to my heart. Dessert is my weakness!" she exclaimed.

"So, stealing my girl's heart, are you, Karl? Well, them there are fighting words where I come from, mister!" Steve said, surprising both Karl and Michele when he came into the kitchen.

"I would put my money on Karl if you two ever did come to blows," Michele said, elbowing her husband as he walked past her.

"Really? You'd put your money on him? Where is the love, Mrs. Michaels?" Steve asked as he got out of the way of her elbow coming at him again.

Karl just looked at the both of them and chuckled. Jim came up behind him, nodding to Karl. "You're lucky you get to leave; I have to put up with this all the time. I'm Jim, by the way. Pleasure to meet you finally," Jim said, extending his hand to Karl.

"Nice to meet you, Jim. I have heard plenty about you from your dad; also, I have something for you. Please excuse me for a minute," Karl said as he walked back out the front door to his car. He returned holding a formal-looking folder that had the crest of the Papal Swiss Guard on it. "Jim, I have been instructed to give you this by the Colonel in Command of the Swiss Guards!" Karl announced, handing the folder to Jim.

"For me? Sure you got the right Jim Michaels, Karl?" Jim asked.

Karl smiled. He knew which side of the family Jim took after; this was what he would expect from Steve as well. Looking at Jim, he saw Michele's features but Steve's height and his determination as well. "Yes, you are the only Jim Michaels in the room, correct?" Karl asked.

"Yes, Karl, I am the only one!" Jim said as he opened the folder carefully. Inside was a richly ornate decree that was written in German. Jim's name was on it; that was all he could read. "Karl, could you translate this for me, please?" Jim asked, handing the decree back to him.

"Certainly, Jim," Karl said as he looked over the decree before he began to read. *"This decree is to announce that Jim Michaels has been given an honorary position in the Swiss Guard for his actions in saving the life of a priest with total disregard for his own personal safety,"* Karl finished reading the decree and handed it back to Jim, who looked at it with disbelief.

"You sure you read that right, Karl?" Jim asked very quietly.

"Yes. Your actions in defense of the fallen priest were quite heroic and should be recognized, Jim. You moved when no one else did and made sure the other altar server got out of the way and took cover. You took the medical actions needed to save the priest," Karl said proudly to Jim.

345

"Thank you, but receiving honors for doing what is right is not how I was raised, Karl. We do it because we are there, and it is needed," Jim told him. *"Humble is the man that succeeds* is what I have been taught, Karl," Jim said, proudly repeating the words that his father had taught him since he could walk.

Karl looked at Jim with pride that he could be so humble yet so proud of what he had done; certainly this must be a family trait. "Jim when you visit the Vatican, as I know you will being the son of a Cardinal, the Swiss Guards will take you and your mother on a tour of the Apostolic Palace where you will get to see sites that the public does not get to see. It is our privilege to have you as an honorary member," Karl said as he shook Jim's hand again.

"Thanks," Michele silently mouthed to Karl as she wiped away the tears that were forming in her eyes. She turned and hugged her son who for once did not object to a display of emotion in front of someone.

Steve came over, shook Karl's hand, and thanked him as well; he too wiped away a tear over what had just happened.

"Mom, I need to go. Karl, thanks again. Will hold you to the tour when we get to go to the Vatican!" Jim said. "My friend Mike's parents are picking me up to take us to a movie so that I can get out of your hair tonight, per Dad! Have a fun night,

Karl," Jim said, winking at him while he ran for the stairs.

"God, that boy is so much like you," Michele said to Steve, wiping away the tears.

"Michele, that man there is a lot like you as well. He shows his father's side, but his compassion comes from you," Karl said, smiling at the both of them.

"Karl, thanks," Michele said as she walked over to give him a hug. Karl was ready for it this time. When she finished hugging him, she turned and threw a punch at Steve's shoulder, saying, "And he is way too much like you!"

The doorbell rang and Steve ran to get the door. Ellen was waiting there, holding a bouquet of flowers and a bottle of wine. "Ellen, so glad you could make it. Please, come in!" Steve said as he opened the screen door and reached out to take the bottle of wine from her hand.

"Colonel, sir, thank you!" Ellen said formally, almost standing at attention.

"Please, tonight it is Steve. Well, for the moment it will be Steve, deal?" Steve said knowing that Karl was going to tell her what really was going on.

"Sir, I don't know if I can do that. You are a Colonel after all, and I am an NCO of the United States Navy. Regs are regs, and you know I follow them without question," Ellen said as she noticed Karl and Michele coming into the living room.

"Ellen, welcome to our house," Michele said after drying her eyes a bit, trying to defuse what was being said between them. "Please, come on in. Steve, get out of her way, would you please?"

"Thank you, Mrs. Michaels, for inviting me here tonight. These are for you," Ellen said, handing over the bouquet to Michele.

"Well, first off, it's Michele. And these are lovely!" Michele said, moving Steve out of the way and leading Ellen to the kitchen, walking past Karl who just waved at her.

"Oh my God, I'm sorry, Karl. How are you?" Ellen said as she started to blush a bit. She walked over to him and got on her tip toes to give him a kiss on his cheek.

"Well, I am doing much better now; I am so glad that you called, Ellen!" Karl said, blushing a bit.

"Umm, you two need some time alone? We can go out to dinner," Steve said as he got out of the way of Michele, who was giving him quite a dirty look.

"Sorry, Steve," Karl stammered as he took Ellen's hand and led her into the kitchen where Michele was putting the flowers into a vase. "Ellen, it is okay for you to call him Steve. True, he is a Colonel of the Swiss Guard, but you need to know the whole story so that you can feel a bit more comfortable tonight around him." Karl led her to the table where he motioned for both Steve and Michele to come as well.

"Karl, would you like me to tell her?" Michele said to him to help.

"Michele, I think this is something I need to do. She is here as my guest, but thank you for asking," Karl said to her rather softly. "Ellen have you seen the video of 'Mr. I Believe' that has been going around lately?" Karl asked.

"I have; that was an amazing feat that he did. We were all amazed how he was able to get the gunman close so he could disarm him. I would not mind meeting him and asking him teach to a class on how to keep calm and do something so decisive to end a conflict," Ellen said in a professional manner.

"Well, you have met the man in that video, Ellen; it is none other than Steve here!" Karl said, pointing to Steve, who was sitting there with a grin on his face.

"No way! That was you? Are you sure, Karl? I thought that guy was taller!" Ellen exclaimed.

"No, I only wish he was taller, Ellen. But it was my dimwitted husband and my son who were in the video," Michele answered with a slight laugh in her voice.

"Oh God, I feel so ashamed that I didn't make the connection before. But wait, Karl you're a member of the Swiss Guard. How did you get mixed up in all of this?" Ellen asked.

Chapter 75

"Well mixed up indeed, Ellen. I was appointed to be his bodyguard by the Pope!" Karl answered, knowing full well the look he was going to get from Ellen.

Her jaw dropped open. Ellen was having a hard time finding her voice until it came out in a soft and almost reverent tone, "You did just say the Pope, correct?"

"Yes. Why does everyone always look at me that way when I say his name?" Karl asked everyone there. "Steve here fulfilled a prophecy with his actions at mass that Sunday that is over one hundred years old and written by a saint."

"Wait a minute. Are you telling me that he—I mean, you were appointed as a bodyguard because of a prophecy? Really, is this on a hidden camera or something? Are you three pranking me?" Ellen stammered out.

Michele started to laugh out loud at the "pranking" reference. When she finished, she just said to Ellen, "No we are not pranking you. There are less than a dozen people who know what I am going to tell you now. My dimwitted husband's actions were foretold in a prophecy by St. Pius X. He was ordered, and I do mean ordered, to Rome — on a Vatican passport, no less — to be handed a letter that St. Pius himself had hand written. The letter was one of four that were kept by an order of monks since they were written in 1914. The third letter was for Steve to open, and it told him what honor he was given and what he needed to do to be able to open the fourth letter. Steve, go and get the box that you showed us when you got home, please," Michele said to Steve while looking into Ellen's eyes and holding her hand.

Karl just sat there smiling, knowing that only Michele could condense this into a believable story and be able to calm Ellen. What a wonderful mother she really must be, Karl thought, for her to be able to sense this and take over immediately without any hesitation. If Steve only knew how lucky a man he truly was.

As Steve brought the box back to the table, Ellen just looked at it, finally getting the nerve to ask, "What's in it?"

Michele first told Ellen that Steve had been given a Pontifical Equestrian Knighthood as a Knight of the Golden Spur for his action in defense of the Church. She took the case out of the box that held the ribbon and medal of his Knighthood to show Ellen, who took it from her with a look of disbelief.

"So this is real? I mean a real knighthood?" Ellen asked.

"Yes, I am sleeping with a knight, and it's not all that it's cracked up to be, let me tell you that," Michele replied, which brought a laugh from the both of them.

"Can you please, Michele — please! — keep all of your comments about me till the end. Please!" Steve pleaded with his wife.

"You have to admit, Steve, that was a pretty good one," Karl said as he began laughing with the girls.

"Funny. Yuck it up, fur ball," Steve replied.

"Ok, you two. Sorry about that one, Steve. Umm, not really," Michele said through her laughter.

"So, a knighthood...but that doesn't mean that he is an officer," Ellen commented as she regained her composure.

"No, you're correct, Ellen," Karl answered quickly. "He was appointed by St. Pius X as a Colonel of the Noble Guard of the Vatican. This unit was disbanded by Pope Paul VI in 1972, and the current Vicar of Christ, Pope Alexander, saw to it that Steve here was named as a permanent Colonel in the Swiss Guard."

"So you being a Colonel is for real then, sir?" Ellen asked as the pieces were starting to fit together for her.

"Yes, Ellen. I am a Colonel, but that is not all, and this is where you can start calling me Steve, okay?" Steve said as he moved the box in front of himself.

"What is in the box, sir?' Ellen asked.

"This is the other gift I was given by St. Pius X, Ellen. The other little honor he bestowed on me for fulfilling his prophecy," Steve said as he took the lid off and removed the ring box. "Please open this," he instructed Ellen.

Ellen took the ring box from his hand and carefully opened the box to reveal the ring St. Pius X wore when he was the Cardinal Patriarch of Venice.

"This is an extremely red ruby. Whose ring is this, sir?" Ellen asked.

"Look inside the band, Ellen, and you will see," Steve informed her.

"*Giuseppe Sarto*. Who is he?" Ellen asked.

"That is none other than St. Pius X himself; this is the ring that he was given when he became a Cardinal," Steve said to her, letting it sink in before he continued. "And this is the hat that he wore as a Cardinal. This is called a—" Steve was about to tell her but was interrupted by Ellen.

"A zucchetto, yes. I know what that is, but why do you have it?" Ellen asked as Karl looked on a bit amazed that his date knew the term for the hat.

"How did you know that? Wait, never mind that. To answer your question, it was given to me when I was announced by a Pontifical Bull as a Cardinal Deacon of the Holy Roman Catholic Church by St. Pius X," Steve said as he put the ring on his finger and the zucchetto upon his head. Karl and Michele just looked at Ellen's face as her mouth dropped open for the second time.

"Oh my God. A Cardinal? Wait…really? This is not a joke, is it?" Ellen almost pleaded with the three of them, hoping that is was.

"No, Ellen. This is the farthest thing from a joke, I can assure you," Karl said as he took her hand and looked into her eyes. "He is a Cardinal and will be announced next Sunday, and I would like you to be there as my guest for the event."

"Your guest? Care to change that to…I don't know…maybe *your date*, Karl?" Ellen said, smiling back at him.

"Well, looks like it is a date then. Steve, how about those steaks that you are going to cook for us?" Karl said as Ellen let what she had just been told sink in a bit.

"Michele, I can call him Steve until he is announced, and then it is his Eminence after that, correct?" Ellen asked.

"Well, I do believe that you will be one of the few that can call him Steve no matter what, Ellen. I'm sure that he'll be grateful for having another woman keeping him grounded. I know I have my work cut out for me there!" Michele said as they both started laughing.

The dinner went off without a problem. Steve was kept in line by Michele the whole evening as Karl and Ellen got to know each other. As both of them left the house, Steve just looked at them talking out front and began to wonder if he looked as goofy as Karl did when he was talking to Michele while they were dating. He stood there smiling as Michele came up behind him, put her arms around his waist, and gave him a hug. He turned and kissed her forehead gently and smiled, knowing that no words needed to be said between them.

Chapter 76

Steve was in Michele's van with Karl driving to O'Hare to pick up the three amigos, which was what Jim had started to call them. As they drove, the talk centered on the plans for Steve being announced that coming Sunday at St. Paul's after the last mass. The plans were coming together as even Elaine was behaving and not making a fuss that this was going to be such a low key event. Karl and Ellen had been out again on their first official date Monday night; well, that was what Michele called it, and they seemed to hit it off pretty well.

As they pulled into the short term parking lot, Karl reminded Steve to let him lead the way and to make sure he followed his lead while they were there. As they entered the international terminal, Steve noticed one of the armed guards walking towards them; he fell in behind Karl, not needing to be told to do so.

"Mr. Michaels, I am to escort you to the VIP waiting lounge. Do you have your passport with you?" the guard asked as he scanned the terminal. Karl handed over his as Steve did the same, keeping to Karl's right side and behind him. The guard took them and spoke into his ear mic; then, he handed them back to the two men without a word.

He gestured to them to follow and walked towards a security entrance to their right. As the three of them entered, they were met immediately by another guard who asked for Karl's weapon and then patted them down. Once done, the man handed back Karl's weapon. The first guard began walking towards another door just ahead of them. When they got to the door, the guard opened it, and they were ushered into the VIP waiting area for international flights.

"Mr. Michaels, I am glad to finally meet you. My name is Ben Olsen, and I am the director of security here at O'Hare. I have seen your video and was quite impressed by your actions. So why do I have the honor of your presence here at the airport today?"

Karl spoke in the very professional voice that never ceased to surprise Steve, "We are meeting three priests coming over from Italy on Vatican diplomatic passports. They are bringing a case with them that is sealed and under the protection of diplomatic agreements between the United States and the Vatican City State. Here are the documents that were sent to me by diplomatic courier yesterday concerning this issue."

"I see," Olsen responded, taking the documents from Karl and scanning them.

"Well, everything looks in order. Thank you for having the documents. I would not want to delay your guests coming into the United States. May I get you something to drink? The plane is on final approached and will be touching down in about fifteen minutes," Ben informed them.

"I am fine, but thank you for the offer," Karl answered while Steve just shook his head. As Olsen left the room, they looked out over the tarmac. They were the only two in the room now. Steve was lost in his thoughts: it was now only five days until he was to be announced, and he went over the plans in his mind once again to see if something might have been missed. Michele had been coaching him nightly on how to walk down the aisle of St. Paul's and hold his sword so it did not sway. She even went to the church to measure the distance so that they could work on the cadence of his steps. She and Ellen had been emailing back and forth about everything. Ellen would meet them at the house Sunday morning. It felt funny how this was coming together so swiftly, and he was grateful that she had taken over the preparations for him. He had known she would take over anyway; that was her nature.

He was smiling to himself when Karl brought him out of thoughts by announcing that the plane was touching down and would be at the gate in a couple of minutes. As it pulled up to the gate, Steve steadied himself and took a deep breath to get ready for what would be the five busiest days of his life.

As the skyway was brought to the plane, Steve noticed how calm he was and that his nerves were completely under control. He was ready to meet his destiny. Karl noticed the calm about him and asked quietly, "Your Eminence, are you feeling okay?"

"First, it will always be Steve to you, and yes, Karl, I'm fine," Steve replied quietly. "For some reason everything is coming together. I just realized that it is out of my control, and I should just enjoy the ride and stop worrying."

"Well, good. It took you only a week to come to your senses. Now let's see if we will be able to get a word in edgewise with Brothers Michael and Angelo in the car on the way back," Karl said as the first of the passengers disembarked from the plane. Karl spotted them first; it was not too hard to see three men in brown robes coming off a plane talking a mile a minute. Well, two of three were. Karl smiled at the three of them being ushered to the VIP room where he and Steve waited for them.

When Olsen opened the door, he was followed by the three Brothers of the Secret in single file with Abbot, now Cardinal, Giuseppe leading the way. Steve walked up to greet him with a warm handshake and a quick but courteous embrace. Brothers Michael and Angelo were all over him seconds later, asking all types of questions as Steve just stood there and smiled back, not knowing whom to answer first.

"Your Eminence and Brothers Michael and Angelo, welcome to the United States; here are your passports back. Please enjoy your visit, and if you will follow me, I will take you to the customs area to retrieve your luggage and the case that you brought," Olsen said, addressing Cardinal Giuseppe with his correct title.

As they walked towards customs, Karl just smiled at Steve, who was totally lost trying to keep up with Brothers Michael and Angelo, who had not stopped talking since they walked off the plane.

"Karl, have you found a good deep dish pizza place for us to eat at? The whole trip over we have been comparing who has the best, and we really need to know," Brother Angelo rattled off without breathing.

"My brothers, please, we have just stepped off a plane, and I would like not to talk about pizza at the moment. You two act like you never go anywhere!" Giuseppe said.

In unison the two answered back, "Well, we never do go anywhere! This is our first time out of Italy in our lives!" Karl just smiled; he knew the ride home was not going to be quiet at all.

Chapter 77

Karl offered to drive as they were putting the suitcases and the case into the back of the van. Steve said in a stage whisper to Karl, "Thanks for offer to drive. I will never be able to keep up with the two of them in the back seat. Thanks a lot, Karl!"

Karl nodded at Steve and began to laugh, realizing he was busted. But he didn't give back the car keys that Steve had given him. As they all piled in, Cardinal Giuseppe took the passenger front seat, which made Karl grin even more. Steve noticed his grin in the rear view mirror and kicked the back of the driver's seat, which drew a laugh even from Cardinal Giuseppe. As they pulled onto I-90 headed west back to the house, Steve endured all of the questions that Brothers Angelo and Michael had about the different types of pizza in Chicagoland.

"Brothers, can you please give it a rest about pizza? Please?" Giuseppe asked with the tone of an order.

"Certainly Abbot, but just one more question, please?" Michael pleaded.

"One more and that's it. Do you understand? I tell you, Karl, it is like traveling with two kids back there!" Giuseppe answered.

"Ok, Steve," Michael asked. "So, is it true that they use more than two kilos of cheese on a deep dish pizza here?"

Steve knew that any answer would have a follow up, so he thought carefully and then answered with a one word answer: "Yes."

Brother Michael began to ask a follow up, but Steve caught him before he could ask and just smiled and said very clearly, "Look, I will sic Michele on both of you if you ask me another question about pizza. Got it?"

Both of the Brothers had heard enough about Michele to know that he was not kidding and nodded in agreement to Steve. "Good. Now that that is settled, my dear Cardinal, anything from the Vatican that you need to share with me?" Steve asked Giuseppe, quickly changing the subject.

"His Holiness sends his best wishes and has informed me to have you email Father Tommaso if you need anything, but from our last email it seems you have everything under control. Cardinal Albani sends his best as well and is preparing to have your announcement broadcast on the Vatican news channel on Sunday night," Giuseppe told Steve, finally looked relaxed as the pizza conversation stopped.

"Thank you, Giuseppe. I would have to say it has been Karl and Michele who have gotten all of the details worked out for Sunday. I am just along for the ride, so to speak," Steve answered, knowing that Karl would be trying hard not to blush from the compliment.

"Do you need help with anything, Karl?" Brother Angelo asked.

"Thank you for the offer; you're very generous. But so far we are all set. I will have Michele give you the itinerary when we get to the house in a few minutes. But I will let you know if anything comes up that I need help with," Karl said.

Cardinal Giuseppe nodded at Karl and now knew that he could control his companions with just a little bit of flattery to keep them in line. They pulled off of I-90 onto Randall Road; the conversation ended as they neared Steve's house.

As they rounded the corner to the house, Brother Michael asked Steve, "So how far away is the closest deep dish pizza place?"

Chapter 78

As they pulled into the drive, Karl honked the horn, which Steve thought was a bit unusual. He started to figure out something was up when Michele came out onto the front porch. She was waving at Karl and giving him the "thumbs up" sign, smiling at all of them. As they began piling out of the van, Michele walked down the steps and went over to greet the Brothers of the Brown Robe, whom she had heard so much about.

"Your Eminence Abbot Giuseppe! Finally, I get to meet you!" Michele exclaimed as she shook his hand.

"Michele, great to finally meet you as well. Let me introduce my traveling companions, Brothers Michael and Angelo of the Brown Robes," Giuseppe said as the two brothers came from the other side of the van to meet her.

"Nice you meet all of you and welcome to Elgin and to our house!" Michele replied. "Now, my dear Cardinal, if I may take these two from you, I have a treat for them inside. Brothers, please follow me." As they followed, Michele looked at Karl, flashed him a smile, and then winked.

"So, Mrs. Michaels, do you have any deep dish pizza places close by? We really want to try them," they both asked at the same time.

"I do believe I can help you with your quest there, my two brothers. And please, call me Michele," she said with a grin. As they entered the front room, the brothers were overcome with the aroma of fresh hot pizza that was waiting for them on the dining room table. "Brothers, let me introduce you to Chicago-style deep dish pizza. Please, get a plate and dig in!"

The brothers stared at the table, which had three different types of deep dish pizza waiting for them to sample; they both had to closed their mouths, realizing that they had both dropped their jaws looking at the table.

"Mrs. Michaels — er, Michele, how did you know? Who told you about this? How did you get it here, and is it still hot?" They asked their questions without waiting for answers.

"Well, it seems that a little birdie told me about your quest, and I thought I would help it out so that you two could avoid tilting at windmills," Michele answered them and began to push them towards the table. Steve and Giuseppe came up behind them and pushed them. Karl stood to the side, grinning at the two of them. Giuseppe smiled at both Karl and Michele, who had put this together as a surprise for the two brothers.

As they gathered around the table, Cardinal Giuseppe joined hands with his brothers, and the three others followed suit, saying grace over the pizza. As they began to dig in, Michele played mother hen to all five of them, explaining how to make the pizza to Brothers Michael and Angelo, who had nonstop questions about everything concerning this feast. After they ate and the brothers were helping clean up, they continued asking questions of Michele, who laughed as she answered. Karl brought the case in from the car and laid it on the now cleared dining room table with help from Steve.

When they unlocked the case, Michele came back from the kitchen with the two brothers in tow to see what was in the case. Inside were four garment bags and two hat boxes, all bearing the logo of Gammarelli's embossed in gold.

"What is Gammarelli's?" Michele asked.

"They are the tailors to the Vatican, Michele," Giuseppe answered. "And these are for Steve, compliments of His Holiness and St. Pius X."

As Karl lifted the first bag up high, he unzipped it to reveal the scarlet choir robe of a Cardinal of the Holy Roman Catholic Church. He took it out and handed it to Steve, who just held it up to see how the length was. Michele stood there, gaping at her husband and the official dress of his soon-to-be office.

"So, Michele, do you think this is a good color?" Steve asked, which brought a round of laughter from everyone there.

"Well, it's a little bright. Think they'll see you coming in it?" Michele asked in return, which brought an even bigger laugh from all of them.

Karl took out the two hat boxes that were in the case as well and snuck a peek inside one of them before handing it to Steve; in it was his scarlet biretta and zucchetto. Both of the hats had his name embroidered inside in golden thread. Steve took both out and tried them on as a hush fell about them. Even the two Brothers of the Brown Robes gaped at Steve. The hush was quickly broken by Michele, who said, "So is there a tiara in there for me to wear?"

"No, but if that is all it would take to keep you happy I am sure we can find one for you!" Steve replied as the room broke into laughter again. He took the second hat box and opened it to find the cover that went with his Knight of Golden Spur uniform. He took off the other two and replaced them with his cover. "Not the same effect as the scarlet one but still, all in all, pretty good, don't you agree?" he asked to all there. All five of them nodded as the reality of what was coming began to sink in.

While Steve put his cover away in the box, Michele asked to see what was in the other three garment bags Karl was holding. The first one held the dress uniform of the Knight of the Golden Spur, the one that Steve helped design. When he took it out, even Karl was impressed by the golden buttons and the richly embroidered crests of the Golden Spur and of St. Pius X. The latter was added by Cardinal Giuseppe as a reminder to Steve of whom he was serving. Steve nodded his approval of the additional crest to Giuseppe, who smiled in approval.

The third garment bag held his dress cassock with a scarlet sash and the fourth two black suits for every day wear with four dress shirts. As Steve carefully put it all back into the bags and laid everything back into the cases, he smiled a sly smile.

"What is the smile for, Steve?" Karl asked.

"Well, I guess the reality of everything is starting to hit home, Karl. Kind of hard to back out now. In for a pound and in for a penny, I think is what they say," Steve answered.

"Well, my dear husband, it's *in for a penny, in for a pound*. I think you had it backwards," Michele chimed in.

"Not really, Michele," Steve answered. "The pound is me, and the penny was the lead of the bullet that hit Father Rick," he said in a strong voice.

"Well, Steve," Giuseppe chimed in, quickly changing the subject. "How about driving us to St. Paul's rectory? I know I could use some rest after the trip."

"Sure, let me get my keys," Steve answered as he went to get them.

Michele mouthed a very quiet thank you to Giuseppe for changing the subject so quickly; he nodded in return. When Steve returned with the keys, holding them for everyone to see, Karl cleared his throat and said, "Your Eminence, I will call you tomorrow to discuss the arrangements for Sunday. Please have a good night."

"I will, and thanks for all you have done, Karl," Giuseppe said as both of the other brothers nodded in thanks as well. "Michele, thank you for your hospitality and for taking care of my two brothers here and their quest. Come, Don Quixote and Sancho. It is time to see if we can find more windmills for the both of you!" Michele came up and hugged all of them and then hugged Karl as well, which made him blush again.

"Michele, please," Karl said as the color rose in his cheeks even more. "I am a professional soldier, and it does not do me well to be blushing so much!"

"Oh, please, Karl. Do you blush when Ellen hugs you?" she asked in a way that only a mother could.

"What? Wait, that is very sneaky of you, Michele," Karl answered as Michele stood there, grinning. "Would it be okay if Ellen comes over tomorrow afternoon while we go through the final schedule? A fresh set of eyes can't hurt."

"Oh, please invite her! Nice to have another woman around here with all this testosterone," Michele said, smiling at Karl.

"Ellen? Who is Ellen, Karl?" Brothers Angelo and Michael asked at once.

"She is a United States Chief Petty Officer who carries a gun and knows how to use it, my dear, nosy Brothers of the Brown Robes!" Karl answered, which brought another round of chuckles from all.

"Ok, enough Karl. Brothers, let's get going." This was all it took from Steve to get them moving because his voice was beginning to carry the weight that he would need in his new life after Sunday's presentation. As they got back into the car, Cardinal Giuseppe thanked Michele again and asked her to wish him luck: he knew that the deep dish pizza discussion was not over by a long shot.

Chapter 79

As they pulled out of the subdivision, the mood in the van was somber. Even the brothers were not speaking.

Breaking the uncomfortable silence, Brother Angelo asked Steve, "What can we do for you Steve? Do you need anything? After Sunday, we will technically be working for you. Isn't that correct, Giuseppe?"

"It is, my brother. As a Cardinal, you will be somewhat in charge, Steve," was all that Giuseppe answered.

"Well, my dear Cardinal, it is I who will be working for you. According to my reading, courtesy of Cardinal Albani, the ranking of Cardinals is based mostly on seniority, and you outrank me," Steve answered, smiling. Even the two brothers did not know that.

"Well, you do have me there, Steve. But let's see what the final letter brings us, shall we? The other three have been nothing but surprising so far," Giuseppe said seriously.

"Is there something wrong, Giuseppe?" Steve asked in the same serious tone.

"Not really. Just a feeling. I know you and Karl have been practicing at St. Paul's for measuring your walk and planning where you could hide during the service, but something keeps nagging at me about all of this," Giuseppe said with much relief that it had finally come out. "I don't know if the world is ready for what is about to be unveiled. I mean, St. Pius X was the most conservative Pope there was, and all of this so far has been a complete one hundred and eighty degree turn from everything that we know about him."

"I have had the same feeling, Giuseppe. From all of my reading, nothing has ever shown this man to think this way," Steve said, grateful that this was finally coming to light now and not after he was announced.

"Sorry to interrupt the two red hats in the front seat who have missed the big picture of what was said in the letters," Brother Michael said with the most force Steve had heard him use since meeting him. "Brother Angelo pointed it out at the Vatican: World War I was about to begin, and he, Pope Pius X, could not stop it. He had predicted the war and knew he would not be alive to see the end of it. I am guessing that he knew what was about to happen and, being powerless to stop it, fell into a deep depression that ended up taking his life. He is known as the Pope of the Holy Eucharist and was instrumental in lowering the age that a young child receives Holy Communion from twelve to seven. This was going to kill many of these bright young men whom he had hoped would follow in his footsteps, become priests, and lead his Holy Mother Church after they had gained the experience needed to do so. That war ended all of his dreams, all that he fought for, and this is his way of helping us recover. I believe that he thought the act that would fulfill his prophecy would come sooner than it did. He has a plan, and it finally will be revealed this coming Sunday."

Steve looked in the rearview mirror while Giuseppe turned in his seat to look at Brother Michael, who wore a determined look. "Could you be a little bit more blunt there, my Brother?" was all Giuseppe said to him while smiling.

"We forget that he knew what he was doing; these letters were his way of helping after the war that he could not stop from beginning. He was a man of unique devotion to our Mother Mary and dedicated his life to her. The useless machine of war was going to change everything; his world was changing, and he was powerless to stop it. I for one am extremely excited to see what he has in store for us and what orders he is going to give Steve to carry out in this brave new world!" Brother Michael said with conviction in his voice.

"Umm, Michael," Steve said sheepishly. "Care to take my place on Sunday?"

All three brothers laughed out loud as Steve and his humor saved the day again.

When they pulled into the parking lot of St. Paul's parish off of Madison Street, Giuseppe reminded them not to talk about any of this. Fathers Rick and George had not been told yet what had happened and what was about to happen on Sunday. Getting out of the van, they were met on the front steps of the rectory by Fathers Rick and George, who still had his arm in a sling.

"Your Eminence, Brothers…welcome to St. Paul's parish," Father Rick greeted them cheerily. He approached Cardinal Giuseppe, looking to kiss his ring, but was greeted by a warm embrace from Giuseppe and then from Brothers Michael and Angelo. Father George waved but did not come forward; he could not risk being hugged with his shoulder still mending. They grabbed their luggage with Father George holding the door open for them all.

As they walked into the foyer, they were greeted by the housekeeper, Angela, who was directing traffic and suggesting where to put the luggage.

"Your Eminence, welcome. May I get you anything?" Angela asked right away.

"Oh, no, I am fine. Thank you. We have already eaten dinner and just need to relax as these next few days will be extremely busy for us all.

Brothers, Father George, and Father Rick, may I see you in your study or meeting room so that we can have a few minutes in private?"

"Your Eminence, the conference room is right this way. Please, follow me!" Father George said, leading the way.

"You too, Steve. You are not getting out of this that quickly!" Giuseppe added with a grin.

As they filed into the same conference room where Steve had taken the call from Pope Alexander, all except Giuseppe and Steve took their seats with the brothers sitting directly across from the two parish priests.

"You are probably wondering why a Cardinal and two Brothers of the Brown Robes are here to visit your beautiful parish and enjoy the gracious hospitality of your rectory. I am also sure that you have plenty of questions, but first I must tell you what I have been authorized to by His Holiness," Giuseppe said in his soothing voice.

"Well, I know I have just a couple of questions, your Eminence," Father George quipped, which brought a slight grin to his face. "But please, continue. None of this so far is making any sense at all!"

"What Steve did at mass after you were shot, Father George, in our opinion, fulfilled a prophecy that was given to the monastery of the Brown Robes for safe keeping by Pope Pius X!"

Both priests exclaimed at once, "Pius X!"

"Yes, Pius X, and what it has revealed so far is earth-shattering to say the least. Father Rick, after your call with Pope Alexander, you knew that he would inform you of events. Well, now is the time," Giuseppe said with only the slightest grin.

"You talked to the Pope?" Father George asked with a surprised look on his face.

"Yes. Why, haven't you? Hmm, seems a pastor has some privileges that younger priests don't!" Father Rick quipped amongst laughter from the others in the room.

"Moving forward…when you left the room, Father Rick, Steve and Michele were informed that Steve was to come to the Vatican and meet with the Pope and us. There he was given a letter written by Pius himself that explained what all of this was about. In short, Steve was made a Knight of the Golden Spur and a Colonel of the Noble Guard for his action in defense of the Church in stopping the gunman. In that letter, he was ordered to receive the rite of first tonsure and then to open an enclosed note from Pope Pius," Giuseppe told them quickly to avoid more questions.

"Whoa there, your Eminence, with all due respect. Did you just say *first tonsure*?" Father George asked.

"Yes," Giuseppe continued. "I helped His Holiness administer the rite along with the Secretariat of State, Cardinal Albani. Once that was done, Steve opened up the note from Pope Pius X, but it was not a note. It was a Papal Bull that ordained Steve as a Cardinal Deacon with all rights and honors!"

Both of the parish priests sat stunned at what they had heard. Brother Michael handed a coin from his pocket to Brother Angelo. Steve noticed and started to giggle when he figured out they had placed a bet on the priests' reactions when they found out he was a Cardinal. Brothers Michael and Angelo smiled as well once they knew they had been busted.

Father George was the first to come out of his stupor and sheepishly asked, "Cardinal Michaels, does Michele know?"

This brought a roar from all in the room. Steve responded while chuckling, "Yes. Michele does know, and thank you, Father George, for your concern."

"Well, with the way she was ready to take on the police at the church after I was shot, I would be a bit concerned for your wellbeing, Steve—er, your Eminence!"

"Thanks, Father George, and it's still Steve until Sunday. By the way, speaking of Sunday, would you mind if I borrowed the church after the 11:30 mass so that I can be announced? Then we all to get to hear what's in the last letter from Pope Pius X."

"There is another letter?" Father George asked.

"Yes. After I'm announced, I'm to open the last letter of Pope Pius X, and no one knows what's in this letter," Steve told him.

"Well, why not? None of this is making much sense to me anyway," Father Rick answered as he stood to shake Steve's hand. "Welcome to the clergy, your Eminence. And please, it will never be just Steve anymore."

"Thanks, Father Rick. Would you two care to say the 11:30 mass and then share in the event with me? We have the itinerary almost complete but could use some help finishing it," Steve asked both of them.

"Yes, your Eminence, we would love the opportunity to help and share in this great event with you. It's funny: whoever would have thought that I would be taking a call from the Pope and then a couple of days later having one of my parishioners being made a Cardinal? I'm sure that whatever is in this letter will be mild in comparison to what has happen so far," Father Rick said as Father George nodded his approval.

"Well, let's just hope so," was all that Steve could add.

Chapter 80

Michele was up early on Thursday morning as Karl and Ellen were coming over shortly to help finish the preparations for Sunday. Karl was beginning to soften a bit being around Ellen but still was diligent in his duties concerning Steve and his protection. Funny, she thought to herself. Her husband was becoming a Cardinal and her son was to be honored as a hero for doing something that she still could kill the both of them for! Smiling as she continued making her cup of coffee, she knew that whatever was in the fourth letter, she was ready to help. She was in for the long haul, so to speak.

Jim was at school already, and Steve was taking the Brothers of the Brown Robes out to breakfast after they went to morning mass.

The doorbell rang, and there stood Ellen with a bag of bagels in one hand and her satchel over her shoulder. "Come on in, Ellen. So happy that you get the time off to help us today," Michele said cheerfully.

"Thanks, Michele. Here, I picked these up. I'm not the friendliest without something to eat in the morning," Ellen said as she hugged Michele. "Karl isn't here yet?"

"No, Mr. Punctual is not here yet. I thought he'd be waiting for me in the kitchen when I came down the stairs this morning," Michele said, both of them grinning.

"You know, just between us girls, I never thought I would fall for another soldier, Michele!" Ellen confessed to her.

"It is something, isn't it? I myself still don't know if I'm going to fall for a Cardinal!" Michele exclaimed, and they both laughed. Once they had composed themselves, they heard the door open. "Hmm, wonder if it's the soldier or the Cardinal?"

"It is the soldier, and what is so funny, you two?" Karl asked as he walked in carrying a bag of bagels as well.

"For me?" Ellen asked, holding up her bag to show Karl.

"Yes," Karl replied as he gave her a hug after putting his bag down next to hers. "Seems I remembered someone saying she's not at her best without one in the morning!" Blushing, Ellen got up on her tiptoes and kissed him, which only made Michele smile even more.

"Oops, sorry about that Michele, but he just does that to me!" Ellen said as her cheeks maintained the redness of her blush.

"No problem. This big soldier here just turns to mush every time he sees you, and don't try to deny that, Karl, or so help me!" Michele replied, shaking her finger at Karl in mock anger. All three of them laughed as they sat down to look over the final preparations for Sunday.

"I really wanted to see you two here today to enlist your help with something," Michele said to both of them.

"Why does this sound like you are going to surprise me, Michele? What have you done? Changed religions and Steve doesn't know yet?" Karl asked, trying to keep a straight face.

"Nothing that dramatic but something even better, I believe," Michele said with a glint in her eye. "I had Father George nominate Jim for the Boy Scout Honor Medal, and it's been approved!" Michele gushed with tears forming. It was the first time she had said the words out loud to someone.

"Michele, oh my gosh!" Ellen almost yelled as she got up to hug her. Karl just looked on; he didn't understand what they were talking about.

"Michele," Karl said rather calmly. "Is this Honor Medal a big award from your Boy Scouts?"

"Yes, it is, "Ellen remarked. "You have no idea what we're talking about, do you, Karl?"

"No, sorry. Remember, I am Swiss!" he said with a smirk.

"Both of my brothers were Boy Scouts. They never achieved the rank of Eagle, but they were in for a long time. Michele, is this the highest award that he can receive from the Scouts?" Ellen asked.

"This is the second highest. Sorry, Karl. I totally forget that you are not an American," Michele told him, smiling. "What I'd like to do is have Father George award him the medal before Steve is announced, just so Mr. I Believe can keep a level head about himself."

"Well, it won't take much to get him to come back to earth. Steve is still embarrassed about the whole thing, but he does seem to be a bit better about accepting his fate," Karl replied. "But to give this award before might be a bit of a problem. How can Steve be there if we are to keep him out of everyone's sight?"

"Well, I think with both of your help, we can carry it off. Here's my plan, but you both have to pinky swear not to breathe a word. Only you two and Father George know about this," Michele said to a confused-looking Karl.

"Pinky swear? Please, Michele. You have to stop with all of this American slang. I am totally lost now," Karl said innocently as the women laughed.

Ellen leaned over and placed her hand on his cheek softly, saying, "Oh, I will teach you, big boy!" This caused them to laugh even louder at Karl's expense, and he began to blush once again. When they composed themselves, both Michele and Ellen stood up and walked behind Karl, kissing him on each cheek at the same time. Karl looked at them both and smiled, knowing when to give up.

As the women stopped laughing, Michele began to tell them her plan to get Steve there to see Jim receiving the award and not spoil the surprise as well.

Chapter 81

Sunday Morning

The next two days moved amazingly slowly for Steve. He took the Brothers of the Brown Robes to downtown Chicago to see the sights and sample yet another deep dish pizza. Michele and Karl hovered about him, trying to keep him busy with marching and presentation drills so that he could look and act like a soldier and just keep him calm. But when he was alone, the fear of what was happening began to creep up on him, which took its toll.

The only joy was having Cardinal Abbot Giuseppe around and his calm demeanor, which inspired Steve. The two practiced how to give his first blessing as a Cardinal. *So much to learn and so little time,* Steve kept reminding himself.

As dawn broke, he sat looking out into his back yard, knowing that life as he knew it would be over in the next few hours.

He grinned to himself about how he was able to trick his fellow brothers of St. Paul's Men's Club into attending the 11:30 mass that day by letting them know about Cardinal Giuseppe being there.

Who didn't want his picture with a Cardinal to brag about later? Little did they know which Cardinal they would have their picture taken with! He smiled to himself about that.

The house was very quiet, and Steve was enjoying his solitude until his cell phone buzzed in the next room. Rising to get it, he noticed that Karl was in the driveway, sitting there in his rental car looking worried. Steve grabbed his cell phone and noticed the text was from Karl but did not read it. He opened the front door and motioned for Karl to come into the house.

"Karl, what's up? You look a bit worried," Steve asked.

"There has been a threat made against you for what you have done. Word has gotten out about Cardinal Giuseppe being at mass today. We are taking the threat very seriously, Steve, and I am going to ask that there are police officers there today as a precaution. The threat was made last night to the Elgin Police department by an anonymous caller simply stating that you, Mr. I Believe, would be no longer if you go to the mass today. They have had no luck in tracing the call. The detective in charge said it probably came from a burner phone that has been discarded," Karl said seriously and straight to the point.

"What do you need me to do, Karl? I have never questioned your ability and will abide by your judgement about this threat," Steve said just as seriously back.

"Well, the first thing I have done is have a police car placed outside of your home since this morning. It will be here only as a deterrent in case someone is checking out the house," Karl said as there was soft knock at the door. "Wait here and do not move," Karl said as he removed his weapon from its holster.

"Karl, it's Paul from across the street. I saw you going into the house. How can I help? Word has gotten around the department about the threat," Paul spoke through the door Karl had opened only slightly.

"Come on in, Paul, and thanks for coming over," Steve said from the kitchen. "So, you two care for some coffee?"

Both Karl and Paul quietly walked back to the kitchen as Steve got cups down to fix their coffees. Only then did he notice that his friend and neighbor was wearing his weapon on his hip in plain sight. Steve poured the coffee and passed each man a cup; all three of them drank it straight black.

"Looks like this is more serious that it seemed, eh Paul?" Steve asked.

"Yes, someone knows that you will be at the 11:30 mass to see Cardinal Giuseppe attend. I believe that this might be one of the folks that Bill Mathers eluded to when he told you about the others that he spoke too about Father George. This is serious, Steve. Karl, how do you want to proceed?" Paul asked as only a police officer could.

"We will have a perimeter set up around the church starting at the 9:45 mass, the church checked, and all entrances guarded as well. Beyond that, we will be relying on an overwhelming show of force to stop them from carrying out their threat," Karl answered with the precision of a professional soldier.

"Have you anyone at the rectory to be with the Brothers of the Brown Robes?" Steve asked.

"Yes, we have a St. Charles police unit there already with an officer inside as well. Father Rick placed the call. He knows the police chief there," Karl said in a somber tone.

"Thank you, Karl. Those three mean the world to me now, and I do not need their security on my mind as well as this threat," Steve said.

"What threat, Steve?" Michele asked sternly. No one had noticed her walk into the kitchen already dressed for a run.

"Michele," Karl said calmly. "A threat was called in about Steve being at mass today. We are taking it seriously."

"I knew it. You and your stupid antics, Steve!" Michele exclaimed, not holding back "So, what do we do, Karl?"

"Well, first we relax a bit. You mentioned that you always run before church on Sundays, so Ellen will be here in about fifteen minutes, and she will go running with you; otherwise, we wait. A good plan is just that: a plan; we have no idea what they have in store for us today," Karl said as calmly as he could.

"Ellen is going to go running with me, Karl? So this is that serious?" Michele asked as it was all starting to hit home with her.

"Yes, it is, Michele. I would go, but I need to organize where and how we are going to handle this threat," Karl answered. "And I would appreciate it, Mrs. Michaels, if you would lay off the 'stupid' comments until this is over, please."

Michele just looked at Karl, who had never taken this tone with her before. She didn't know if she should apologize or rip into him. Choosing a compromise, she touched his arm and said quietly, "Thanks for the help. I will try to refrain from saying what I want to, but when this is over, I am going to kick his you-know-what from here to there," she said, pointing to the back of their yard.

"Deal. I will look the other way. Steve, you are on your own, then!" Karl said, trying to stifle a grin.

"Great. Paul, can I borrow your weapon, please?" Steve pleaded.

"Umm…no, you may not. Michele, okay to sell tickets to the neighbors for the ass-kicking that is to come?" Paul asked as he moved away from Steve.

"Funny, you two. And don't even begin to laugh, Mr. Professional Bodyguard. I know your boss," Steve said.

Chapter 82

Ellen was there within five minutes; as the boys were finishing their coffees, Michele started a load of laundry to keep herself busy until she could run off the nervous energy that she had from the threat being announced. As Ellen walked in the door, she was greeted by Karl, who gave her a quick kiss and an update on the situation at hand. She was in her running outfit, looking quite remarkable, and it took all of Karl's training to keep himself focused on the task at hand while looking at her. Michele caught the look and lightly punched him on his arm as she walked by him saying, "She does look quite sexy, doesn't she, Karl?"

Karl just stood there blushing, wishing that these two women would leave him alone about everything. Smiling, he walked back into the kitchen, seeking help from Steve and Paul.

"Don't look at me, Karl. She owns me as well; not a thing I can do about it," Steve said, throwing his hands up in mock surrender.

"Don't even go there with me. Sorry, Karl," was all that Paul said, laughing.

It was only when the girls left to go running that Steve noticed Ellen was armed and ready for anything that might happen on their run together. Grateful for the protection for the love of his life, Steve settled into his chair and picked up his book, reading a bit more about Pope Pius X and who the man was. Paul walked back towards his house after talking with Karl about where he needed to be and when. Karl walked over and sat down, waiting until Steve had finished the chapter before suggesting, "We can call this off today and tape it so that you will not have to face the public and this threat."

"We don't even know who the threat is from. I have to face this thing head on, Karl, or I'll be looking over my shoulder my whole life," Steve said with conviction.

Karl just looked at this man who a week ago was not even sure if he wanted to read the last letter or not; to say the least, he was impressed. After pondering a minute, he asked Steve if he would be willing to take any extra precautions at mass.

Steve looked up from his book and asked, "Like what?"

"Would you wear a vest under your suit today?" Karl asked.

"Would that be a three button or a two button one, Karl?" Steve asked with a gleam in his eye.

"Geez…someone is trying to kill you, and you're making a joke. Will you wear it?" Karl asked, almost pleading.

"Tell you what: let's ask the girls when they get home. I will take their advice, but if it's up to me, then no, I will not wear one," Steve said and went back to his book, leaving Karl with his thoughts.

Steve knew his stubbornness was making him treat Karl very rudely, and after a few minutes, which seemed like hours to Karl, Steve looked at him and said softly, "I trust you, Karl. But it was idiotic people like this that put me in this predicament in the first place. If I give in to them, they win. I believe that my fate has already been foretold, and I must see what it brings me."

Karl just stared at Steve, not knowing how to respond to him. This was a first for him. "So, should I tell the girls about the vest or just let it go, Steve? Your choice…" Karl asked.

Steve reflected. Accepting his fate was a far cry from being reckless, especially since he had already caused his wife a great deal of stress and anxiety. "Karl, I trust you and put my life in your hands. Tell the girls, and let's see what they say. After eighteen years of marriage to Michele, I can't say no to her. Ever!" Steve said, smiling, already knowing the outcome but not wanting to make the decision for himself.

"Okay, but you are turning into a sly guy, your Eminence," Karl said with a laugh.

"It will always be *Steve* to you, and don't you forget it," Steve responded, laughing.

As they chuckled, the doorbell rang, which caused Karl to jump up and motion to Steve to stay put. Walking toward the door cautiously with his hand on the butt of his gun, he noticed that it was an Elgin police officer at the door holding a package.

"Are you Karl?" the officer asked.

"Yes, I am," he replied, not letting his guard down.

"I have been asked by Paul Roberts to drop this off," the officer said, holding the package up for Karl to see. In the package was a bulletproof vest that Paul had arranged to have brought over.

"Thank you for the delivery service; sorry to make you come all the way over here to drop this off!" Karl said very gracefully.

"No problem; please tell Mr. Michaels that we will be watching the house until this threat is resolved," the officer said as he nodded and left the front porch.

Karl carried the bag holding the vest back into the living room and asked Steve to stand so that he could check to see if it fit. As Steve rose he noticed the police car out front and Paul talking to the officer sitting the front seat; he reminded himself that he owed his friend a huge debt of gratitude for all of this.

The vest fit snugly and was military grade; it was one that the Elgin police department used to protect visiting VIPs. He wore it and sat down to get used to the feel since he already knew that Michele would make him wear anything that could protect her husband. Looking at Karl, he commented, "I do not want you to put anyone else in harm's way today, Karl. If something happens today, protect Michele, Jim, and Ellen. I can take a shot wearing this. They won't be expecting me to be wearing one. I'm sure they will get only one shot off before the police take them down."

"I will do as you have requested, Steve, but it is you whom I am here to protect. Please never forget that," Karl said, not knowing where this discussion was leading.

"I know, Karl. But Michele, Jim, and now Ellen are more important to me than my own safety. Just protect them in case anything happens to me today. Do you understand, Karl?" Steve said in a stern manner that Karl understood all too well.

"I will do as ordered, Your Eminence," Karl answered, knowing that Steve had accepted his fate whatever it may be, and nothing could change his mindset now.

"So let's get going with how to tell Michele that I am going to wear a bulletproof vest. By the way, does this make me look like I have a bigger chest?" Steve said as his humor took the edge off what was just said.

"Umm, not really, Steve," Karl answered, which brought a smile to both of them.

Chapter 83

As they were finishing their run, Ellen asked if all was set with Jim to receive the Boy Scout medal. Michele just smiled, nodded, and gave her the details for what she had worked out with Father George. The medal was to be awarded to Jim during the time that the homily normally would be given by Father Rick, who was going to be the main celebrant at the mass. Ellen then asked how Karl was going to get Steve into the mass to see the presentation.

"That was the easiest part; Steve will be attending mass today and will be going to get into his Knight of the Golden Spur uniform after he receives communion. This way no one will know that he is gone, and with you and Jim by my side, it should go off without a hitch. Karl will be at the back of the church and will escort the Scout district executive to the pulpit. It's all so exciting to be able to pull something off like this even with this threat!" Michele said, trying to contain her emotions.

"Well, it is exciting, and thank you for letting me be a part of all of this; I mean, you must so proud of both of them even if you will never tell them," Ellen said, which made both of them start to giggle.

As they made their way around the last corner, they both noticed the police car in front of the house and Paul standing by it. As they began their cool down, Paul nodded to both of them and smiled. The reality of what was happening hit Michele with both barrels as she touched Ellen's arm and asked, "Is this because of the threat?"

Ellen nodded and turned her fanny pack around to show the quick access panel from which she could withdraw her weapon. Michele stared at it, now knowing that it was all for real, which made her even more determined to make sure that nothing happened to her family that day.

As they made their way up the drive to the house, Steve was at the front door, wearing what looked like a vest over his shirt.

"Is that a bulletproof vest you have on, Steve?" Michele asked.

"Yes. Karl here thinks is gives more definition to my pecs. Do you agree?" Steve asked Michele, trying hard to defuse the worry on Michele's face.

"You might want to get another opinion on that, Steve. It really doesn't do a thing for you," Michele said, which brought a smile to Ellen's face.

"And what are you laughing at, young lady?" Steve bellowed at Ellen, which only made her laugh out loud.

Between fits of laughter, she finally replied, "Oh nothing, Steve. But if you want, we could get you some bra cup inserts to help. I'm sure we can pick some up on the way to church if that's the look you're going for!"

Michele burst out laughing as Ellen's line made Steve stop in his tracks without a comeback at hand. The women high fived each other as they moved past Steve, who stood there, dumbstruck, holding open the front door.

"What are you laughing at?" Steve yelled without looking back at Karl, who was in the middle of the room hugging Ellen.

"Who me? Oh, nothing..." Karl said, positioning Ellen between himself and Steve.

Steve turned. "Do you think she will stop me, big fella?" Ellen, realizing how she was maneuvered in between them, quickly spun around behind Karl and pushed him toward Steve. Michele, who was standing to the side watching them, laughed as she got between the two of them and hugged Steve, which made him stop advancing.

Karl stood there, looking at the two of them, when he felt Ellen's arms wrap around his waist and heard her say softly, "I need to take a shower and get ready for mass. Okay to use your hotel room?" Karl just smiled and began reaching for the room key.

"Oh no, you go ahead and get ready here, Ellen. Leaving me with the two of them is a just bit unfair," Michele said as she smiled at both Karl and Steve.

"It's a deal. Let me go and get my things out of my car. Karl, care to carry my bag for me?" Ellen smiled at him as she walked toward the front door with Karl following, leaving Michele and Steve alone.

"Thanks for wearing the vest, Steve; you knew I would make you, given the chance, didn't you?" Michele asked sheepishly.

"Well, Karl kind of made it a no brainer for me, and I knew I couldn't say no to you, Michele," Steve said as he hugged her again.

"Finally learning after eighteen years! Not bad, Mr. I Believe," Michele said as she moved to open the front door, catching Ellen kissing Karl on the porch.

No one noticed Jim coming down the stairs. He also caught Ellen and Karl kissing and said in a not-so-quiet stage whisper, "Geez, you two…get a room, will ya?"

Steve just stood laughing; this was what he needed to relieve the stress that was building for what lay ahead in the next couple of hours for him.

Chapter 84

All five of them were ready to leave for the church with Steve, who wore his uniform slacks, crisp white shirt, bulletproof vest, and tie. He left the suit coat in its garment bag as he would be attending mass before changing. His uniform coat, presentation sword, and cover, along with his zucchetto, would be put into the sacristy so that no one could see him after he changed until he was about to be presented. It was decided that Father George would inform the parishioners at the mass of what had happened, but it would be Cardinal Giuseppe who would introduce him as a Knight of the Golden Spur and then read the rest of the third letter from St. Pius X and the Papal Bull. Elaine and her camera crew were already in place to record this for posterity. Once that was done and Steve was officially announced, the last letter would be opened and its contents revealed to all.

To say that nerves were building for Steve would be an understatement, but with Michele and Jim at his side, he knew that he could make it through. As long as the threat did not rear its ugly head…but even if it did, he knew that somehow he was going to make it because the best of the best were there to protect him and his family.

Karl and Ellen had driven together, and they were responsible to get the rest of his uniform into the church without anyone knowing what was really going on. *Funny,* he thought as he drove. *Whoever thought this would be happening to me and that I'm going to be announced as a Cardinal priest today in front of my friends and family?*

As he pulled into the church driveway, he noticed a police squad car in the circle drive and another at the end of drive as well. He knew there would be plain clothes police in the pews at mass and that Karl was there, but would that be enough to stop those who had made the threat? *Well, in for a pound,* he said to himself as he pulled into a parking spot by the kitchen. As they got out, Michele came over to Jim and tried to fix his hair, but in his usual way, Jim protested. He knew he wouldn't win when his mom took out her brush to fix it as she had done all of his sixteen years. Smiling at the two of them, Steve walked through the kitchen and into Dempsey Hall, which led to the side vestibule of the Madison Street church.

He was greeted by members of his Men's Club who were waiting to be introduced to Cardinal Giuseppe. Bizarre, he thought, that a Cardinal was right there amongst them, and they did not know. Catching him smiling, one of the members asked what was so funny; Steve just smiled and walked on to find the Brothers of the Brown Robes.

Locating them in the main narthex of the church, he found them talking to a small crowd around them. Giuseppe was even wearing his scarlet zucchetto, which surprised him as well. As he got near them, Brother Angelo grabbed him and pulled him into the center of their group. He and Brother Michael were asking more questions about deep dish pizza to whomever would answer them.

He excused the Brothers of the Brown Robes and motioned for them to follow him to the other side to meet his fellow brothers of the St. Paul's Men's Club. As he got near they formed a straight line and all at once bowed before Cardinal Giuseppe, who was impressed with the formality of their greeting. Steve stood smiling as he introduced each member by name proudly. The Brothers noticed this and were grateful; this little act took some of the nerves away from Steve's face. As the introductions finished, Karl came up behind them with Ellen by his side and motioned for Steve to come with them.

"Steve, we believe that we have located the source of the threat; the police were able to trace the call after all. It came from a relative of the man who shot Father George, and it was meant to stop you today. The police have arrested the man, but his son, who also is a suspect, has not been found. We have his picture in every officer's hand here today but wanted you to know the latest. Your neighbor, Paul, called me, and a squad car came by with the picture, which we have handed out as I said. Knowing who we are looking for is huge, but we have to keep our guard up. I see that the Brothers and His Eminence are taking all of this in…" Karl finished speaking as Steve stood looking at the picture.

"So, all of this is about revenge, then. Correct, Karl?" Steve asked, still looking at the picture.

"Yes. They do not share any of Bill Matters's beliefs; they just wanted to *make things right* is how the dad put it. The parents of Bill Matters pleaded with their relative to give up his son, but he was not having any of it. They do not hold you responsible for the outcome as you were just protecting everyone here that day, Steve," Karl said in his very professional manner.

"Okay. So how do we proceed from here?" Steve asked.

"Well, we have a good plan to catch him. We know that he has a hand gun and not a rifle. He will have to get close to do anything, and we have extra police stationed on the edge of the church property, forming a perimeter ring. If he shows up, we will get him, Steve. Do not worry," Karl answered him directly.

"Okay, then let's get going. Mass is about to begin. Oh, and Karl? Thanks for everything," Steve said as he grasped Karl's hand and gave it a firm shake.

Karl came to attention and gave Steve a crisp salute, adding in a whisper to him, "Your Eminence, it is my privilege to serve you."

Chapter 85

As the mass began, Steve took up his regular seat, second pew on the right-hand side. He was there with Michele, Jim, Ellen, and the three Brothers of the Brown Robes. Father Rick began the prayers of the day as all seemed quiet. As the first Epistle was starting, Michele squeezed Steve's hand lightly, smiling at him, which eased his worry a bit. Karl was in the back of the church, keeping his ever-present vigil for the threat and also putting the rest of Steve's uniform into the sacristy as planned. When the second Epistle was finished and Father Rick rose to read the gospel, Steve stood proudly next to Michelle as Father George came up and stood next to the seat that Father George had just vacated. Steve thought about how strange it was that he was still in his sling and yet would be there on the altar today.

As the Gospel finished, Steve noticed Father George crossing the altar after bowing in front of the tabernacle and standing next to the pulpit with Father Rick. As he took the pulpit, Steve was expecting a homily that only Father George could give but instead was in for the shock of his life.

"Good afternoon, and welcome to St. Paul's," Father George warmly greeted everyone. "As some of you have heard, we have some rather outstanding brother clergy visiting us today from the Vatican. I would like to introduce to all here today Brother Michael and Brother Angelo from the Monastery of the Brown Robes in Northern Italy." As they stood, there was a very nice round of applause for them, and the two of them took it all in.

Jim looked over to his mom and whispered, "Would you look at those two hams?" Michele just smiled and tried to hold back a laugh, which brought a stern look from Steve.

"It is also my great honor to welcome His Eminence Cardinal Abbot Giuseppe of the Brown Robes as well!" When Giuseppe stood, the whole parish stood to greet him as well.

At this time, Karl walked down the center aisle with the representative from the Boy Scouts who was holding a presentation case in his hand along with a file folder. When they arrived in the front of the altar, a tear formed in Michele's eye; Ellen handed her a tissue, already dabbing at her own eyes as well. Father George nodded to Karl, who turned and smiled at Jim as he walked back to his station at the back of the church.

"I would like at this time also to introduce Mr. Alan Bridgeman from the Three Fires Council of the Boy Scouts of America," Father George said as

Mr. Bridgeman made his way to the pulpit. As he adjusted the microphone, he opened his file folder and cleared his throat, beginning his presentation.

"I am Alan Bridgeman, the district representative for the Boy Scouts of America for the Three Fires Council. As most of you know, and as Father George can attest to, there was a little incident here at St. Paul's that has been brought to the attention of the leaders of the Boy Scouts at the national level." As he spoke, it started to register with the Michaels men that Michele had totally pulled the wool over their eyes. Mr. Bridgeman continued, "The events that day, while tragic, have been brought to our attention due to the actions of one young man, an Eagle Scout and a member of Troup Three. James Michaels, if you would come up here by my side, please?"

Jim rose, looking very surprised. He was greeted by a hug from his mother and his father's large hand on his shoulder. As Steve and Michele sat, Steve looked at his wife, smiling, knowing that she had set this entire thing up.

Mr. Bridgeman continued reading from the file folder, "The events of that day and what this young man did during the shooting of Father George were remarkable, to say the least. James here crawled over to assist and give first aid to Father George, all the while making sure that the other altar server serving with him that day was out of harm's way.

407

When his own father came up to help, it was James who gave orders in caring for his patient, who was rendered unconscious after being shot. For keeping a clear head and acting in the manner of a Boy Scout carrying out the motto of being prepared, James Michaels is hereby awarded the Boy Scouts of America Honor Medal for his lifesaving first aid of Father George."

As Mr. Bridgeman finished and came down from the pulpit, he took the medal out of its presentation case and draped the ribbon over Jim's head, adjusting it around his neck. The whole church stood and began to applaud wildly for Jim, who looked very embarrassed by what had transpired. As he shook Mr. Bridgeman's hand and accepted the presentation case and the file folder containing the speech that was just read, he looked at his parents, smiling.

Michele was holding onto Steve, crying unselfconsciously. Steve beamed at his son, who was looking for a place to hide. This all was totally unexpected and quite embarrassing. He posed for a picture with Mr. Bridgeman; then, he came down from the altar and went back to the pew with all in the church still standing and applauding. He waved as he sat down, and Father Rick returned to the pulpit, trying to regain a bit of order before the mass could continue.

Steve leaned over to his son and very softly said, "Your mother hoodwinked both of us, Jim."

"Yes, she did, and she really got us good. Seems like she's starting to forgive us for putting ourselves in danger. Well, maybe just a bit, at least!" Jim took his dad's hand and shook it man to man.

As Father Rick continued with the mysteries of the mass, Steve began to get a bit edgy, knowing that an even bigger surprise than Jim's award was going to be revealed in a few more minutes. As the final prayers were said over the bread and wine, the communion song started, and Steve stood to receive communion. He knew that this was it.

Chapter 86

As Steve stood in line to receive Holy Communion, Michele whispered to him, "Karl and Ellen will meet you in the sacristy to help get you ready. Try not to trip when you walk back up." This was greeted by a smile, and Steve rolled his eyes at his wife.

Walking to the back of the church after receiving Communion, he noticed a young man intently staring at him. Steve slowed down a bit and stared back at him with the same intensity. The young man smiled and reached inside his suit coat very quickly; this action made Steve stop, not knowing what he could do if this was the young man they were looking for. Karl noticed that Steve had stopped as well and was looking at someone in the pew. He rushed up the center aisle of the church with his weapon drawn and by his side.

The young man stood up, pulled his gun, and shot Steve square in the chest, the sound of the gunfire deafening everyone nearby. Steve fell as the bullet struck him, the breath leaving his body. Karl returned fire from the end of the pew, striking the young man in the center of his back, killing him instantly.

As he fell over the people next to him, screams began but in slow motion. Time seemed almost to stop.

Ellen was steps behind Steve and began running at the sound of the first gunshot, looking to see where it came from. Jim grabbed his mother and pushed her down in the pew, covering her with his body. As Ellen got to Steve, she saw Karl kill the gunman, who was still pointing his weapon at where Steve had fallen. Brother Michael got up to run to Steve's aid as Brother Angelo covered Giuseppe with his body to protect him as well.

Elaine and her camera person took all of this in as they followed Steve's progress up the aisle after receiving Communion. She gasped when the gunman rose and shot Steve and then watched Karl return fire. She turned to her camera person, Linda, who had been at the house when they interviewed Steve. Almost begging, she asked Linda, "Please, tell me you got all of this. Please!" Linda nodded zooming in on what was happening.

Ellen reached Steve first as Karl made his way through the parishioners in the pew to get to the gunman and make sure that he could not harm anyone else. Ellen slowly turned him over after noticing that there was no exit wound on his back. She was greeted by Steve opening his eyes with what could only be described as a look of disbelief.

He spoke but very softly to her as he got his wind back, "God, that hurts. I think one of my ribs is broken. And would you look at my shirt? Michele is going to kill me over that." Ellen started to laugh at him as Brother Michael came up to help.

"Is he okay? Did the vest stop the bullet?" Brother Michael asked quickly.

"Yes, it did its job, but he got the wind knocked out of him, and he thinks he broke a rib," Ellen answered as if relaying info on an injured soldier, calmly and professionally. "He also needs to be evacuated since Michele is going to kill him for ruining one of his shirts!"

Brother Michael laughed at that response as Karl yelled over to Ellen, asking if Steve was all right.

"He's fine, Karl. Nice job getting him!" Ellen answered, pointing at the gunman "Is he dead?"

"Yes, he is. Can you move him?" Karl asked. He didn't want to leave the gunman until the police could take over the scene.

"I can, but he's more worried about his shirt and what Michele is going to do to him," Ellen said back, which got a smile from Karl.

The police had the section of the church cleared minutes after the gunman went down. An EMS squad had been called and would arrive in a minute as well. Michele was still being covered by Jim in the pew and was struggling to get free from her son.

"Would you let me up, Jim?" she yelled at him.

"Oh, sorry Mom. Here, let me help you," Jim said as he uncovered her and stood to help her.

"Ellen!" Michele screamed. "Is he okay?"

"Yes, he's good. The vest saved him!" Ellen yelled back to her.

"Well, good, because now I'm going to end it. Let me out of here, Jim!" Michele directed as both Brother Angelo and Cardinal Giuseppe got up as well.

"Mom, sit and stay here. Do you understand? Here, hold this for me, please," Jim said, pushing his mother back into the pew as he handed her his medal. "Brother Angelo, keep her here while I go check on my dad," Jim said authoritatively. Michele looked at him, disbelieving that her son would say that to her. As Jim crawled over the pew to get to his dad, he pointed at her and said, "Stay here!"

Michele just sat there, looking at Angelo and Giuseppe, not knowing what to say until Giuseppe took her hand and said, "Hmm, wonder where he gets his authoritative side from?"

"If you weren't a Cardinal, I'd show you where he gets it from!" Michele answered, and all three of them chuckled.

Brother Michael and Ellen were helping Steve to his feet as Jim came up and grabbed his dad's side to steady him.

"Looks like it hurts. How bad are you?" Jim asked.

"Well, I think I broke a rib. Where's your mom?" Steve asked softly, his voice shaky.

"Back in the pew. I made her stay there until I could make sure you were fine," Jim said sternly.

"Oh boy, are you in trouble, young man. She will kill you for that one!" Steve said as a smile came to his face; it became a wince from the pain in his ribs.

"Only after she's done with you; I have Brother Angelo and the Cardinal watching her now," Jim said, solidifying his position in charge of the scene.

"Well, let's get back to her now. No need to stay my execution any longer," Steve said as Ellen and Jim held him up and Brother Michael led the way back down the aisle.

"Clear the way!" Jim called. "Here he comes!" Ellen began to laugh, but Steve could only smile, for the pain was too much. As they made it to the pew where Michele was still being guarded by the other two Brothers of the Brown Robes, she got up with Angelo's help and walked toward Steve.

"Michele, he is going to be bruised pretty badly but will make it. Please, go lightly," Ellen pleaded with Michele as she got close to them.

"Steve, are you okay?" was all Michele asked, not knowing if she could hug him; the pain was very visible on his face.

Chapter 87

Sensing her reluctance to hug him, Steve leaned forward and pressed his forehead to his wife's. For a moment, they simply stood there, Steve reassuring her wordlessly that he was in one piece.

"Here, sit down. You look terrible," Michele said finally as she motioned for him to sit.

"Not yet…can someone help me get this vest off?" Steve asked. Michele started to unbutton his shirt as Jim began to tug it out of his pants. As they removed his shirt with much effort not to hurt him, they gasped at the bullet in the center of the vest. Jim started to undo the Velcro straps that held it in place as Paul came up to them from behind.

"You know we are going to have to charge you for that, don't you?" Paul asked as Steve smiled and mouthed *thank you* to him. "Well, maybe we can make an exception just this one time," Paul added as he moved to help Jim remove the vest. The bullet had not penetrated the vest, but on Steve's chest was a massive bruise, already turning purple as it was exposed.

"God, it looks like Michele really did a number on you this time, Steve," was all Paul could say to him as he handed the vest to another officer who had come up to them at the front of the church.

"Mr. Michaels, you'll need to be seen by the EMS squad. That does look quite bad," the police officer informed Steve, who nodded at him in return.

"Karl, did you get him?" Steve asked, still not sure of his voice.

"Yes, the threat has been eliminated," Karl answered quietly as Ellen came up to him.

"Okay. Was anyone else hurt at all?" Steve asked weakly.

"No, just you and the gunman. We have the situation under control. We have evacuated the church, and everyone is fine," Karl replied as Ellen squeezed his hand.

"Okay. God, does this hurt. I think I need to sit," Steve said as he slumped into the pew, looking quite exhausted from everything. "Well, Giuseppe, I hope this ends the discussion with those two about deep dish pizza for a while. I've given them something else to talk about now."

Everyone laughed as the EMS tech asked if he could see Steve for a minute or two. As he began looking Steve over, Karl motioned for the three Brothers of the Brown Robes to come over with him and Ellen for a minute.

"Nice shot there, Karl," Giuseppe said quietly so that only the five of them could hear.

"He is really busted up, your Eminence; he should be taken to a hospital to have x-rays, at least. Also, what do we do about the last letter now?" Karl asked, knowing that he spoke for all of them.

"Well, the letter can wait. I agree that he really needs to be looked at somewhere other than here. Do you think there was anyone else with the gunman or was he alone?" Giuseppe asked Karl.

"He was alone; the police have verified it with his father, who is in custody," Karl replied.

"Let's see what the EMS tech says about him before we decide anything about the letter. Think anyone in Rome will believe what has happened?" Giuseppe asked to those around him.

"With what has already happened, I doubt it, your Eminence," Karl answered, knowing that he was having a hard time believing it himself.

"Karl and Giuseppe, can you come over here?" Steve called out, his voice still a bit weak. As the two walked over, Steve was being attended to by the EMS tech who informed him that without x-rays, there was no way to tell if he had a broken rib.

Michele just looked at Steve and mouthed quietly to him, "Your call."

"Steve, what do you need?" Karl asked with Giuseppe next to him.

"Let's get this over with; no need to wait. I will go and get my ribs checked out after. With Elaine here, we can record it and then have it released publicly. Karl, can you go out and see if the guys from my Men's Club are still here?" Steve asked with Michele nodding her approval.

When Karl returned within minutes, with him were fifteen men who belonged to the St. Paul's Men's Club along with their families. A few asked Steve how he was, and he laid out the plan for what he needed them to do. Like a bunch of kids getting ready to play a pick up baseball game, they took their positions in the pews as Elaine moved her camera up to the middle of the center aisle.

With Karl's help, Steve made it back to the sacristy and put back on the shirt with the bullet hole in it.

"Michele didn't seem too upset by the bullet hole in the shirt; I might not get into too much trouble for that one, Karl!" Steve said as he tied his tie very gingerly.

"You're funny, Steve. You get shot, and you're worried about you shirt. Here, let me help you with that before you hurt yourself more," Karl said, not seeing Ellen behind him.

"Here, Karl, you get his jacket and cover. Let me do this," Ellen said, moving Karl out of the way and beginning to sound a lot like Michele.

"Thanks for the help, Ellen; you really are a blessing to us all. Well, mainly to him," Steve said as he jerked his thumb over at Karl.

"Yeah, I might keep him around if he stays for a bit. Do you know when your protection detail is over?" she asked nonchalantly.

"I will see what I can do to keep him around for you, Ellen," Steve answered with a wink, which made her blush. As they finished getting him ready, Ellen made sure to have his tie centered over the bullet hole. The two of them watched Steve place the zucchetto on his head and motion for his cover. Ellen and Karl just stared at him, which almost made him blush. "What? Is there something wrong?" he asked.

"No, Steve. But this is the last time that you will be you. Your zucchetto fits you, and no matter what, you have earned it!" Karl said as he reached out to shake his hand. Ellen kissed him on the cheek and adjusted his cover so that none of the watered scarlet could be seen under it. They both helped him on with his scabbard and then handed him his sword to place in it.

"Okay, Karl. Let's go see what Pope Pius X has in store for me!" Steve said, and they left the sacristy.

Chapter 88

Ellen opened the door to the church carefully so that Steve could not be seen and walked down to take her seat with Michele. As she sat, she nodded to Father Rick and to Father George who had come back into the church after helping make sure that everyone who left was okay. Father George got up to the pulpit, and everyone seated in the pews came to attention to see what this was all about.

Father George began, "Well, first I would ask how you are doing, but we know how you are: excited over what has happened and wondering what is about to happen here today. Let me first tell you that St. Paul's own Steve Michaels has been given a great honor by the Vatican but not by Pope Alexander IX. To tell you that story, I would like to introduce to you His Eminence Cardinal Giuseppe of the Brown Robes." Father George walked down from the pulpit and led a very polite round of applause for Cardinal Giuseppe as he made his way up the stairs.

"Thank you all," Giuseppe exclaimed as he motioned for the applause to die down. "You all know what transpired here at St. Paul's parish with Father George being shot and what Steve did to protect everyone afterward, but now I am honored to tell you what happened to him after the shooting. In 1914, Saint Pope Pius X created a prophecy that a man from the Americas would be faced with death for his beliefs but would not let it sway him. He would triumph, and it would be recorded for the whole world to see. He would win this fight on his beliefs alone." As he finished reciting the prophecy, Brothers Angelo and Michael came up to the altar, carrying the wooden box that contained the letters of St. Pius X and the metal box. Brother Angelo took out all four of the letters and laid them carefully on the altar, with the fourth letter still sealed in the wire rope and the wax impression of the seal of Pope Pius X. Cardinal Giuseppe motioned to Brother Angelo for the third letter and was handed it by him.

"This letter is the one that Steve read after he was summoned to the Vatican by St. Pius X per the directions of Pope Alexander IX. Pope Pius X had left us four letters; the first one I opened at our monastery in Italy; it commanded us to take the letters to see the current man who sits on the Throne of St. Peter. Once there, the second letter was opened, which ordered the current Vicar of Christ to have Steve brought to the Vatican to open the third letter. This third letter is the one that I will read to you now," Giuseppe took a breath and noticed that all eyes were riveted to him as he looked down at the third letter and began to read, mimicking the words Steve himself had read just days earlier.

As Giuseppe finished reading the third letter, Steve marched up the center aisle, looking very formal in his uniform as a Knight of the Golden Spur. He stopped in front of the altar, sharply saluting the flags of the United States and of the Vatican. He stood at rigid attention as those in the pews rose to applaud him for receiving such an honor. Steve smartly turned to face all of them while still remaining at attention. As the applause gradually died down, Steve turned slightly to look at Michele and Jim and smiled as he knew he was going to make it now.

"As you can see, Steve is in his dress uniform as a Knight of the Golden Spur; his sword belonged to a Knight Templar and was made in the year 1200," Giuseppe stated clearly for all to hear while Steve remained at attention.

"In the third letter, there was a reference to Steve receiving first tonsure, and in 1914 it was considered the first step in becoming a member of the clergy. Today it is when a man is ordained a Deacon. As this letter was written in 1914 as a Pontifical Order, it is as valid now as the day it was written. Along with myself, His Holiness and the Secretariat of State for the Vatican issued the rite of first tonsure to Steve by taking four tufts of his hair and blessing him in the name of the Father and the Son and the Holy Spirit." Giuseppe took a breath and looked at Michele, who smiled back and gave him the thumbs up sign.

"The reference to the 'other envelope' caught us all off guard. Brother Angelo, may I have the other envelope?" Giuseppe asked.

Brother Angelo brought the folded up Papal Bull and then stood alongside Giuseppe as he began to unfold it.

"This is a Papal Bull, and I will read it in English as I was asked to read it for Steve at the Vatican. A Papal Bull is basically an order or a patent that is a formal proclamation made by the Pope and only by the Pope," Giuseppe explained. He took a deep breath and read the Bull.

When he was finished reading the Bull, a loud and audible gasp escaped from all who were present as Steve took off his cover to expose for the first time publicly his watered scarlet zucchetto. The members of his Men's Club and their families who were present stood while giving a rousing round of applause to his Eminence Steve Cardinal Michaels.

Chapter 89

As Steve turn to face the altar again, he bowed and made his way up the stairs toward the pulpit. There he was greeted by Brother Michael, who put the ring of St. Pius on his finger, and by Brother Angelo, who place upon his head the scarlet biretta. He then walked towards Father Rick and Father George, who both bowed and kissed the ring of the Cardinal. As he walked up to the pulpit, Cardinal Giuseppe gave him a hug and said softly to him as they embraced, "Welcome to the club!" He then moved away with a slight smirk on his face.

As Steve stepped up and adjusted the microphone, he motioned for all to sit so he could address those present. "I for one am more shocked and surprised than you are over what has happened to me since the day that Father George here was shot," Steve began. "When the Papal Bull was read, all I could think about was how I was going to tell Michele and who was going to be there to stop her from killing me." This remark brought a ripple of laughter as all there knew Michele and what she was capable of with Steve. "But seriously, my friends," Steve continued. "I am at peace with all that has happened and have placed my trust in my beliefs and in Pope Pius X for having the courage to do what you have just witnessed here today!"

Steve nodded toward Brother Angelo to bring the fourth letter to him. "This is the letter that His Holiness and I have been waiting to open to see what orders a saint is going to give me here today!" Steve was handed a small knife by Brother Michael to break the seal, and then he untied the rope that bound the letter. Handing back the knife, he unfolded the letter to find that is was, as he and Giuseppe had feared, another Papal Bull handwritten by a saint. "As this is written in Latin, I would like to ask His Eminence Cardinal Giuseppe to please read it for all to hear for the first time." As Steve got down from the pulpit, Giuseppe took the step up and after a very deep breath started to read the Papal Bull:

"*Pius, Bishop, Servant of the Servants of God, herby decrees to you, my protector of the faith, having been announced as a Cardinal, my last Pontifical Orders for you to carry out to serve mankind.*

"*As I cannot stop the war that is about us and since I know that I will not be alive to see it end, you must do my bidding to help the world after this most terrible conflict is over.*

"*Since a whole generation of young men will be slaughtered, and there will be nothing left at the end but countries claiming victories and rights that do nothing to help heal, you will be my healer.*

425

"As of this day, I command that you take your place as the new leader of priesthood, an usher into our ranks of any man who wants to be a priest and serve our Church. The rule of being single and celibate is hereby abolished; men who are married and those who are Deacons serving the Church may now take the steps that you see fit to begin their road to full priesthood.

"Our Holy Mother Church will help rebuild the world, and by having more men serve as priests, we can only then begin the healing that is needed. No more will local parish priests need to travel for hours to serve their flocks. Every church will have a priest to serve it, and those that are lucky enough will have even more.

"Tend to the flock, my dear Cardinal, and lead this new way of priesthood in the same manner as you have defended our Holy Mother Church.

I command this day of the Epiphany in the year of our Lord 1914. Pius X pp."

As Giuseppe finished reading the Bull, not a word was spoken, and a pin drop could be heard. Brothers Michael and Angelo just looked at each other, as did Father George and Father Rick. What was just read was slowly registering to all present as the words of a saint reverberated in their minds.

Steve looked at Giuseppe in disbelief and asked quietly, "You didn't make that up, did you?" which brought a smile to Giuseppe's face.

"No, Steve. You can have Brother Michael read it again for you to verify, but my Latin is very good," he answered Steve, who didn't have a comeback for the first time in his life. "So, my dear Eminence, I was not expecting that out of St. Pius X!"

Steve just stood there, silently shaking his head and mouthing to Giuseppe, "No, I was not either!"

Brothers Angelo and Michael, along with Fathers Rick and George, came up to look at the Papal Bull just to make sure what they all had heard. Steve returned to the pulpit, and after clearing his throat to get everyone's attention, he spoke to all of those present.

"What we have witnessed here today is earth shattering for us as Roman Catholics but not for what has transpired over the course of these last couple weeks for me. We must now embrace what a saint has ordered us to do and face this brave new world that he has given us. The traditions that we all have had will change, and under the direction of His Mother, Mary, I ask each of you for your help to do what we have been ordered to do. If you all will rise, please," Steve motioned with his hands as he said this. Giuseppe and both of the Brothers were listening intently to him and moved to stand on either side of the pulpit, amazed at how Steve was dealing with this. "There is only one way to end this today: by asking for your prayers as God only knows I will need them.

427

I bless you in the name of the Father and of the Son and of the Holy Spirit." Steve made the sign of the cross three times, first to his left and then the center and finally to his right as he was taught by Giuseppe. All present made the sign of the cross as well, having been witness to Steve's first actions as a Cardinal, and then they broke into applause again as Steve just smiled.

When he stepped down from the pulpit, he took the biretta off his head and placed in back in the metal box that it came from, walking down from the altar to begin what a saint had laid out for him: to begin the healing of his Holy Mother Church, just some one hundred years later than Giovanni Sarto had expected!

Thanks for reading Mr. I Believe; I hope you have enjoyed it as much as I did writing it!

I would like to thank all of the Priests, Nuns and Lay Teachers at St. Albert the Great Grade School in Dearborn Heights, Michigan and Dearborn Divine Child High School in Dearborn, Michigan. I guess with all of the religion classes I took something did stick with me!!!

If you would to comment on Mr. I Believe please let me know at mribelieve@gmail.com

Thanks Again,
Sean